SPLINTER THE BONE

DI DREW HASKELL & PROFILER HARRIET QUINN DETECTIVE SERIES BOOK 3

BILINDA P. SHEEHAN

Copyright © 2020 by Bilinda P. Sheehan

All rights reserved.

No part of this book may be reproduced in any form or by any electronic or mechanical means, including information storage and retrieval systems, without written permission from the author, except for the use of brief quotations in a book review.

Version 2

***

Please Note: this book contains text speech, which is written as it would appear on a phone. Therefore, it is not grammatically correct, and words are spelled differently.

ALSO BY BILINDA P. SHEEHAN

Watch out for the next book coming soon from Bilinda P. Sheehan by joining her mailing list.

A Wicked Mercy - DI Drew Haskell & Profiler Harriet Quinn Detective Series Book 1

Death in Pieces - DI Drew Haskell & Profiler Harriet Quinn Detective Series Book 2

Splinter the Bone - DI Drew Haskell & Profiler Harriet Quinn Detective Series Book 3

Hunting the Silence - DI Drew Haskell & Profiler Harriet Quinn Detective Series Book 4

All the Lost Girls-A Gripping Psychological Thriller

Wednesday's Child - A Gripping Psychological Thriller

SPLINTER THE BONE

CHAPTER ONE

ONE YEAR AGO

FURZEY LANE STRETCHED AHEAD, a muddy, gravel path that wound its way through the woodland, a stark contrast to the kinds of walks Carol was used to taking. Hiking was not exactly at the top of her list for favourite activities, but James had insisted they needed to get out of the house. And then, of course, there was Skipper. Carol had never seen him so excited to go for walkies.

Rain pattered down around them gently, the large droplets hitting the muddy ground formed growing puddles that became increasingly difficult to avoid.

"Skipper!" Carol's voice rang out through the small woodland area. Just why James insisted on letting the dog off the lead was beyond her. Why couldn't he just do as she wished, for once? If he had, they wouldn't be stuck out here in the middle of the trail searching for a little four-legged beast.

"Skipper! Come on, boy!"

"I think I can hear him," James said, sounding a little excited as he moved ahead towards the tall, spindly looking trees that lined the gravel pathway.

Carol tilted her head to the side and listened. Sure enough, she could hear the telltale sound of Skipper in the distance as he rooted around in the heavy undergrowth.

"Perhaps you should go in after him," she said. "I mean, what if his collar gets caught on a tree branch, or--"

"He'll be fine. Stop fussing," James said.

Even though she knew he didn't mean to sound so uncaring, Carol couldn't help but feel the sting of his words. He was always telling her not to fuss, but she couldn't help it. Skipper could be a right pain in the behind, but he was her pain in the behind, and the thought of him ever coming to grief filled her with the kind of dread that threatened to send her crashing into the undergrowth in search of the spaniel.

As though he could sense her continued discomfort, James walked toward her and drew her into a tight hug. "You'd swear he was a small child, the way you fret over him," he murmured against her hair.

"Don't," Carol said, sliding free of his hold. "Somebody might see."

"So what?" James shrugged, his *laissez-faire* attitude grating on Carol's nerves.

He studied her for a moment, before his expression darkened. "You know, I'm getting bloody sick of your constant mood swings. You're up and down all the time. I don't know where I stand."

"I don't want to talk about this here," Carol said stiffly, straining to listen to the sounds that made up the backdrop to their walk. "I can't hear him anymore." Panic laced her words.

"You and that bloody dog," he grumbled. "I'm going to keep moving before my muscles cool down too much."

With his long stride, it wasn't long before James was so far ahead on the path, he was practically out of sight.

"Come on, Skipper, I'm not messing around anymore. Time to go home!" Carol called.

Silence closed in around her, as her words faded into the trees. She glanced up at the clouds gathering overhead. It wouldn't take long for the evening to close in. Despite it being August, an autumnal chill that had slowly crept into the air. And in the evenings, the temperature was gradually inching down. She shivered as a drop of water slipped beneath the collar of her rain jacket and slithered down her cold skin. It was a typical British summer.

"Skipper!" Exasperation coloured her voice as she crossed the path and stared down at the undergrowth. It would be all too easy to trip, twist an ankle on a thick tree root, or a fallen branch. Glancing back at the path, she sighed. James was now completely hidden from sight. She hadn't honestly believed he would leave her here, but here she was, on her own.

You sure can pick 'em.

"Please, Skip..." She whispered the words. Silence followed. There was no cheerful yip, no rustling sound to tell her he was on his way back. Maybe he was hurt. What choice did she have? Swallowing down her unease, she stepped off the path. Mud squelched beneath her new hiking boots as she clambered through the undergrowth.

Beneath the trees, it was much darker, the evening light only filtering through in patches. Carol crashed around in the undergrowth, pausing every couple of minutes to call her dog. It was during one of these pauses that her worst fears were realised.

She stepped over what appeared to be a large tree branch, and her foot sank into a water-filled hole on the other side. She teetered for a moment, arms windmilling in the air as she fought to stay on her feet. Something crunched beneath her heel, driving her foot deeper into the hole, and it was then that she lost her balance entirely. She went down hard, her body slamming into the churned up, muddy undergrowth. Her cry cut off as she raised her hands to protect her face from the fall.

It was the smell that told her something was terribly wrong. It spread up around her, the foetid air clinging to her skin and hair.

Pushing upwards, she gagged as her hand pressed into and then passed through something gelatinous. Putrid air chased up her nose, bringing vomit racing up the back of her throat.

She rolled away from the mess she'd fallen into and scrambled to her feet. Her boots slipped from beneath her again, and she hit the ground with her hands. Her fingers tangled in something dark and stringy before she finally clambered upright again.

The smell clung to her, an inescapable odour that burned the back of her throat, making her think of the dead badger Skipper had once had the misfortune of finding in the park during one of their walks.

Shaking her hands, she tried to clear the stringy material from her hands, but it had tangled around her fingers, and caught on the sleeve of her *North Face* jacket. Until that moment, her brain had tried to shield her from the truth of her discovery, but as she pulled the strands of dark hair from her hands, Carol realised what she was looking at.

She glanced back at the hole she'd fallen into as a scream built in the back of her throat. Dark hair splayed out from the clear plastic bag someone had wrapped it in.

Carol's scream rent the air, carried on the stillness of the dark evening.

DI MELISSA APPLETON stared at the scene. They had brought floodlights in, to give the forensics team enough light to carry out their work. It had been a race against the clock to get some sort of cover up over the area, protection against the rain that had lashed from the sky.

Even now, rainwater puddled around the perimeter of the crime scene, making the excavation of the site that much harder. There was only so much evidence that could be rescued from the human soup that the patch of ground had become.

Melissa sighed and dug her face down lower into the collar of the Tyvek suit she wore. It wasn't much protection against the rain, but it was better than the light jacket she'd been wearing when she'd received the call.

"Guv, they've found another body," DC Ayesha Javed said, her voice muffled behind the white mask she wore over her face.

"That makes how many?" Melissa asked.

"Three so far. They think they might have at least one more." The constable stepped carefully across the platforms they'd embedded into the dirt to keep the worst of the foot traffic off the ground.

Melissa sighed. "All women?"

Ayesha nodded. "They think so. Clothes, and the size of the bodies, certainly seem to indicate the gender of the victims is female."

"What has the pathologist said?"

"Forensics haven't cleared him to enter the site yet," Ayesha said tightly. "They're still gathering evidence."

"For fuck's sake," Melissa growled. "What am I supposed to tell Templeton?"

Ayesha shrugged. "It's not like he doesn't know what goes on at a crime scene, guv. And the weather isn't exactly on our side, he can't hold that against you."

Melissa bit back the retort that hovered on the tip of her tongue. The constable couldn't possibly be expected to understand the kind of relationship she shared with Templeton. He would view the lack of information as *her* fault, as though she could control all the different variables involved in the crime scene examination.

A shout went up, a few feet deeper into the woodland.

"What was that?" Melissa asked, sliding her mask back up over her face as she followed Ayesha over to the edge of the cordon. One of the crime scene analysts carried something dark, wrapped in a plastic evidence bag, towards them.

"This needs processing," the woman said. Only her eyes were visible above the top of her mask, and

Melissa couldn't help but notice the smudging along the woman's mascara. "We found a fourth body, and this one had ID."

"How do we know it belongs to that body?" Melissa asked, craning her neck to see into the plastic bag.

"We don't. At least not yet. But it's too important to ignore."

Melissa nodded. "Fine. Who does it say it is?"

"DC Anna Spencer."

Melissa's heart skipped in her chest. "Excuse me? Could you repeat that?" Heat flushed over the surface of her skin, making her body feel stifled beneath the white forensic suit. The urge to rip free of it, to feel the cool kiss of the night air on her feverish skin was overwhelming.

Instead, she clenched her gloved hands into a fist, flexing her fingers in and out as she waited for the forensic technician to correct her mistake.

"It's a Southampton ID for DC Anna Spencer." The woman glanced down at the bag, before lifting it into the air. The artificial lighting hit the plastic and bounced off the surface, making it almost impossible to ascertain anything through the glare. Then, the plastic shifted, and the ID came into focus, sealing the air inside Melissa's lungs. The serious, unsmiling face of Anna Spencer stared back at her.

"I need to see the body," Melissa said, her

stomach rolling violently, threatening to bring the contents of her last meal back up her throat.

"That's not possible right now. We--"

"I don't care what you think is possible. You've just told me we've potentially got the body of a fellow police officer in there. I need to see it. I need to know." There was an edge to Melissa's voice that brooked no argument.

The forensic investigator shook her head. "It's not possible, DI Appleton. There's a protocol..." As an afterthought she added, "As soon as I can let you in, I will. But I'm going to have to insist you wait, until then."

Melissa's shoulders sagged, and she nodded. "Of course." It grated on her nerves to agree with the other woman. The last thing she wanted to do was wait around in the dark for what could be hours, or maybe even days, to get a look at the body they'd found. "I want to know the moment I can see her."

The woman opposite her nodded. The sound of her Tyvek suit rustling against her hair only seemed to add to the absurdity of the situation. They were wrong. They had to be wrong. They'd made a mistake. It wouldn't be the first time that had happened. Somehow, Anna had lost her ID, and it had ended up in the unmarked grave of some poor soul out here in the New Forest National Park.

"Are you all right, guv?" Ayesha asked, following her back to the roadside. "Did you know her?"

"What?" There was an unintentional sharpness to Melissa's voice that she regretted the moment she uttered the word. "Sorry, I just need to make a call."

Ayesha nodded, her gaze unreadable beneath the mask. Melissa turned from her and walked away down the gravel path. She avoided the worst of the puddles as she unzipped the front of her suit and pulled her phone out from the inside pocket of her jacket.

It took a couple of moments for her fingers to stop shaking long enough for her to dial Templeton's number. He answered after the first ring.

"How's it going down there?" he asked, sounding far more relaxed than he had any right to be.

"They've found something important," Melissa said. She hesitated. It was probably just a mistake, like she'd thought. Anna was fine.

"What?" The question was loaded, and all traces of relaxation were gone from Templeton's voice in that one simple word.

"They've found an ID buried with one of the bodies, sir." Melissa sighed, and pressed her hand against her face. This wasn't happening. It couldn't be happening.

"Who is it?"

"Detective Constable Anna Spencer," Melissa breathed. The line was silent, and she pulled the phone away from her ear, glancing down at the screen to make sure they were still connected.

"Are they sure it's her?" A bitter note laced Templeton's voice.

"Sir, with all due respect, they've only just found the body. It might not actually be..."

"When will we know for certain?"

"I don't know," Melissa said helplessly. "They won't let me in there to see her... it.... the body I mean."

"The moment we know for certain, I want you to call me," he said, and the line clicked dead. Melissa tugged the phone away from her ear and contemplated hurling it into the undergrowth. Not that it would do her much good. She shouldn't have expected anything better from him. He'd view her behaviour as nothing more than sentimental nonsense.

She closed her eyes, seeing Anna's smiling face superimposed over the inside of her eyelids.

Her fingers hovered over the screen of her phone again. Chris—Anna's husband—needed to know. He would be heartbroken. They'd been married less than a year.

A lone tear tracked down Melissa's cheek, and she scrubbed it away violently with the back of her hand. Nothing was certain, yet. Anna was still alive. She had to be. Whoever was in there with Anna's ID was just some poor sod who'd met a grizzly end, but it wasn't Anna herself. It wouldn't be her friend. Life wasn't that cruel.

TWO DAYS LATER, Melissa stood on the other side of the metal table in the morgue. She stared down at the covered body, and contemplated turning on her heels and leaving, but she couldn't bring herself to be so cowardly.

Somebody had to identify the body. Well, that wasn't exactly true; the pathologist had already confirmed ID with dental records. DNA would take a little more time, but as far as the rest of the force was concerned, the ID was a done deal.

But not for Melissa. She needed to see her with her own eyes. She couldn't bring herself to believe it was true until she did that.

"Okay," she said, softly. The morgue technician folded the sheet back, revealing light brown hair that beneath the fluorescent lighting appeared darker than it had been in reality. The face was bloated, and discoloured almost beyond recognition, but Melissa could see through the decomposition that had caused skin slippage, the disfiguring ante-mortem, and perimortem bruising to the face of her friend.

"Thanks," she said, her voice cracking as she turned from the body and hurried from the room. She made it to the hall before her legs betrayed her and buckled beneath the crushing grief. Melissa slid down the wall and buried her face in her hands as the tears she'd been holding at bay for days finally tracked down her face.

"Crying isn't going to bring her back." Templeton's icy tone cut through Melissa's grief, and she tilted her chin up to meet his gaze.

"You're a cold and heartless bastard," she hissed. "She was one of ours, and you don't even care. You didn't even know she'd gone missing."

"Neither did you." His voice betrayed the barely restrained rage that bubbled beneath the surface of his impassive exterior. "She knew the risks."

Melissa got to her feet and drew her hand back to lash out at the man in front of her.

At the last second, she pulled herself up short and shook her head. "She didn't deserve this. We failed her. We failed her, and now she's dead." She sighed, the rage abandoning her as quickly as it had arrived, leaving her feeling exhausted. "Did you know she was pregnant?"

Templeton's expression shifted, and he dropped his chin on to his chest as though the floor had suddenly become the most interesting thing in the world. "I heard."

"Someone robbed her of her future."

"It's what they do," the DCI said. "Anna wasn't the only one who lost her life out there. Three other women also lost theirs. Well, I say women, but I don't think I can even call them that. The youngest was fourteen."

"Do you think Anna was trying to get them out?" Melissa asked.

Templeton nodded. "It's probably what got her killed. She always was sentimental. The officer in charge of her undercover operation said she'd got close to some newcomers who match the descriptions of the women we found out there with her."

"Trafficked?"

"That's the general consensus." Silence stretched between them, and Melissa found she couldn't bring herself to meet his gaze any longer.

"We've got to stop them," he said heatedly, and it was then Melissa caught the first glimpse of his true feelings. "They can't be allowed to continue."

He cut off, his voice breaking.

"Sir, I'm sorry..." She hesitated before speaking again, this time in a much lower tone. "Anthony, I'm so sorry." Melissa took a step forward, placing her hand on his arm, the briefest of touches but enough to convey the depth of her feelings.

He glanced up at her, his eyes glassy with unshed tears. "No one is supposed to bury their children, you know?"

Melissa nodded. "I know."

He coughed, clearing his throat violently as he straightened up and dashed a lone tear that had dared to trickle from the corner of his eye. "Sentimentality won't bring her back," he said hoarsely.

"They're not going to let you anywhere near the investigation," Melissa said.

"If they know what's good for them, they'll let me do my job." He turned away, staring at the door that led to the morgue, and to the room where Anna's body lay. Melissa contemplated asking him if he'd seen her and then dismissed the idea as unnecessarily cruel.

Without another word, Templeton strode away down the corridor, leaving Melissa alone.

They wouldn't let him near the investigation, of that much she was certain. But she also knew he would move heaven and earth to bring those responsible for his daughter's untimely death to justice.

And if the powers-that-be knew what was good for them, they would stay out of his way while he did it.

CHAPTER TWO

PRESENT DAY

HEY, beautiful!

Zara glanced down at the phone in her hands, and read the message she'd just received, careful to ignore Poppy's overly dramatic eye roll.

"That isn't Noah *again*, is it?" Poppy asked, placing all the weight of her displeasure into that one small word.

Zara felt the heat creep up into her cheeks as Poppy flopped back on the bed, her tiny body barely putting a dent in the mattress as she cast her hands toward the heavens dramatically.

It wasn't Noah. At least, not this time. But Poppy didn't need to know that. It was Zara's little secret, hers and Jacob's. It was nice to finally meet someone who understood what she was going through. Someone who knew what it was like to be let down by everyone in your life.

"When are you going to learn; that boy only wants one thing from you. You know that, right?" Poppy propped herself up on her elbow, her long fingers playing in her sandy coloured hair.

"You're wrong," Zara said, moving out of her spot on the bed. She crossed the cosy, disordered space of Poppy's bedroom and paused in front of the vanity mirror over the dresser.

Despite the small size of the room, Zara still felt the faint prick of jealousy she always felt when she was here.

Poppy had a bedroom to call her own, and parents who—despite Poppy's protestations to the opposite—loved her madly, and who would have done anything to please their wilful daughter. Zara knew this because it was easy to spot it when you didn't have it yourself.

Poppy didn't understand what it felt like to have the only people in the world who were supposed to have your back, no matter what, turn away from you.

Scooping up one of Poppy's beaded necklaces she'd found draped over the small, silver necklace tree, Zara held it up to her own slender throat.

"What do you think?" She glanced over her shoulder and caught Poppy trying to unlock her phone.

"What the fuck do you think you're doing?" She dropped the necklace and stormed across the room, snatching the phone out of Poppy's hand.

"When did you change your pin-code?" Poppy asked.

Zara couldn't be certain, but there seemed to be a note of hurt in Poppy's voice.

"When the creep started trying to read my phone messages at night while I was asleep." Zara tried to stuff the memory down. Finding her foster father, Matthew, looming over the top of her in the dark—her phone clutched in his sweaty palm while she was supposed to be asleep—was a memory she'd much rather forget. He hadn't tried it on with her or anything, nothing like that, but as far as she was concerned it was probably just a matter of time.

Bouncing around from care home to foster families had taught her more than a few valuable lessons, not least of which being that she should always trust her instincts. And her gut told her Matthew was a creep.

"Oh, my god, why was he doing that? If my parents so much as—"

"Pops, it's dinnertime!" Poppy's mother called up the stairs.

Poppy rolled her eyes and sighed. "The jailer is calling. I suppose I'd better make an appearance down there tonight. You're welcome to stay, if you'd like." Her voice lifted hopefully.

Zara contemplated rejecting the offer, but the thought of returning to a cold, dark house with nobody waiting for her didn't exactly fill her with joy.

"Sure, if your Mum is all right with that."

"She won't care," Poppy said airily, sliding her arm through Zara's. "She'll be happy to have you around, anyway."

"Oh? Why's that?"

"I suppose she thinks you make me happy or something, I don't know." Poppy wafted her hand lazily around in the air.

That drew a small smile from Zara. The joy she felt was short-lived, though, as she remembered Jacob's words when she'd told him about Poppy. He'd been right, of course; Poppy wouldn't understand what they shared.

She let Poppy pull her out the door and down the stairs. Like Jacob said, the girl was spoilt and childish, and she definitely didn't understand how lucky she was.

Poppy released her hold on her arm as soon as they reached the kitchen doorway. "Smells good, Mum!" she said, sidling into the room.

"It's just a few bits I had left over in the freezer," her mother said from her place near the sink, as she scrubbed her hands. "I didn't have time to get the food shop in yet."

As far as Zara was concerned, she couldn't smell

anything other than the eye-watering scent of bleach that hung in the air.

Her gaze drifted to the woman's hands, and the reddened appearance of her fingers as she ran the nail brush back and forth over them, with a viciousness she didn't seem capable of.

It wasn't the first time Zara had seen the woman behave like this, and any attempted to question Poppy about her mother's seeming obsession with cleanliness was usually dismissed with a finger gesture Poppy made along the side of her head, indicating her mother was crazy.

"It's all right if Zars stays for dinner," Poppy said, taking up a place at the table. It wasn't, Zara noticed, a question. She hated it when Poppy called her Zars, but no amount of trying to make her stop had worked.

She watched as Mrs Taylor's back stiffened. The woman raised her attention from her assault on her hands. "Oh, I didn't see you there, Zara," she said, her voice a little more strained than usual.

"Sorry," Zara said. "I can go—"

Mrs Taylor pulled her hands from beneath the water spray as though it were particularly difficult for her and shook her head. "Don't be daft, love. You're more than welcome to stay for dinner. I just hope I've made enough, now. Pops, you should have told me sooner that we were going to have a guest."

Poppy shrugged, not bothering to shift her attention away from the phone in her hand. "It's fine. I don't want to eat much, anyway."

"Oh? And why is that?"

"I've got a competition coming up in a week, and Mrs Lewis said I have to be in tip-top shape if I'm to stand any chance of getting on the podium."

Mrs Taylor tutted and turned back to the sink, where she grabbed a cloth and began vigorously scrubbing the counter.

"I'll never understand why that woman is allowed to get away with the things she says."

Zara darted her gaze over to where Poppy sat and waited for her friend to fire back an answer. But Poppy seemed utterly oblivious to her mother's displeasure. Mrs Taylor caught Zara's eye and smiled kindly.

"You go and take a seat at the table, Zara."

"I can help you get things ready if you'd like." Zara said. It always made her uncomfortable to sit around as others waited on her. She'd lived her whole life always taking care of herself, unlike Poppy who allowed her mother to fuss over her like she was the Queen of Sheba.

"You're too kind, but really I've got it all under control. You sit yourself down and, I'll get everything served up."

Zara did as she was told and surreptitiously pulled her phone from the pocket of her hoodie. She quickly scanned down over the messages Jacob had sent her and did her best to ignore the way her heartbeat sped up over his compliments on her appearance.

Unlike Noah, Jacob was a genuinely nice guy. Not to mention the fact that he was drop dead gorgeous, at least if his videos on Tik Tok were anything to go by. Why anyone like him would be interested in someone like her, was something she couldn't quite fathom. But Poppy had told her she was far too critical of herself. Perhaps she was right.

"Earth to Zara," Poppy said, as she irritatingly shoved her hand under Zara's nose and waggled her fingers to gain her attention. "What are you so engrossed in, anyway?"

"Nothing," Zara said, shoving the phone back into her pocket in order to give her friend her full attention. The last thing she wanted, or needed, was for Poppy to figure out the truth.

Poppy sighed dramatically and shoved her hair back from her face as her mother approached the table with two plates piled high with wedges and what looked like chicken nuggets.

"Those are the vegetarian ones, right?" Poppy eyed the plate her mother placed in front of her suspiciously. "Because I told you last week, I'm not eating meat anymore."

Her mother nodded. "I remember."

Poppy relaxed visibly and beamed up at her mother before she picked one of the breaded nuggets up with her fingers. She bit into it and her face crumpled in disgust before she spat the partially chewed nugget back onto the plate.

"Oh, God, these are disgusting!"

Zara didn't have any such compunction about the food, and she started to eat with enthusiasm as Poppy complained loudly. There had been far too many days in the not-so-distant past when Zara hadn't known where her next meal was coming from. It was amazing what a little scarcity could do to rid someone of being too picky.

"Well, Zara seems to think they're all right," Mrs Taylor said.

"Zara's like a dustbin, she'll eat anything you put in front of her," Poppy said. "And anyway, she can eat crap like that. She's not on the team, so she doesn't need to watch her weight."

Zara shifted uncomfortably in her seat and tugged self-consciously at the front of her hoodie. At the best of times, she wasn't exactly comfortable with the soft curves of her body. And not even Jacob telling her she was beautiful had helped to put her fears to bed. When she looked in the mirror, she could see all of her flaws, even if he couldn't.

She let the sound of mother and daughter bickering fade into the background as she munched through the food on her plate. When Poppy shoved up suddenly from her place at the table, she started.

"What's—" She never had the chance to finish

her sentence as her friend stormed out the room and stomped up the stairs. A couple of seconds later the sound of the bedroom door slamming shut echoed through the house as Mrs Taylor sighed and dropped down into the chair her daughter had vacated.

"Don't ever have kids, Zara," Mrs Taylor said. The woman looked utterly exhausted.

Zara wondered if perhaps she should ask her if everything was all right, but she couldn't quite bring herself to form the words. Instead, she smiled awkwardly, and pushed her empty plate away.

"Thanks for the food, I really appreciate it." It was the truth. She did appreciate it. She could count on one hand the number of adults who had ever taken any kind of interest in her wellbeing. Well, apart from her new foster parents, Rebecca, and Matthew, but that was just crap. Jacob had said they were just playing her, in it for the money, and he was probably right. After all, they were always arguing about cash, and the lack of it when they thought she couldn't hear them.

"There's plenty more if you want it." Mrs Taylor said wryly, as she eyed Zara up and down. The urge to accept the woman's kind offer hovered on the tip of her tongue but, Poppy's harsh words rose up unbidden in her mind and she shook her head.

"I'm fine, I've got to head home, anyway."

Mrs Taylor nodded. "Of course. How are things at home now?"

Taken aback, Zara felt heat rise up her face as she stuttered through a half-hearted answer about everything being just fine. There was only one reason Mrs Taylor would ask her about her life at home, and that was because Poppy couldn't keep her mouth shut.

"Well, I'm glad to hear that," she said.

Zara couldn't be entirely sure about it, but Mrs Taylor didn't seem as interested as she'd first feared.

She made it to the door with no further questions.

"Thanks again," she said, as she pulled open the front door, and stepped out into darkness without waiting for a reply.

AN HOUR LATER, Zara hid beneath the thin duvet on her bed, and shivered as the cold air in the house slowly seeped into her bones. At least there had been no need to field any questions about her whereabouts this evening.

That was the good thing about having the place to herself most evenings. Of course, the downside of that was that she didn't have access to any heat.

Then again, living here was still better than living with her mother; not that she'd ever admit that aloud to anyone. As much as she loved her mother, she understood that getting away from her was for the best. Because no matter how much Zara tried to help her, or prove her love for her, none of it was ever reciprocated.

Not that it could be helped. Mum was ill, plain and simple. Addiction was an illness. One that made you selfish, and a poor judge of character, and Mum was all of those things and so much more.

Sorry, I've been AWOL. Was over at Poppy's house. Zara's thumbs flew over the screen as she typed the message.

The reply was almost instantaneous.

Cool. You 2 have fun?

I suppose. Missed chatting with u though. Zara's finger hovered over the send button before she finally built up the nerve to send it. What would he think of her?

The silence was almost deafening as she waited for a response, something, anything to let her know that he didn't think she was weird for saying it.

I missed u 2.

The response when it came made her sigh as her heart did a small flip in her chest. Her phone vibrated in her hand, and she glanced down at the screen.

Maybe we should meet? U know, in reality.

Zara's breath caught in the back of her throat.

Been 8 wks now. I want to c u. I want to kiss u 4 real.

She set the phone down and laid back on the

pillow, as her heart continued to hammer in her chest. Was this what she wanted?

She knew the answer, of course. Jacob was everything all the other boys weren't. He was sweet, and smart, and for some reason he genuinely seemed interested in what she had to say. But she wasn't a fool either. She'd heard enough horror stories to know what happened to girls who met people from the internet.

Not that Jacob was a creep.

Picking up her phone, she flipped through the pictures until she came to the one she wanted.

The black and white screenshot of the boy in the video grinned back at her, his dark hair artfully tousled. And even though his face was heavily made up to reflect his Tik Tok OC, his eyes still sparked with the mischievous personality Zara associated with him.

Not yet, but soon. x. Zara typed the message quickly and hit send before she had the chance to bottle it.

U don't trust me?

As soon as the message arrived, she knew she'd hurt him.

I do trust u. I'm just not ready.

K. I understand. Got 2 Go. Talk later. x.

Deflated, Zara scrubbed the back of her hand over the corner of her eye to brush aside her tears. She'd blown it. The urge to reply and tell him she was wrong was overwhelming, but she bit it back. It would do nothing but make her look desperate, and if there was one thing she had learned after going out with Noah, it was that guys did not like desperate girls.

Wrapping her arms around her chest, she curled up in the bed and closed her eyes, allowing her salty tears to run into the pillow.

CHAPTER THREE

SURREPTITIOUSLY, DS Maz Arya slipped into a seat near the back of the room. It was just typical that he'd got here so late. If he was lucky, then DCI Templeton's hawkish gaze wouldn't notice his tardiness. Of course, if the DCI's recent behaviour was any kind of gauge, then Maz knew he wouldn't be so lucky. The man was like some kind of terminator, and nothing slipped under his radar.

"I know many of you believe that here in North Yorkshire we don't have a problem with human trafficking. But it's that kind of sloppy attitude that has seen the scum who run such operations flourishing." The conference room remained silent as Templeton carried on with what could only be described as a diatribe.

Maz sank lower in his seat and let his eyes roam over the grouping of people who had been hand-picked for the new task force. As far as he was concerned, there was one very obvious officer missing; not that Templeton cared what he thought.

Maz caught sight of Olivia. Her warm honey hair reflected the overhead lights, and he wondered why he'd never noticed how pretty she was.

"And that's why I've decided we're going to go back to basics here. I want you out, pounding the pavements, and getting to know the local people." Maz's attention snapped back to Templeton. The man had clearly lost his mind. This might be how they worked down south, but this definitely wasn't going to fly with the locals up here. One look at their lot, and the locals would have their guts for garters. Not a chance would they want to discuss anything with a bunch of coppers.

He crossed his arms over his chest and contemplated the match scores from the night before as Templeton started to wind up his speech.

Maz waited until everyone else in the room moved, before he too climbed to his feet. Before Olivia could leave, he pushed through the crowd and paused next to her. "What did you make of that?"

She turned toward him, her hazel eyes widening in surprise before a smile flickered to life on her face. "I'd never thought we had such a huge problem here," she said honestly. "I knew it was an issue, but I thought it was more nationwide."

Maz nodded. "If he thinks we're going to get anyone to talk to us..."

"It sounds a little off the wall, but he's right." The woman next to Olivia spoke up. Her platinum hair brushed against the collar of her white shirt as she rolled her shoulders.

"Melissa, right?" Maz asked, inwardly hoping that he'd got the name correct. It would just like him to get tongue-tied and screw it all up.

"DI Melissa Appleton," she said brightly, holding her hand out toward him. "I don't think we've been formally introduced."

Maz took her hand in his, surprised at the strength of her grip as she met his gaze head on with her icy blue eyes. Only the smile she wore told him it wasn't a challenge, but he'd seen her type before and knew how easily that could change. "I guess around here we're not really supposed to be formal. We're all on the same side..." He let her hand go and cursed inwardly at his own stupidity.

Melissa smiled politely. "Like I was saying, Templeton might sound a little zealous, but his heart is in the right place."

Maz caught Olivia side-eyeing the woman next to her and found himself wishing that Dr Quinn was here to break down the thoughts of those around him. He wasn't the doctor's biggest fan, but there were times when her uncanny perceptiveness about her fellow teammates came in handy.

"You knew him from before?" Olivia asked, as she shrugged into the navy jacket she'd slung over the back of her chair.

"Only by reputation," Melissa said with a small chuckle. "Everyone knew he was going places. And he'd moved up by the time I joined the team down in Southampton," Melissa said, lowering her voice as though concerned those around them might hear her confession. "But that was a long time ago, and from what I can tell, he doesn't seem to have changed much. He was just as interested in trafficking then."

"Arya!" Templeton's voice cut through the melee. Maz's heart sank as he met the DCI's gaze across the room. Shit, he knew. How did he always know when he was late?

"You know, maybe you should set your alarm to go off earlier," Olivia said with a smirk.

"Was I that obvious?"

She grinned at him. "Oh yeah. I thought Templeton was going to blow his top then and there." She nudged him toward the DCI. "Best just to get it over with."

Maz hung his head and crossed the room. When he'd worked with Drew, nobody had cared that he was sometimes a few minutes late. But since he'd joined the task force, it seemed to be the only thing Templeton was interested in.

"Sir, you wanted to see me?" Maz kept his voice low but met the DCI's intense scrutiny head on.

"My office, Arya."

Maz followed the DCI into his corner office without another word. He bit his tongue as he shut the door and then took the seat the DCI indicated he should have. Maz fought the urge to knit his fingers together in his lap. His mother had always told him it was a bad habit, not to mention the fact that it gave away just how nervous he was feeling, and Templeton really didn't need any more ammunition against him right now.

"Do you like being here, DS Arya?" Templeton's tone was mild, and if Maz hadn't seen the man in action before, he might have been fooled into believing the DCI didn't really care to hear his answer.

"I'm thrilled to have the opportunity, Sir."

"Your actions don't exactly say that. In fact, I don't think you really want to be here."

"Sir, I want to be here."

"There are other police officers—better police officers—who would have given their right arm for the opportunity you're currently pissing up the wall. So, you can see why I'm finding it so hard to believe you, Arya."

Maz nodded. It would be easier to tell him the truth; to just come clean, but Maz found the words sticking in the back of throat. "Sir, I'll make a concerted effort to prove to you that I want this position."

Templeton seemed to contemplate his words before he finally gave a curt nod. "Fine. Consider this your final warning, Arya. The next time you won't find me so accommodating."

Maz pushed onto his feet, but Templeton waved him back into his seat. "Am I right to believe you know York, and the surrounding towns well?"

"Well, as much as anyone can..."

"I want you to get Appleton up to speed on what you know of the area." Templeton placed his elbows on the table and leaned toward Maz. "This is important, Arya, I don't want you to mess this up with your lackadaisical attitude. We've been led to believe there is something going down here in the next few weeks. I want us to get ahead of it, but we'll only do that with local cooperation, do you understand?"

Maz nodded and pressed his fingers together in his lap. He'd always wanted more responsibility, but now that it was being given to him, he suddenly wished he didn't feel so exposed. If Drew were here, he would know exactly what next move to make. If anyone could coordinate something so complicated, it was DI Haskell.

"I won't let you down, sir." Maz pushed onto his feet and made his way to the door. He paused, hand on the door handle.

"Is there something else, Arya?" Templeton asked.

Maz contemplated confronting the other man about his refusal to hire on DI Haskell to the team. But he was already on thin ice. If he went out on a limb for Drew, he might be condemning his own career. It was a risk he couldn't take, at least not right now. There would be time enough for questions when Templeton didn't view him with such abject contempt.

"Nothing, sir." Guilt washed over Maz as he left the office and re-joined the others who had gathered at a set of desks in the corner of the room. He was being a coward, but simply admitting that to himself wasn't enough to make him march back into Templeton's office and confront his SIO. It seemed he would be a coward a little longer. Tomorrow might be a better day to try.

As he reached the desk, he realised Melissa had already laid a couple of maps covering York, Scarborough, Whitby, Loftus, and the surrounding areas out on the desk. Maz opened his mouth to ask her how she'd known and then changed his mind. He might not be as perceptive as Dr Quinn, but he wasn't a fool either.

When Melissa had said she'd known of Templeton in the past, Maz had the uncomfortable feeling that she hadn't been entirely honest about everything.

"Templeton wants me to get you up to speed on the area," Maz said lightly. Perhaps if she admitted to her prior knowledge, then it would at least give him a reason to trust her now.

"Great," she said. "Looks like my hunch was correct." She gestured to the map she'd laid out. "I guess no time like the present. Shall we break this down into something more manageable?"

Maz nodded as his stomach sank into his boots. She hadn't admitted that she'd known what Templeton was planning, and it set alarm bells off in his head.

As he settled into the seat opposite her, he couldn't keep his mind from straying back to the disturbing discovery he'd made over her lies. Aside from an uncomfortable feeling, he didn't have much to go on.

But there was one thing he did know for certain: working with an SIO he suspected of deceit wasn't going to be easy. But until he was in possession of more substantial evidence regarding the game DI Appleton was playing, he would just have to play along, and hope that nothing happened in the meantime to threaten the safety of the rest of the team.

CHAPTER FOUR

THE BLACK HOOD over her face scratched and tickled her skin. Naomi longed to reach a hand up and relieve herself of the maddening itch that threatened to send her already frazzled mind into hysteria.

She'd barely clung to sanity as it was.

The drugs they had given her were fading, leaving only the cramping in her stomach and the pain in her head for company. Oblivion had been better than this. Whatever this was?

The men who owned her spoke in hushed tones around her, the sound pulling her further from her comatose state.

One stupid mistake. That was all it had taken for the world to come crashing down on her head.

There had been a time when Naomi hadn't been afraid of bad things happening. She'd felt invincible, as if nothing could ever touch her.

Fool! The thoughts were bitter as they swirled in her mind.

She shuddered, the cold metal of the van floor against her exposed skin bringing a flush of gooseflesh to the surface. How long had she lain here? The drugs had addled her mind, but even now she longed to feel the pinch of the needle and the sting of nothingness it offered. It was easier that way. Always easier that way.

She tried to remember how long she'd been here, but found her mind failed her in even this simple task. A small whimper wriggled out past her dry, chapped lips and her fear skyrocketed.

"Shut it," the voice in the dark taunted her, and she instinctively cringed inwards in anticipation of another vicious blow.

Thankfully, it didn't come... this time at least.

"Just apologise." Grace's words echoed in her mind. It was the smart thing to do. English wasn't her strong suit, but she'd learned the word 'sorry' quickly enough. It was amazing what you could learn when your survival depended on it. But Naomi had a feeling that no simple apology would get her out of this.

The van jolted and juddered over rough terrain. She'd felt the difference the moment they had left the road behind. It was now or never. *I'm sorry...* Her voice rasped, and the words came out as an unintelligible moan. Pain erupted in her mouth as she tried to move her lips. Her throat burned, a vicious combination of dehydration and the punishment they'd inflicted on her.

"I said shut up." Something hit her in the dark, and she cringed, rolling her body in on itself to shield herself from anymore blows.

Even if she'd known the words to form, she knew she wouldn't be capable of speaking to them; they had seen to that.

Despite the darkness surrounding her, Naomi squeezed her dry, gritty eyes shut in an attempt to drive out the horror of the memories that plagued her. They had known just what to do to break her. And as much as she tried to keep the memories of what had happened from her mind, she couldn't. Without the safety of the drugs in her system, she was like a raw nerve; exposed over and over to the harsh reality of what had happened to her.

Even now, she could feel their weight on her small frame, feel their moist, eager breath on her feverish skin.

Panic clawed at her, threatening to overwhelm every last rational thought she had left.

No!

She shut the memory out, sealing herself inside her own mind. No matter what happened, she didn't have to be a part of it. She tried to think of simpler things, happier times; anything just to cure herself of the vile imagery that danced on the inside of her eyelids.

She tried harder to block it all out, concentrating instead on those she loved.

The sound of her sister's laughter; crystal clear, high-pitched and gleeful. Marissa was always laughing...

It had been so long. Months... Maybe longer since she had held her in her arms. Would she ever see her again? They had stolen so much from her already.

She shivered, the cold of the van interrupting her thoughts. No, she could do this. She could take herself away from here, to another place. A place where nothing they did to her mattered. With her eyes closed she tried to imagine the cold receding, replaced by the touch of a summer breeze. The pain in her mouth and throat became the bitter tang of a not yet ripe plum—

Something touched her leg, ripping her from her memories, and she cringed, drawing her knees toward her chest. The laughter in the van mocked her terror, and she longed for the ability to cry. But her tears had long since dried.

"This is not the end. This is not your end." Naomi repeated the words over in her mind like a mantra.

It took her a moment to register that the van had stopped moving.

"We can't give her anymore, or we risk killing

her." The men, as they argued, intruded on her thoughts.

"And if we don't? Then what?"

"There's four of us, and one of her. It wasn't such a problem holding her earlier, and she fought like a wildcat, then."

The van door opened, bringing with it a fresh blast of air. There was something familiar about it, something that tugged on the dark corner of her mind. She knew the scent in the air, knew it as it stung her bruised skin.

Strong hands grabbed her legs, and she struggled instinctively, kicking and lashing against the unwanted touch.

There was a grunt of pain as the heel of her bare foot struck something soft and vital, and she found herself hoping it had done him some damage.

Cold metal pressed against the back of her neck, and she froze against the floor of the van.

"Do that again, and I'll make sure Marissa pays for your misbehaviour."

Naomi would have known his voice anywhere, she'd heard it echo often enough in her nightmares, and it was seared into her memory. He pressed the gun against her skin, as though to emphasise the seriousness of his words, but more than the kiss of the metal against her neck, it was the threat that caused her to cease her struggling.

He'd been the one who had promised her a better

life. It felt like an eternity ago since she had agreed to the plan. The worst mistake she'd ever made. It didn't matter that her reason for agreeing to his terms were so her family could have a better life, that she would eventually fulfil her dream and go to school to study teaching. But to think that he might do to Marissa all the things he had done to her. It was too horrible to comprehend, and Naomi felt the last of her sanity crumbling beneath the weight of his words.

She wanted to scream at him, to beg him to leave her sister be, but her words were incomprehensible. Blood and saliva drooled from her mouth as she moaned into the hood covering her head.

His laughter was cruel. "Didn't I tell you? Marissa is coming to join you... Well, she *was* going to join you, until you screwed everything up." He leaned over her, the gun digging into the base of her skull. "Remember the fun we had? How do you think Marissa will do? I hope she learns faster than you did. Getting you bitches over here isn't cheap, and you've turned out to be a complete waste."

The memory of it now felt like a fever dream, something so far away, so improbable that it was impossible to believe it had ever been real. He had been the one to turn her dreams to ash. He'd been the first to press her into the stinking mattress back in the dank basement; he'd said it was necessary to test the merchandise. To think of him doing the same thing to her innocent little sister was too much to bear. She contemplated fighting him, but it was a fruitless task. Instead, she needed a plan.

A hand grabbed her upper arm and jerked her painfully upright. She went with them without a fight, her numb legs buckling beneath her as they dragged her from the van. She hit the hard ground without so much as a whimper.

Naomi recognised the sound of the sea before she recognised the scent of the seaweed and salt. That was why it was so familiar. She'd been to the beach once when she was a child, swimming and floating in the cold greenish grey waters. What had once been a pleasant childhood memory, was now an alien landscape fraught with unseen dangers, and certain death.

"Get her off the ground and down to the boat."

The sand beneath her hands bit into her palms and knees. But that didn't bother her. Hearing him speak of putting her on a boat, however, had struck pure terror into her heart. They would not take her home. They would not let her go when her debt was repaid, as they'd promised. The realisation hit her like a punch to the stomach, and Naomi knew she would never see her sister again. Never hear her cousins' voices as they chattered excitedly.

Never feel the warmth of her mother's arms around her shoulders as she turned to her for comfort. A part of her had known it was impossible the moment Dimitri had pressed the tip of the needle into her skin. She had known everything she'd ever held dear was gone the first time they'd forced her to bed with a large, unshaven man who stank of cheap alcohol and body odour.

But when the opportunity had presented itself, in the form of a person she had believed to be a sympathetic businessman who had treated her with kindness, she had taken it. Despite the warning they'd given her that if she ever spoke the truth, they would kill her.

Despite the risk, she had told him her story in what little broken English she had. And his shock had given her hope. Brought her the first shred of foolish optimism that her ordeal would soon be over. And then Dimitri had come for her with his silent, seething rage that had ravaged her body.

The part of her that hoped for rescue knew now that if she got on the boat death would follow, and at Dimitri's hands it would be slow and agonising. And then he would have her sister. Use Marissa up, just as he had done her.

The realisation hit her like a ton of bricks, and she felt the air disappear from her lungs as though somebody had punched her.

They dragged her onto unsteady feet, their fingers digging into her soft bruised flesh. The pain helped to clear her head, helped to solidify the plan in her mind. One last chance to escape. One final moment to risk it all.

Her heartbeat thudded in her ears, as the darkness the hood offered became a suffocating tomb.

"Shit, who the fuck is that?" One of the men nearest to her whispered furiously.

Someone urged her to move a little faster, but the grip they had on her wasn't as secure. The moment she felt their fingers slide from her, she willed her body to move, to run in any direction she could.

"Fuck!" The muttered curse from behind her as she slipped out of their grasp and ran blind. She darted in the direction of what she hoped was safety, but the moment she felt the cold water of the sea against her bare feet, she knew she'd calculated incorrectly.

Something heavy slammed into her back, tackling her to the ground. Salt water soaked through the hood, pouring into her nose and mouth as her attacker's weight pressed her into the surf.

Gagging, she kicked and lashed, desperate to catch her breath. He lifted her free of the ground, and bile raced up the back of Naomi's throat as she choked on the sea water, which had very nearly drowned her.

Her father had once told her it was possible to drown in a teaspoon of water. She hadn't believed him at the time, but now she wasn't so certain.

"Get her on the boat, and I'll deal with him," Dimitri said. His callous words struck a chord within her, leaving her colder than the freezing waters ever could have. Out of them all, he was the one who truly frightened her because she knew he was capable of anything.

"Leave him. He's just a druggie, he's probably so high he won't even remember this in the morning."

"We can't leave any witnesses." Dimitri's words sent a chill down her spine that had nothing to do with the icy water which had soaked through her clothes.

"Get her in the boat now. I'll join you once I've got things here squared away."

The man holding her jerked her off the ground, and she fought against him. His grip was unrelenting, but still she struggled.

"Here." Dimitri spoke again, only this time he was closer. "This is a kindness, Naomi, for all the fun we shared once." Rough fingers jerked her arm out straight, and the sting of a needle sliding beneath her skin caused her to cry out silently. This wasn't what she wanted. Tears squeezed out between her dry, gritty lashes as the effects of the drug they had administered swept through her body.

It spread to her limbs, causing them to go limp. Her skin felt feverishly hot, and she shivered uncontrollably, but her mind remained—at least for now—untouched by the drug.

The arms holding her seemed to melt away; the ground passing swiftly beneath her, and she was only vaguely aware of the splash of salt water against her exposed skin.

When she came to, the bobbing of the water beneath the boat rolled her stomach. Acid like vomit raced up her throat, and she struggled to sit up, but her body refused to cooperate.

The image of her mother's face—tear streaked and grief-stricken—danced in front of her eyes; mocking the state she found herself in. Marissa's desperate and pain laden cries echoed in her ears.

"Get her up before she chokes." The voices were far away, and for that Naomi was grateful. They lifted her upright, propping her against the side of the boat, but she was only vaguely aware of the push and pull of their hands on her body.

"Hold on to the edge. There, have you got it?" Were they talking to her? The feel of them placing her hands on the guide rail felt as though it was all happening to someone else's body. Some other poor unfortunate who had found herself caught up in this mess. Not her. It wasn't real. It couldn't be real.

The hood was tugged off her head, and the cold air slapped her in the face, bringing with it a momentary burst of clarity. Blinking against the surrounding darkness, it took her a moment to realise it was nighttime, and that they were in fact on some kind of boat. The red light at the end of a pier blinked at her in the distance, as it swam in and out of focus.

She stared over the side of the boat, down into

the inky waters. It would be infinitely easier to give up now. To just let go and drop over the edge into the waiting oblivion. But she owed Marissa more than that.

The hands holding her let go. It only took a moment. Using the last of her strength, Naomi tilted forward, letting gravity do the rest.

She hit the water, and the icy shock seared through her. She opened her mouth.

Darkness clawed at her, and she let it. With the last vestiges of strength, she fought against the pull of the water. But Dimitri and his drug filled needles had robbed her of that. There was no fight left in her body, just the overwhelming joy that she had at least thwarted Dimitri of his prize. The plans he'd whispered in her ear, of all the pain he would inflict on her, would now never come to pass

She sank, letting the water pull her down. At least here she was safe at last.

CHAPTER FIVE

HARRIET STARED down into the cup on the counter in her kitchen. While she wasn't entirely certain that today was in fact the day that Drew returned to North Yorkshire CID, it seemed the most likely. The last time she'd spoken to him, he'd seemed more withdrawn than usual, and she couldn't help the nervousness that fluttered in her stomach.

She had no illusions that he would be the same man he had been before his run in with Nolan Matthews. Experiencing something as traumatic as that would undoubtedly leave scars. She could only hope that he would talk about it. If not to her, then to someone who could help him understand and develop coping skills.

It was hypocritical of her to think like this. After the traumatic situation she'd found herself in, she hadn't sought out the help of anyone. It was probably foolish of her, and no doubt it would come back to bite her in the behind somewhere down the line.

But for now, at least, she felt as though she had a handle on the residual panic, and fear she'd been left with. She consoled herself with the idea that it was easier for somebody like her to cope. After all, she'd read all the books, done the training necessary. If she couldn't figure out her own trauma, then how could she expect somebody else to do it?

Arrogant. Shaking her head, she lifted the cup to her lips and drained the last of the coffee as the phone on the marble counter next to her rang. Harriet contemplated allowing the machine to pick it up. Glancing down at her watch, she noted the lateness of the hour. Being late again would do nothing to win her any favours with Martha.

Then again, she'd long since concluded that there wasn't much you could do to change the mind of somebody who had already formed an opinion of you. Setting the cup down, she picked the receiver up and pressed it to her ear.

"Yes?" Habits it seemed died hard, and despite Martha's pleadings with her, she still had done nothing to improve her abrupt phone manner.

"Dr Quinn?" The voice on the other end of the line was silky and gentle. "Is that Dr Harriet Quinn?"

"Speaking. Can I ask who this is?" Harriet fought

the suspicion that rose within her. It seemed she hadn't quite resolved all the negative emotions associated with her past trauma, and it chose now to resurface like a bad penny.

"I'm so glad I caught you." The stranger sounded relieved, and the small laugh she emitted made Harriet want to smile right along with her. "I was worried you would already have left. My name is Dr Chakrabarti--" There was a pause on the other end of the line, as though the woman expected Harriet to fill in the rest of the information.

The name rang a bell in the recess of Harriet's mind, but her thoughts were too focused on Drew and his potential mental state that she found herself incapable of figuring out why the name was so familiar. "I'm sorry, do I know you?"

Dr Chakrabarti laughed again, creating an image in Harriet's mind of somebody who took great pleasure in their lives. The sound was easy, and left Harriet in no doubt that this was something the strange doctor did quite a bit. "I suppose it's foolish of me to think you would know who I was. Considering the work you do with Yorkshire CID, I imagine you're a very busy woman, and in heavy demand."

Harriet bit her tongue and wished she had let the machine take the call after all.

"I'm one of the psychiatrists the defence assigned to Nolan Matthews' team."

The blood in Harriet's veins ran cold, and she gripped the counter with her free hand. She should have been expecting a call like this. If she allowed herself the luxury to think about it, a call like this was an inevitability. After all, she had been the one to promise Nolan that she would visit him in prison. Had she not promised him help to control his darker impulses? She had created a rapport with him, told him a secret that she had shared with nobody else. It only made sense that someone would come looking for her sooner rather than later.

"I'm not sure there's anything I can do to--"

"I was rather hoping there was something you could do for me; or rather Nolan." Dr Chakrabarti cut Harriet off before she could make an excuse to worm out of the conversation. "Nolan would like to see you."

"I don't think that would a good idea."

"Actually, I, and the others, believe it would be very helpful if you did come to see him. He seems quite taken with you. It was, after all, you who saved his life, Dr Quinn. An experience like that can create quite an intense bond, and to ignore something like that in somebody such as Nolan Matthews would be foolhardy."

"It's for that exact reason I believe it would be a mistake if I were to visit Mr Matthews," Harriet kept her tone brusque and professional; it was the only defence she had against the memories Dr

Chakrabarti's call had brought to the surface of her mind.

Facing down your own possible demise was harrowing. But when she'd walked into Drew's plastic covered living room and saw him secured to the chair, his body bloodied and battered, it had cut her to the core. The powerful emotions she'd felt as a direct result had taken her by surprise. He'd become somebody important to her, and that knowledge had crept up on her.

"Nolan has suggested that you made some kind of bargain with him, that you--"

"You have my answer, Dr Chakrabarti."

"Think about it."

"I'm a busy woman, Dr Chakrabarti, as I'm sure you are too. I don't want to waste your time by making you think there is hope of my visiting Nolan when I really have no intention of it. Please take my refusal for what it is. I have no intention of changing my mind." Before the other woman could say another word, Harriet ended the call.

Setting the phone down, she pressed her head into her hands and sucked a deep breath in through her nose. It never ceased to amaze her how memories could trigger such intense emotional responses. The phone started to ring again, and Harriet stared down at it as though it were some large hairy spider that had just tried to scuttle over her foot.

Pushing it away with the tip of her finger, she

climbed to her feet and moved to the door. Grabbing her bag, she cocked her head to the side and listened as the answering machine kicked in automatically.

With her keys in one hand, Harriet stepped out into the brisk winter morning and let the door slam shut behind her, effectively drowning out Dr Chakrabarti's message.

CHAPTER SIX

PC LYLA PEARSON stared down at the display of pastries and cakes that filled the cabinet in *Bothams*. Not that she needed something so calorie laden. Just the week before, Greg had told her she was getting a little thick around the middle.

Not that he was one to talk. She couldn't remember a time when he'd ever bothered with the ever-expanding nature of his waistband. But that was the problem, it was different for blokes. They could do whatever they wanted, eat whatever they wanted, and nobody would ever bat an eyelid. But God forbid she enjoyed one too many lemon buns...

"What'll it be, love?" the woman behind the counter asked, her smile broad and welcoming.

"I'll have two of the lemon buns," Lyla said. Damn Greg and his opinions, anyway. "And two coffees to go, please."

The woman behind the counter nodded. Lyla stared out the front window of the shop, studying the faces of those who passed up and down the rain slicked street. If something didn't come in soon, then Lyla was certain the day would be little more than a washout.

Not that she really minded. No news was often good news. But she missed the frisson of excitement she'd had when she worked in Manchester. There was always something happening there.

"There you are, love." The crinkle of the paper bag with the lemon buns inside brought Lyla back from her reverie. With a grateful smile, she took the proffered items and pulled her money from her pocket as the woman behind the counter totted it all up.

A few moments later, Lyla pushed out onto the street. The icy rain slapped into her face, and she pushed her nose down inside her collar as she walked into the wind. Balancing her cup on the top of the car, she clamped the paper bag between her teeth and tugged open the car door. Heat rolled out toward her, and she slipped into the passenger seat. The air vents directly in front of her blasted against her skin, making her face feel tight and dry. It was just one of the many things she disliked about winter.

"What did you get me?" PC Kai Blake—or Nippy, as he was more affectionately known by his friends on the force—tried to grab the paper bag of buns from her. Jerking her head away, she thrust the still hot cup of coffee out toward him. "You didn't want anything."

"Yeah, well, I changed my mind."

"Nippy, if you say you don't want anything, then I'm just going to take you at your word."

He pouted, his lower lip thrust out; an attempt to make himself appear as pathetic as possible. And just like always, Lyla felt a grin slide across her face. "Fine, you can have one of my buns."

"Ace!" Before she could stop him, he snatched the packet from her and tore open the paper. Despite not yet figuring out where the nickname 'Nippy' had come from, Lyla suspected that it stemmed from his ability to always get the best food before anybody else got a look in.

"Would it kill you to act like a normal girl for once and get something smothered in chocolate?" He lifted one bun free of the packaging and sniffed it disdainfully. "You know I'm not keen on lemon."

"Nobody said you had to eat it."

Nippy shrugged and rammed the bun—whole—into his mouth. Rolling her eyes, Lyla turned her attention to the street as she took her own lemon bun out and nibbled delicately around the edge. The sweet enriched dough melted against her tongue, the sultanas adding an extra layer of spiced flavour that complemented the sweet icing smeared across the top. From the corner of her eye, she spied Nippy licking his fingers clean.

"For someone who says they don't like lemons, you sure finished that off in a hurry."

"I've learned to eat at speed," he said. "Can't risk a call out in the middle of my elevenses."

As though just by saying it aloud could conjure a job out of thin air, the radio crackled to life and the voice of the operator filled the car as she directed them to a job in Newholm.

"See, told you," he said smugly as he started the engine.

With a sigh, Lyla eyed the rest of the bun and considered saving it for later. Instead, she followed Nippy's example and stuffed the last of the bun into her mouth.

"Get in!" Nippy grinned from ear to ear as he steered the patrol car out into the street. Lyla clamped her hand over her mouth and tried to stop the crumbs from escaping as she grinned in response.

HALF AN HOUR LATER, Lyla stood on the doorstep of a one Ms Dunsly. The two-storey cottage was silent as she rapped on the bright blue door. Nippy disappeared around the side of the house, as Lyla took a step back and peered up at the darkened windows. At least the rain had stopped.

Grabbing her radio, she called it in and waited for the operator to respond. The sound of a bolt being drawn back pulled her attention toward the door. A small gap appeared, and a wide-eyed woman appeared wrapped in a red dressing gown.

"Ms Dunsly? My name is PC Pearson."

"Can I see some identification?" Despite the pallor of the woman hiding in the doorway, Lyla was surprised to find her voice was steady. The uniform was usually enough to allay any fears the public had, but clearly Ms Dunsly was badly shaken up and required extra reassurance.

There was a rattling sound from the back of the property. Lyla didn't think it was possible for Ms Dunsly to get any paler, and she gripped the door until her fingers turned white. "What was that?"

"That's just my partner," Lyla said, hoping she was correct in her assumption. "PC Blake is just ensuring the property is secure. You have nothing to worry about."

The frantic sound of a dog barking from deeper within the cottage drew Ms Dunsly away from the door. "Freddy, no!"

Lyla pushed the door open with the toe of her boot and watched as Ms Dunsly disappeared down the hall. She followed her inside carefully. "Ms Dunsly, if you have a dog loose on the property, please secure it."

Silence greeted her, and she paused in the hall,

unsure about going any deeper. If an angry dog came around the corner, she would only have a split second to get back out the front door and the corridor was quite narrow, which would hamper her escape. A noise from deep within the property caused Lyla's heart rate to speed up. Tentatively, she took a step back toward the front door. She'd been bitten by a dog once when she was a child; a severe enough encounter that it had required fourteen stitches to close the ragged wound on the calf of her leg. If she could help it, she would avoid a similar outcome.

"I've locked Freddy in the back room," Ms Dunsly said, appearing at the bottom of the hall.

"And Freddy is your dog?" Lyla asked. It was always safer to clarify things, that way if something went wrong, she could at least be prepared.

"He's a good boy, but he gets spooked..." Ms Dunsly glanced down at herself. "I think he's upset because I was. You know dogs are very sensitive creatures."

Lyla nodded sympathetically. "Do you want to tell me what happened?"

Ms Dunsly's head snapped up, irritation reflected in her eagle-eyed gaze. "Didn't they tell you? Somebody tried to break in--"

"They mentioned that," Lyla said. "I just want to hear it in your words..."

"Whoever it was is long gone," Nippy said from the doorway. Lyla fought the urge to jump. She'd been so intent on Ms Dunsly she hadn't heard him return from his initial inspection of the property.

"That's because it took you lot so long to get here," Ms Dunsly said, her temper now evident in her tone of voice. "I can't believe they didn't tell you about the break-in."

"I can assure you, Ms Dunsly, we were informed about the break-in. I'm merely trying to a hear the facts from you."

Ms Dunsly glanced up at her, and beneath the angry facade, Lyla could see that the other woman was terrified. The way she gripped her dressing gown, drawing it tighter around her body as though that alone could keep her safe. Lyla had never been in the kind of situation Ms Dunsly had just experienced, but she'd been involved in her share of incidents when she'd worked in Manchester. Enough to know it must be terrifying to feel so vulnerable. Ms Dunsly had the same look in her eyes as the other women involved in the recent spate of burglaries in Scarborough and York.

"I can make you some tea," Lyla said, hoping that a strong cup of sweet tea would restore some of Ms Dunsly's equilibrium to her, at least enough of it that they could get the facts of the matter.

"The kitchen is through there," Ms Dunsly said, waving her hand in the general direction of the end of the hall. "If it's all right with you, I'd much prefer to get dressed. I feel ridiculous standing here in my nightclothes."

"Of course," Lyla said with a warm smile. "You get dressed, and I'll make some tea."

Ms Dunsly hesitated, and Lyla wondered if the unnerved woman was about to change her mind. Instead, she nodded abruptly and turned on her heel and disappeared up the stairs.

"Did you find anything?" Lyla kept her voice low as she turned to Nippy, who was still standing in the doorway.

"There's significant damage to the patio doors 'round back," he said, taking his lead from Lyla and keeping his tone low. "I found a discarded screwdriver in the grass. I've left it where it is. Hopefully, the SOCOs can lift some decent prints from the handle."

Lyla swallowed past the lump in her throat. There was something so disconcerting about a stranger trying to invade the place where you were supposed to be safe. Just thinking about it made her shiver. Pushing the thought away, she inclined her head toward the kitchen. "Are you coming in?"

Nippy ducked his head and glanced up the stairs before he shook his head. "I'll stay out here, take another look around, and wait for the SOCOs to get here."

Lyla grinned at him. "She said the dog was locked up so you're safe."

Nippy feigned innocence. "I'm allergic to dogs, not afraid of them."

"Could have fooled me," she said. She let him go without teasing him too much and proceeded into the kitchen. If she was being honest, she enjoyed working with Nippy. When they'd first met, she hadn't been entirely convinced about his seriousness, or even his suitability for the job. But now that she'd worked with him for a while, Lyla couldn't imagine a shift without him by her side. She knew that no matter what happened, Nippy would always have her back, and she would have his.

Finding the kitchen was easy, and she set about making herself acquainted with the layout of the room as quickly as possible. By the time Ms Dunsly came down the stairs again, Lyla had a cup of steaming hot sweet tea ready and waiting.

She popped her notepad out as she watched Ms Dunsly pick at the already raw skin which ran down the side of her nails. "If you're up for it, I'd like to start at the beginning."

"I'm not sure what you expect me to tell you," Ms Dunsly said defensively. "I didn't see him."

"But you know it was a 'he'?"

Ms Dunsly sighed. "Well, of course it was. How many women do you come across breaking into people's houses?"

Lyla kept her thoughts to herself, and fixed her

expression into a blank, unreadable mask. "Ms Dunsly, I only want to help."

"Caroline," she said quietly as she took her cup and leaned against the sink.

"Excuse me?"

"My name is Caroline," Ms Dunsly said. "Calling me Ms Dunsly all the time just sounds odd. Please, just call me Caroline."

"Fine then, Caroline, can you tell me when you knew somebody was at the door?"

She tilted her head to the side as though she could see, or hear the scenario playing out in her mind; maybe she could. "Freddy woke me up around half six," she said. "At least I think it was half six, but he'd barked on and off during the night, so I try not to pay too much mind."

Ms Dunsly sighed. "There was more to it this time, though. He was frantic, acting completely out of character, and I just knew there was something really wrong."

"And what happened then?"

"I got up, pulled open the bedroom door, and that's when I heard him trying to get in."

"Did you see anyone?"

She shook her head. "No, I didn't get a look at him. Frightened me half to death, and Freddy tried to get out, so I grabbed him and dragged him back inside the bedroom."

"And then you called us?"

Ms Dunsly nodded, brushing her hands over her face. "I told him I'd called you, and I know he heard me."

"What makes you so certain?"

"Because the noise stopped..." She hesitated, and Lyla could see there was something she was holding back.

"Is there something else, Caroline?"

Caroline's fingers automatically went to her mouth, and Lyla watched as she chewed at the frayed and damaged skin which lay alongside her nail beds. She cringed, gripping her pen a little tighter. Apparently, there was a comfort in chewing your fingernails, but Lyla had never fathomed it out.

To her, the idea of chewing your fingernails was abhorrent; probably rooted in some deep-seated psychological issue from her childhood.

"He tried harder when I'd told him I'd called you lot," she said quietly from around the side of her finger.

Alarm bells triggered in Lyla's head. "What do you mean he tried harder?"

"He was more frantic," she said. "I could hear him scrabbling at the windows and doors, far more frantic than before." She closed her eyes, as though that action alone could block the memory from her mind. "And then it just stopped."

"Did you leave your room at any point to check if he'd gone?"

Caroline shook her head, her expression incredulous. "Do you take me for a fool?"

Lyla said nothing. Staying put had been smart, but she knew there were plenty of people who would have risked a peek.

"Do you have an alarm system on the property?"

Caroline glanced down at the table. "No. I've been meaning to get one, but I just haven't had a chance to get around to it."

Lyla's smile was kind. "Do you know if any of your neighbours have CCTV, or...?" Lyla cut off as Caroline shook her head.

"I wouldn't know," she said. "We don't really have a relationship outside of a quick wave if I pass them on the road. I suppose you think that's awful."

"Of course not."

Caroline's expression soured as she pushed onto her feet and proceeded to turn around to face the kitchen sink. She flipped on the taps, the noise loud enough that she was forced to raise her voice just to be heard. "I always thought I was safe, that I didn't need any of those things." Steam rose from the water gathered in the sink, and Caroline thrust her hands into the water. Watching her scrub at the non-existent dirt on her cup, Lyla half wondered how she could stand the heat. "I really need to get ready for work..."

"I've just got a few more questions--"

"There's nothing else I can tell you," she said abruptly. "I've told you everything I know."

Lyla could tell that she was losing her. "I'll go and have a word with PC Blake," she said, as she left Caroline alone to process her thoughts.

AS SHE STEPPED out through the front door, Lyla wondered if it was cowardly of her to walk away. Caroline was obviously distressed, wasn't she supposed to say something to comfort her? Anything to help take the edge off the fear she so clearly struggled with? No amount of training could prepare you for the real world. Not really.

Instinctively Lyla knew there was nothing she could say or do to make Caroline feel safe. If she was lucky, time would help to take the edge off it all.

"Anything?" Nippy asked as she found him near the car.

"No alarm system, and no CCTV. She didn't see anything either. So hopefully he was an idiot and left his prints behind."

Nippy nodded, but Lyla had worked with him long enough to know there was something more he wasn't telling her. "Spit it out."

"What?" He glanced up at her, surprise etched into the lines of his face.

"Whatever is going on inside that head of yours?"

He cast a glance around at their surroundings. "It's very isolated out here."

"Is that all you've got to say?"

Nippy smiled. "I'm not imagining it though," he said. "I wouldn't want to be out here. I mean it's nice in a wide open, exposed kind of way."

"But it's too isolated," Lyla mused. "You're right. There's nobody around. At least none that will prove useful for our investigation."

"Doesn't that tell you something about this?" He was right. It wasn't just a random occurrence. Or at least as far as Lyla was concerned it couldn't be. "And I found something else odd," he said.

Lyla rolled her eyes. "Talk about burying the lead, Nippy." Ignoring her well-intentioned teasing, he gestured for him to follow him around the house.

The back garden was obviously Freddy's domain, the yellow chequered lawn proof of all the nights Caroline had let him outside to do his business.

Lyla and Nippy traversed the garden in silence, the dew-soaked grass sticking to her boots with every step she took. Nippy paused next to a tall evergreen tree in the corner of the garden. As she followed Nippy into the undergrowth, fighting her way through the thick branches, Lyla fought the icy shiver that slithered down her spine.

"There," he said, pointing to a spot where the fence line had crumbled. Although crumbled was the wrong word, Lyla realised as she studied it a little more closely. The fence panel had been freed of its moorings, held in place on one side only. She followed the direction of Nippy's hand and found the trampled grass littered with cigarette butts. The icy feeling of unease she'd been fighting took hold of her now, and she wrapped her arms around her upper body as a gesture of comfort.

"Do you think it's connected?" Nippy asked, and Lyla knew he was hoping she would dismiss his concern as nothing more than an overcautious personality.

"There's no way to know for certain, but we definitely need to get somebody out here to look at it..." She hesitated, as the memory of two other recent break-ins rose unbidden in her mind. "It looks like the last two places," she said finally.

"That's what I thought..."

Relief rocked Lyla on her feet at hearing Nippy's agreement. She wasn't imagining it. She wasn't jumping to conclusions where there wasn't proof.

"Did you call it in?"

Nippy nodded. "I'd already asked for SOCOs to come down here because of the door, but I called them back and asked if somebody higher up the chain could come and take a look."

"Good," Lyla said. But the knowledge that this wouldn't be their problem for much longer didn't bring her the relief she'd hoped for. "I should go back in..."

Nippy nodded, but his attention was still fixed on the evidence scattered over the ground. "You know what this means, right?"

"Yeah." Lyla didn't want to say it out loud. Doing that would only make it real, and she really didn't want to admit to something so bloody creepy.

"If it's connected--"

"Then he's been watching her," she finished the sentence for Nippy.

"Shit," Nippy said.

"Yeah," Lyla said. "Shit is right."

CHAPTER SEVEN

DREW SAT behind the wheel of his car and stared up at the building in front of him. It seemed like a lifetime since he'd walked through the doors. Of course, that wasn't true. It was weeks, really, but it still felt like a lifetime to him. All that time wasted on recuperating, and then there had been the visit to the counsellor to sign off on his return to work. She'd spoken about the invisible toll his encounter with Nolan Matthews would take on his psyche. Not that he needed her to tell him that.

He hadn't been able to bring himself to return to the house he'd shared with Freya. Just thinking about it made him feel like a coward. It had been their home, their refuge, and at the first bit of trouble, he'd deserted it. He would have to get back on the horse sooner rather than later...

But first he had a job to do.

Steeling himself, Drew pushed out of the car. He stood, the keys dangling from his fingers as he tried to control his breathing. He knew he could do this, he'd convinced himself of it. So why was he now standing around outside like a dick?

Sliding his keys back into his jacket, Drew made for the front door. The moment he pushed it open, the familiar scent of stale coffee and disinfectant assailed his nostrils. The front desk was unchanged, only the uniformed officer sitting behind it seemed unfamiliar. It was amazing how quickly things changed.

Drew made for the side door and quickly typed in his code. The door gave an angry beep, and he glanced over at the desk, only too aware of the surreptitious glances cast his direction by the officer on duty.

"Haskell, good to see you back!" The voice from the room behind the desk was familiar, and Drew turned to find Sergeant Harris bearing down on him. Before he could react, the sergeant had clapped a beefy hand on Drew's shoulder. He winced, the force of the blow ricocheting down through his body.

He'd healed up perfectly fine according to the doctors, but that didn't mean he wasn't still a little achy.

"Sorry, sorry," PS Harris said, withdrawing his hand hastily. "It's just good to see you back. For a while it seemed like it was touch and go..."

Drew had practiced the smile he now wore in the mirror. He'd known there would be well-wishers, and the last thing he wanted to do was appear ungrateful in any way. Because he was very grateful to be alive, to still have a job... There were so many things to feel gratitude over. And yet, despite that knowledge, Drew couldn't shake free of the anger he felt. Why him? Hadn't he gone through enough? Why had Nolan chosen him above everyone else? Why not pick Dr Connors to exact his revenge upon? After all, he'd been the cause of so much heartache to begin with.

Drew pushed the destructive thoughts aside and tried instead to focus on the present moment. Harris stood staring expectantly at him, and Drew realised with a jolt that the man had asked him something and he was now expecting an answer.

"The door..." Harris gestured toward the keypad. "They didn't issue you with your new code, did they?"

Drew shook his head and tried to ignore the flicker in the DS's eyes which signalled his curiosity over Drew's odd behaviour. "You know what it's like, they'd forget their heads if they weren't screwed on properly." It was a weak reply, and Drew knew it, but he straightened his shoulders and did his best to broaden his smile.

Sergeant Harris stepped past him and quickly typed a code into the security pad. The door gave a small grateful bleep, and Drew tugged it open.

"You take care of yourself now, son," Harris said, as Drew made his escape down the corridor. "We need you around here."

"You too," Drew said, feeling utterly impotent in his response as he hurried toward the stairs that would take him up to the next floor. What was wrong with him? He was behaving like a complete fool. If he didn't get a grip, then the Monk would take one look at him and send him home with a flea in his ear.

Drew paused on the landing between the floors and scrubbed his hands over his face. He ignored the curious glances from the other members of the force who scurried past him on the stairs. His hand slipped inside his jacket and he patted the packet of cigarettes he'd bought fresh that morning. After his run in with Nolan, it had been all too easy to fall back into old habits; not that it had taken much to do it. Drew knew he'd already been teetering on the edge, and Nolan was simply the excuse he used to soothe his guilty conscience.

He contemplated slipping out the side door to have a sneaky cigarette before facing the monk, but changed his mind at the last second. He was better than this, stronger than this. Freya would be so disappointed in him...

Drew knocked the thought aside. Freya wouldn't care; couldn't care because she'd opted off the merry-go-round and left him alone.

Squeezing his eyes shut, he swallowed past the

bile that seemed to sit permanently fixed in the back of his throat nowadays. But he wasn't alone, was he? He had Harriet. She'd been there when it had counted, and it had been Harriet who had saved him from Nolan and his wickedly sharp craft knife. She'd risked her own life to save his, and that was a debt he couldn't ever repay. The knowledge didn't sit comfortably with him, but Drew—for now at least—knew he could live with it.

He made it into the office with no more run-ins or—to his relief—almost breakdowns. The office was quieter than he last remembered it, and he glanced over at his empty desk. All of his stuff was still sitting there just waiting for his return, but what struck him then was Maz's desk. Apart from the computer, it stood empty, and a thin film of dust covered the keyboard.

"The dead rises!" DCI Gregson's voice cut through his thoughts, and Drew turned to find the DCI standing in the doorway to his office.

"Good to be back, sir," Drew said. The relief that washed through him was surprising, but not unwelcome, and he followed the Monk into his office.

"Grab yourself a seat." The monk dropped down into his worn leather chair, causing it to let out a long protesting groan of metal as he made himself comfortable. "I didn't think you were coming back for another week, or two?" The monk cocked an inquisitive eyebrow in Drew's direction.

"I couldn't sit around at home twiddling my thumbs any longer, sir. Not when I knew you'd be short staffed here..." Drew left the unspoken hang in the air between them. There was a reason the office was as quiet as it was, and it wasn't because all the criminals in North Yorkshire had hung up their leather gloves and gone away on holiday.

Gregson's expression darkened, and Drew knew he'd stepped on a potential landmine. "That bastard gutted us here," the monk said. "Took everyone worth a damn, and whisked them off for training, leaving me with only a skeleton crew." The monk closed his eyes as though that action alone could block out the terrible truth of him being passed over in favour of an outsider.

"I was sorry to hear they hadn't moved you over to the task force," Drew said quietly. "I can't imagine what they were thinking. You were the DCI in charge of bringing down one of the biggest serial murderers in British history."

"You and me both," the monk said. "But I wasn't the only one screwed over."

Drew hung his head, shame burning his cheeks. The wounds Nolan had inflicted on him might have healed, but there were some wounds that would never close, no matter how much time passed. And getting passed over for the promotion of a lifetime because that prick had put him in the hospital was definitely one of those wounds.

"It's fine, sir. I heard Maz is settling in well." Drew glanced up and found DCI Gregson observing him.

"He would. The little shit always lands on his feet."

"Sir, I don't think that's entirely fair."

"I know." Gregson sighed. "Arya is a damn fine officer, but it still chaps my hide to think he was picked up and they left you behind." Gregson held his hands up. "Not that I'm complaining."

Drew cracked a smile at the DCI's colourful language. "I heard they brought in a lot of new officers from further south."

"Nepotism, if you ask me," the monk said. "Templeton brought most of the officers from his previous team, therefore cutting out the potential to take on more officers from here. I mean, what do those soft bastards from down south know about Yorkshire? Send them out and about, and they'll be lost in an instant."

Drew couldn't disagree with his SIO. There was only so much a map could tell you about an area, and the officers who had worked their way up through the ranks in Yorkshire CID certainly had the upper hand when it came to knowing the place. You couldn't dismiss the value of experience, especially when it came to the police force.

"You heard he didn't even want to take Dr Quinn onboard?" Gregson said, his gaze sharp.

"I hadn't actually," Drew said, noting the subtle shift in the monk's shoulders that signalled some kind of relief.

"So, you haven't been talking to Dr Quinn then?" The phone cut the conversation off before Drew could answer him. The monk held a hand up, signalling to him to remain seated while he scooped up the receiver.

"DCI Gregson," he said. The air of authority Drew associated with the other man was back. "Where?"

Drew scrubbed his hands together, anticipation singing in his veins. All he wanted to do was jump back into the job with both feet. Of course, if Gregson thought for a moment that he wasn't yet ready to take on a job in the field, Drew knew he would find himself chained to a desk. That couldn't happen. Things were bad enough, without adding to the depressing turn his life had taken after he'd been passed over for the promotion onto the task force.

"Fine, I'll send someone down there now." Gregson set the phone down and closed his eyes. Drew held his breath, observing the other man.

"It's not good then?" Drew swore inwardly as the monk's eyes snapped open and his gaze zeroed in on Drew's face.

"Have you been signed off?" Gregson asked. The sudden change in conversation caught Drew off guard. But the monk was good at doing that; with him, you had to always be on your guard. It was a talent he'd obviously honed during his years with CID.

"Yeah, got the all-clear yesterday."

"Great," Gregson said, his smile grim. "They've got an attempted break-in over at Newholm."

"Sir, I'm not sure if--"

"They want one of our lot to head down there and take a look." Gregson said ominously. "And you've said you're all signed off."

"Sir, it's just a break-in..." Drew left the words hanging unspoken in the air between them. He didn't want to say it aloud, but to him it felt like a demotion.

Gregson shuffled the papers on his desk before he glanced up at Drew. "They don't have many details, so I want you to go and give it the once over. It'll be a nice easy way to get back in the saddle."

Drew kept his mouth shut as he pushed onto his feet. There was nothing about the situation that felt like a nice way to get back in the saddle. In fact, it felt like a kick in the bollocks, but telling that to the monk probably wouldn't win him any favours from his SIO.

"And Haskell, I want you to take a DC with you."

Drew sucked a breath in through his teeth. He'd thought it couldn't get any worse, but it had. Getting sent out to a burglary was one thing, being sent out there with a DC for a babysitter was something else entirely. "Sir, I'm capable of doing this on my own."

Irritation coloured Drew's words more than he'd expected.

Gregson's eyebrows disappeared up toward his thinning hairline. The expression told Drew he was skating on thin ice.

"Of course, sir, did you have somebody in mind?"

"Much better," Gregson said, with a broad smile. "I'll let you decide."

Keeping his thoughts to himself, Drew headed for his old desk. He paused and glanced at the empty desk next to his. Getting to know another partner was the last thing he wanted to do. He'd only just got used to working with Arya and his quirks. The idea of learning about somebody else brought Drew out in a cold sweat.

He scanned the room. It was slim pickings. It seemed Gregson hadn't been lying when he'd suggested that Templeton had all but cleaned them out. Couple that with the fact that he'd brought more officers from down south and that told Drew that the new task force was huge.

And yet, despite all of that, he'd been locked out by Templeton. He didn't want to take it personally, but there was a part of his ego that still smarted over the perceived slight.

"You," Drew said to the young man bent over his desk as he studied a haphazardly put together file. "What's your name?" There was something vaguely familiar about the young fair-haired officer who stared up at him through milk bottle glasses.

"Sir?"

"Name?"

"Tim—Timothy, sir." He swallowed hard and shoved his glasses back on his nose toward his eyes. "DC Tim Green. I started here last week. Brought up from the traffic division, and--"

Drew shook his head, and the young officer clamped his mouth shut. "I don't need to hear your life story," Drew said, not unkindly. "You all right to come out on a job?"

DC Green glanced back at the files scattered across his desk. Was he going to be turned down in favour of paperwork?

"Sure, sir." Green climbed to his feet, awkwardly shoving his chair back out of the way while he tried to grab his jacket.

"Great," Drew said dryly. The day was off to a cracking start already.

THE JOURNEY PASSED in uncomfortable silence. The moment he'd sat into the car, Drew had pulled his phone out and found himself calling Harriet. He'd told himself it was just his way of checking in. He'd left it too long already, and after Gregson had said Harriet too had been passed over for the task force, he'd felt compelled to talk to her.

Getting her voice mail had been the kick in the pants he'd needed. Calling her up was utterly inappropriate. If she didn't want to mention to him that Templeton hadn't taken on her services, then that was her business. It certainly wasn't his place to go poking his nose in where it didn't belong.

As he pulled into the driveway in front of the cottage, he spotted the marked car that sat at the front door.

"What are we looking for in particular, sir?" DC Green asked as he unbuckled his belt slowly.

"Anything that might be of use," Drew said sharply. He pushed out of the car before the young DC could ask anything else, and as he slammed the door, he prayed that this wasn't DC Green's first case.

A rake thin uniformed officer straightened up as Drew approached the car in front of the house.

"DI Haskell, and this is DC Green," he said, gesturing to the young detective who scrambled after him. "What are we dealing with here?"

"Good to see you, sir. I'm PC Blake, and my partner PC Pearson is currently inside with the lady who owns the property." He took a breath and glanced back at the house. Drew noted the tension that coursed through his body.

If Harriet had been here, she'd have had some kind of useful insight into the man's behaviour. Drew cast a surreptitious glance at the man next to him and sighed. If he was hoping DC Green would somehow take Dr Quinn's place, then he would be disappointed. DC Green's expression was blank. It seemed he was green in more ways than one.

"The resident interrupted a would-be intruder," PC Blake said.

"Have the SOCOs been by yet?" Green's question took Drew by surprise, and he took a second glance at the young detective. It grated on him that the newly recruited officers had taken to calling the forensic teams by the acronym CSI. As far as Drew was concerned. It all sounded a little too Hollywood for him, especially when there was absolutely nothing wrong with the word SOCO. That Green had used the shorthand phrase SOCO pleased him. Perhaps there was hope for him after all.

"No. We called them as soon as we arrived, but last I heard they were stuck at a job over near York."

Drew nodded. "Anything else we should know?"

Something in the uniformed officer's behaviour told Drew he was holding back on him. And pushing him to answer might not have the desired effect he wanted. Not everyone wanted to be pushed, he'd learned that the hard way.

"Sir, perhaps I'm reading more into the situation than I should. But I found a number of cigarette butts in the tree line behind the house."

"You think somebody was surveilling the property prior to the attempted break-in?"

"It looks that way." PC Blake shifted awkwardly, as though he was expecting Drew to laugh in his face.

"Good work," Drew said, noting the relief on the uniform's face. "Tell forensics what you've found when they get here. They'll appreciate the heads up." Drew started toward the cottage.

"Sir, if it's not too bold, can I ask why you're here?"

The question brought Drew up short. "Excuse me?"

"Well, this is a burglary. We rarely see your level down here for something like this."

Biting his tongue, Drew held his thoughts in check. It would be all too easy to snap at the unsuspecting uniform, which would be too unfair. The anger Drew was harbouring didn't need to be visited upon unsuspecting PCs. "I go where I'm told," Drew said, with as little emotion as he could muster. However, judging by the flinching around the corners of PC Blake's eyes, he knew he'd failed to keep his cool as much as he'd wanted to.

"Very good, sir. I didn't mean to intrude."

Drew contemplated an apology, but changed his mind at the last second. It would do nobody any favours to draw out the conversation longer than it needed to be right now. The best thing he could do for both himself and PC Blake was to walk away.

DC Green caught up to him as he reached the

open door to the cottage. "That seemed a little rude," Green said.

Drew looked the other man over as blotchy colour crept up Green's neck. It clashed with the smattering of freckles which covered the DCs face, but it wasn't embarrassment that caused the DCs reaction. Drew struggled to smother a smile as he realised it was pure indignation that had given rise to the bright colour which marched up toward the young man's hairline. "That's your opinion," Drew said.

"It is my opinion," DC Green said. "And in my opinion, that was rude... sir."

Perhaps the young DC had a backbone after all. Drew pushed the thought aside and covered the smile that threatened to appear with a frown. "And why do you think that?"

"Because I know how hard it is to be a PC," Green said. "When you're a PC, you get treated like dirt by those who outrank you. Nothing more than a general dogsbody, when all you want to do is your job. PC Blake didn't deserve that back there."

"PC Blake is a friend of yours, is he?" Drew cocked an inquisitive eyebrow in Green's direction. It was the most conversation he'd got out of the junior detective since they'd left the office, and it surprised him to hear Green get so passionate about the supposed mistreatment of his fellow officers. Perhaps he was planning on becoming a fed rep?

"No. But he doesn't have to be. I just don't like it when I see others throwing their weight around."

"And you think that's what I was doing?" Drew asked mildly.

"Well, maybe not exactly. But there was no need to be so abrasive. Would it kill you to be a bit more approachable?"

Drew shook his head and stepped into the cottage, leaving Green to follow him inside.

Voices drifted toward them from the depths of the house, and Drew followed the sound.

"Ms Dunsly, would you not prefer to take a seat while we discuss this?" The unfamiliar voice held a note of authority, and Drew stepped unnoticed into the kitchen as a second uniform officer tried to steer a woman toward a seat at the table.

"If I don't get this done now, I won't be able to get it clean later--" The woman's voice cut off as Drew cleared his throat by way of announcing his presence.

"I'm sorry to intrude," he said. "The front door was open. I'm DI Drew Haskell, and my colleague here is DC Green."

The uniformed officer gave him an appraising glance before she took a step back toward the wall. Drew appreciated the unspoken gesture and gave a tight-lipped smile in response.

"Ms Dunsly, I was hoping we could have a little chat about what happened here this morning?"

"I don't want to talk to anyone else about this. I told the other officer here everything that happened. I don't know anything else, so why can't you lot just do your jobs?"

Drew nodded sympathetically and gestured toward the chairs at the table. "Do you mind if I take a seat?" He was only too aware of his training, as Ms Dunsly studied him with barely veiled hostility. He couldn't blame her for her reaction.

As police officers, they were taught to approach everyone with compassion no matter the situation. And that was something Drew tried to uphold. At the end of the day, a situation like this for him was a normal occurrence, simply a run-of-the-mill day, but for Ms Dunsly this was anything but ordinary.

For police officers it was simply a job, a day like any other, but for the people who needed them it was often as a result of the worst day of their life, and Drew tried to never forget that when he interacted with the public.

Ms Dunsly nodded miserably, and she took a seat opposite him, before she buried her face in her hands. He gave her a moment to compose her thoughts before he spoke. "Would you mind running through the events of this morning with me?" He kept his voice gentle and was rewarded for his patience when Ms Dunsly lifted her face.

"Like I told the other officers, Freddy woke me up..."

Drew glanced over at the uniformed officer. "Freddy is Ms Dunsly's dog," she said hastily. "He's been secured in another room."

The tension which had gathered in Drew's shoulders slowly released. The last thing he needed was to deal with an overly excited dog on top of everything else.

"So, Freddy woke you. Does he often do that?"

Ms Dunsly paused and seemed to consider his question before she shook her head. "No, he's a good boy. He knows to wait for me to get up. He's always been very even tempered."

"But last night was different?"

Ms Dunsly chewed her lip, and Drew knew there was something she was holding back. "Well, he's been restless for a while now."

Drew sighed and tried to keep his patience in check. Just because things weren't running smoothly in his life, didn't mean Ms Dunsly deserved to fall victim to his ire.

As though she could sense his irritation, colour flooded up Ms Dunsly's face. "I don't see why I have to go over this again. I didn't see anything, so it's not as though I can help you. Everything you're going to get out of me you've already had. Can't you just leave me be so I can go to work and try to get back to some semblance of normality?"

With a tight-lipped smile, Drew nodded and

climbed to his feet as a male voice drifted through from the front drive.

"What's going on in here?" The voice was instantly familiar, and Drew felt the tension he'd recently managed to shake free from returning to his body. He turned in time to see DS Perry erupt in through the kitchen door. "What are you lot doing here?" There was no denying the evident hostility in Perry's voice as he gave Drew a once over. "I thought you lot were too good for us?"

"I'm going to have a word with DS Perry," Drew said, returning his attention to Ms Dunsly's face. "If there's anything else you can think of—anything at all—then this is my number." He pulled a card from the inside pocket of his jacket and slipped it across the table toward Ms Dunsly. She eyed it as though it were some form of deadly snake, rather than the harmless piece of white card it was.

When Drew turned to Perry, he discovered the other man had already gone ahead of him.

A couple of moments later and Drew found the DS waiting for him outside the house. "There's no murder here for you lot to go poking your noses into, so I don't know what you think you're doing here."

"I go where I'm told, Mike, you know this."

Perry rolled his eyes and moved away, causing Drew to go after him.

. . .

"PERRY!" Drew hurried after the retreating man. "Mike, wait." Using his first name was enough to bring the stockier man up short. He turned and cast a withering glance in Drew's direction. The corners of his mouth drew down, as though he'd set eyes on something particularly unpleasant. He probably had; it was no secret that there was no love lost between them.

Despite entering the police at the same time, Drew had been the one to move up through the ranks, while Perry had lagged behind, stuck in uniform until very recently, when he'd made the move to detective.

"What do you want?" The Yorkshire man's accent only grew thicker, and Drew recognised that as a sign that he was particularly upset.

"I didn't mean to step on your toes, mate. But you know what it's like, I'm only doing my job. There's nothing malicious in it."

"What's North Yorkshire's golden boy doing here, anyway? I'd heard you were being promoted to that new team. If I'd known the best way to get fast tracked around here was to allow a serial to get the jump on me in my gaff, I—"

"You always were a bitter prick," Drew said, cutting him off before he could finish his sentence.

For a moment, silence stretched between them and Drew wondered if he'd made a serious mistake.

The thought faded from his mind as a smile broke out across Perry's weathered face.

"I might have been bitter, but at least I'm not an arrogant bastard like you."

Drew rolled his eyes in mock irritation as Perry held his hand out toward him.

"What brings you round these parts, anyway? Surely a half-arsed burglary is beneath your lot's consideration."

"Like I said already, I go where I'm told, and they told me to come here. What makes you so sure it's just a straight up attempted burglary?"

"Come on, it's obvious, isn't it? She disturbed the bastard before he could get his hands on anything of value. But that doesn't change the facts of the matter. Don't tell me all that time you're spending with the head doctors is turning you soft?"

Drew shook his head and fought the grin that spread across his face. "So, you heard about that then."

Perry returned his grin with one of his own. "Aye, everyone has heard of your lady friend. I've seen her around, she's as pretty as they said too. You and her aren't getting down to business?" A lascivious wink accompanied the latter, leaving Drew in no doubt as to his old colleague's meaning.

"It's strictly a working relationship," Drew said, his voice tighter than he would have wanted. "How's Joan these days?"

"She's great," Perry said. The bitterness crept back into his voice. "Left me for a mechanic so she did, and they're expecting their first little 'un in the next few months."

"Christ, I'm sorry to hear that."

"Don't be, I'm not. She was a psycho bitch, anyway. It's good riddance, as far as I'm concerned."

There was a moment of awkwardness, broken only by the drone of a van making its way up the isolated lane.

"That'll be the SOCO lads." Perry seemed as relieved as Drew felt for the forced change of subject.

There was an awkward beat that passed between them as they watched the van amble down the lane. "You can leave the rest of this to me," Perry said. "I can handle it from here. I'm more familiar with the protocols, anyway."

Drew contemplated arguing with the other man, but changed his mind at the last second. There was no point pissing Perry off more than he was already. If he insisted on hanging around, it would only create a much larger rift between them, and the investigation would only be hampered by such a situation.

"I'll let you coordinate here once you have their report. I'd like to go over it with you before we decide our next move."

Perry nodded, and the relaxing of his shoulders told Drew of the relief he was feeling.

"Of course."

Drew started to turn away when Perry called after him. "I'm glad you didn't bite the big one."

Drew gave a sharp jerk of his head in response and returned to the car to find DC Green was already waiting for him.

"Finished already?" Drew couldn't help himself. He knew he was needling the other man, and really there was no need for it. None of what was happening was DC Green's fault.

"We're done, aren't we?"

Drew gave the other man a once over before he shook his head. "No. I want you to stay here and lend a hand to DS Perry."

"You mean keep an eye on him?" Green quirked an eyebrow in Drew's direction, which only served to increase his ire.

"That's not what I'm suggesting," Drew said, barely managing to contain his temper. It was happening more and more these days. Ever since the situation with Nolan, Drew was finding it increasingly difficult to keep a lid on his darker emotions. "I just want you to do your bloody job."

"What am I supposed to do?" There was a whining note in Green's voice that unsettled Drew. Just what the hell was he supposed to do with such a milquetoast officer?

"Follow orders," Drew said sharply. "Mike will give you instructions, and I expect you to follow them to the letter."

"And what are you going to do?" Drew couldn't be certain, but it almost sounded as though there was a note of challenge in Green's voice. He dismissed the idea completely.

"There's somewhere I need to be." Without waiting for Green's response, Drew slipped in behind the steering wheel and started up the engine. As he reversed out of the driveway, he caught sight of Green's petulant expression as he watched him drive away. It seemed Templeton really had gutted the force. It struck him then just how much he actually missed Maz. "Let it go." He muttered the words beneath his breath as he put the car in gear and the wheels spun in the gravel before finding purchase and causing the car to jump forward. Maz was gone, and there was not a damn thing he could, or should, do about it.

CHAPTER EIGHT

THE DARK PANELLED door that separated Harriet's office from her secretary's area swung open and Martha poked her head inside. Where others would have looked chagrined to have interrupted; Martha appeared unbothered.

"Your morning appointment has arrived," she said, her voice as frosty as usual.

"I—" Harriet started to respond, but Martha merely rolled her eyes and indicated the computer screen.

"I sent a reminder this morning, and you've already rescheduled twice this week."

"Fine, of course. Send them in." Harriet pushed aside the thoughts of Nolan Matthews from her mind. Receiving the phone call from Dr Chakrabarti had thrown her for a loop, but it was time now to put it out of her head.

The tentative knock on the door at that moment tugged her from her own thoughts, and she straightened up behind the desk.

"Come in!"

The young female student who slipped into the office was petite, her mousey hair pushed back behind her ears. The rucksack she carried was very nearly as big as her and forced her to stoop forward as she shuffled across the carpet toward the vacant seat.

"Thanks so much for this," she said, dropping her bag gratefully onto the floor.

"No problem…"

"Misha," she said with a small smile. "If you don't mind me saying, I'm really happy to be here."

"Oh, why is that?" Harriet tried to keep her tone upbeat as she clicked through the files on the computer in search of the appointment details.

"Because you're the reason I'm here…"

Harriet's head snapped up in response, and she found herself taking a renewed interest in the young woman in front of her. "I know you… What did you say your name was again?" Something about the girl's eyes tugged at a long-buried memory in Harriet's mind. One that she had deliberately buried all those years ago.

When the girl smiled again, it brought the memories flooding back, and Harriet felt a shiver travel down her spine.

"You're Louise McDermid's daughter, aren't you?"

The girl looked uncomfortable for a moment and glanced down at her hands clasped in her lap. "I didn't know if you would remember."

Harriet's stomach dropped into her shoes as she watched the girl squirm across from her. Sympathy flooded her system as she studied the young woman. "I wouldn't forget something so important."

Misha straightened her shoulders and glanced up at Harriet through her dark lashes.

She was pretty, Harriet thought, as pretty as her mother had been. Now that she knew the truth, she wondered why she hadn't seen the familial similarity the moment she had walked in the door. After all, Louise, and everything she represented to Harriet, was never far from her mind.

"It's her birthday next weekend, you know?" Misha said. Harriet was left with the feeling that she was speaking to herself in order to break the awkward pause which had sprung up between them. "But that's enough about Mum." She fidgeted with her hands in her lap.

"You've picked a research topic?" Harriet knew how important it was to respect the boundaries put up by those who were grieving.

Misha smiled gratefully, and doubled over at the waist, her dark head disappearing below the edge of the desk as she practically climbed into her rucksack in search of her papers. "I thought I might examine the relationship between childhood trauma and violent crime in adulthood."

Harriet nodded, a smile hovering at the corner of her mouth as she watched Misha straighten up with a biro and spiral notebook in hand.

If she believed in the supernatural, or reincarnation she might have been able to convince herself that it was in fact Louise who sat opposite her, but when Misha spoke, the moment was broken. Louise was gone. Murdered. And it was Harriet's fault.

The moment the realisation struck, Harriet felt her mouth go dry. It wasn't that she had forgotten the part she had played in Louise's death; it was just with everything else that had happened down through the years, the trauma of her colleague's brutal murder had become somewhat blunted in her mind. *A necessary survival tactic of compartmentalising some terrible things she had borne witness to.* It was a lie she used to try to assuage her conscience, or the guilt would suffocate her beneath its weight.

"Have I said something wrong?" Misha asked, her blue eyes—so like her mother's—searched Harriet's face for confirmation of her guilt.

"It's nothing you've done, Misha. Really. I just—" Harriet pushed onto her feet, and the memories of Louise's gurgled last breaths clouded her mind. "I just need to get a glass of water. I'll be back in a minute—"

Crossing the room, she was at least pleased to discover that she didn't have to run. Pushing out into the reception area, Harriet ignored Martha's curious and watchful gaze.

Reaching the door to the small toilet which sat just off the reception area, Harriet secured the solid white door, and gratefully leaned back against it with her eyes shut. It was there she struggled to get her breathing back under control, but her mind—just as it always did—was determined to conjure all the images she had long thought safely squirrelled away in the back of her mind.

Just get a grip. It was a long time ago.

Gritting her teeth, Harriet moved to the sink and ran the cold-water tap. Avoiding her own reflection—she already knew what she would find there, and she didn't need to be reminded of how little sleep she was actually getting—she splashed the freezing water up onto her face. It was the jolt she needed. Sucking down a deep breath, she buried the memories of Louise back where they belonged in the darkest recesses of her mind. It was in the past, and there was nothing she could do now to change what had happened.

Louise was gone, and no amount of wishing and hoping it were different would bring her back.

. . .

FIVE MINUTES LATER, she was back in the office. Misha sat in the same spot she had been in when she'd left, but Harriet could tell the young woman was perturbed by her behaviour.

"I didn't think you would mind me coming here—"

"I don't." Harriet tucked a stray strand of damp, dark hair behind her ear as she settled into her chair on the other side of the desk. It was right that Misha was here. Her mother would have been overjoyed to see her daughter succeed in life. "Your mother would be so proud of you."

Misha ducked her gaze, a dark expression crossing her face, but it was gone so quickly Harriet found herself wondering if she'd imagined it. She contemplated asking her about it, but changed her mind. It wasn't her place to go prying into Misha's personal thoughts and feelings; no matter how much she longed to understand what was happening behind the young woman's unfathomable gaze.

Instead, Harriet plastered a smile onto her face and leaned forward, placing her forearms on the desk in front of her.

"So, tell me, what you've found out about childhood trauma and violent crime."

Relief filtered across Misha's expression, and Harriet knew she'd made the right choice by not prying. The young woman would come to her own conclusions, and if she ever wanted to talk privately, then Harriet would be here. But she wouldn't make the first move. She'd made the mistake once before, and she was damned if she would allow history to repeat itself.

CHAPTER NINE

MARTHA SAT with her head engrossed in whatever item she was reading on the computer screen. From his vantage point outside the office door, Drew watched as she bit into a sandwich she had set out on a tissue on her desk. The ghost of a grin played across his lips as he watched her glance jealously about, her shoulders hunching subtly as she carefully raised it to her mouth and took a substantial bite. He chose that moment to push the door open, and stride into the open office space.

A momentary flicker of consternation crumpled her features at his disruption before she rammed the remains of her sandwich into the open desk drawer at her side. The audible click of the drawer as she slammed it shut broke the silence in the space.

"Is she in?" He inclined his head in the direction of Harriet's closed office door. Without waiting for

Martha to reply—not that she was really in any position to do so without running the risk of spitting her lunch out onto the desk—Drew reached for the door handle.

"There's someone in there." Drew wasn't sure how she managed to form the words around the obstruction in her mouth. He sighed and took a step back from the door.

"I can wait."

Martha dabbed delicately at her lips with the hankie she'd pulled from the box of tissues on her desk. "I can't say how long they'll be. It'd be better if you came back later, or perhaps made an appointment like everybody else has to?" There was a steely edge to Martha's words.

"Don't mind me," Drew said. "You can eat the rest of your lunch."

"Excuse me?" Martha leaned away from him, as though he'd just shown her something particularly unpleasant that she was concerned would somehow transfer to her if she got too close. "I don't know what you mean."

But Drew could tell from the colour that mounted her cheeks that she knew exactly what he was referring to.

"Your sandwich," he said, gesturing toward the desk. "You were eating it as I came in here. Don't stop on my account."

Martha narrowed her eyes. "Even if there was a

sandwich, I wouldn't behave so vulgarly. I get a proper lunch break just like everybody else." She made it sound like an accusation, and Drew felt laughter bubbling in his chest. "But it sounds to me as though you were trying to catch me out, DI Haskell?"

"Not trying to catch you out," he said. "I know what it's like sometimes."

She furrowed her brow. "What?"

"To not be able to wait until lunch. Some days I can't wait either and I eat my lunch before elevenses. It's this cold weather," he said, rubbing his hands together as though to emphasise his point. "It makes us all want to eat like bears going into hibernation."

Martha stared at him horrified, but before he could say another word the door to the office swung open, and a young dark-haired woman who looked barely old enough to be high school, never mind college, appeared in the doorway. "I really appreciate your insight."

Drew gestured to Martha's desk, and the still visible crumbs that decorated the surface. Martha's gaze dropped to the desk, and she frantically swiped at the crumbs as Harriet followed the young woman out. He smothered his laughter with a fist pressed against his lips and pretended to clear his throat. From the other side of the office, Martha paused her cleaning long enough to watch him with barely veiled hostility.

The righteous rage reflected in her eyes threatened to destroy what little self-control he had left.

Harriet caught his eye, and her smile widened. "It was my pleasure, Misha. I'll see you again on Friday?"

The girl nodded and seemed surprised when she glanced up to find Drew standing in reception. She blushed and hoisted her rucksack higher over her shoulder. "Sorry for keeping your waiting," Misha said to Drew before she escaped from the reception area and re-joined the rest of the students who littered the corridor.

"Are you free for a chat?" Drew asked, noting the way Harriet seemed to stare longingly after the young woman who'd just left. Harriet tore her gaze away from the door as it swung shut.

"I'm sure I can squeeze you in?" The statement was directed toward Martha, who proceeded to roll her eyes.

"Is that your none too subtle way of asking me to cancel the rest of your appointments?"

Any guilt Drew had felt over his teasing of Martha earlier vanished. Harriet nodded, seemingly oblivious to the barbed insult thrown her direction. How could she do that? He'd heard the phrase 'turn the other cheek', often enough from his parents when he was growing up. But there was turning the other cheek, and then there was allowing somebody to treat you like dirt. Drew bit his tongue. Harriet wouldn't take kindly to him intervening, no matter how well meaning it might seem.

Not to mention the fact that Harriet was a grown woman, and not some damsel in distress who needed saving from a dragon.

"I'm not sure," Harriet said, turning back to Drew. "Is this a social visit, or?" She left the question hanging in the air.

"Just a social call," he said.

Harriet glanced down at her watch. "Perfect, then we can get something for lunch."

Martha's expression shifted. "I was hoping to take my lunch now," she said. Drew glanced up sharply, but Martha ignored him entirely.

"That's fine," Harriet said. "I'll just lock up when I leave."

"But what if someone needs you?"

Harriet's smile was kind, and her tone of voice gentle. "Anyone who needs me can always come back after lunch. I don't suppose there will be too many emergencies on campus that will require my skills?"

Martha seemed to take this onboard before she gave a curt nod of her head. "Suit yourself."

Harriet beckoned Drew into the office as Martha got her coat and gathered her belongings. "Have you been here long?" Harriet asked.

"Just a couple of minutes," he said, watching Martha from the corner of his vision as she pretended to busy herself with locking her desk drawers. She seemed to linger over the action, and Drew could tell she was subtly listening to everything they said.

"What's wrong?" Harriet asked, as she slipped her coat on, and fluffed her dark hair over the top of her collar.

He inclined his head in the direction of the reception area, and Harriet raised her eyebrows questioningly before his meaning sank in. Harriet rolled her eyes before she called out to the other woman. "Bye, Martha!"

Martha jumped and grabbed her bag from the chair. Without a backward glance, she left the reception, allowing the door to slam behind her.

"You know she's lying to you?" Drew tried to keep his voice casual as he leaned against the door frame and watched Harriet chew her lip as she studied her computer screen.

"Lying to me? That seems a little extreme, don't you think?"

"She had her lunch while you were in your meeting."

Harriet glanced up at him then. "What do you mean?"

"I mean, when I arrived, she was eating lunch at her desk."

"And that's your proof, is it?" Harriet's smile was gently teasing.

"I'm just telling you what I saw."

"Oh please, don't tell me you haven't eaten food at your desk, and still gone out for lunch during your break?" She quirked a dark eyebrow in his direction. "You can't go around accusing people of lying just because they do that."

"She doesn't behave properly," Drew said, feeling suddenly irritated. Just because he wasn't a big shot psychologist, and he couldn't quite put his finger on the exact reason he thought Martha was lying, didn't mean his feelings weren't valid. He'd been a DI long enough to know the signs when he saw them. "She treats you like you're the one working for her."

"And sometimes I think maybe I am." Harriet sighed. "Don't worry about it. Martha might have a few rough edges, but she means well."

"Well, for who?" Drew asked.

"The university," Harriet replied honestly, as she clicked off the computer and grabbed her handbag from the desk. "You needn't worry, I'm under no illusions as to where Martha's loyalties lie. If she thought selling me down the river would somehow help her get ahead in life, she'd do it in a heartbeat."

"So why do you keep someone like that around?"

"Because I know exactly where I stand with Martha. She can't hurt my feelings, and I definitely won't hurt hers when I don't ask her for a rundown on her personal life because I'm preoccupied calculating the statistical results for a peer review paper."

For Drew, the idea of keeping somebody who

could betray you like that around seemed preposterous. Trusting people in general didn't come easily to him. It was probably some kind of side-effect of the job he did. But it was vital to his ability to do his job that those he allowed into his inner circle were people he could trust.

When Harriet had kept her involvement in Freya's care a secret and it had all come to light, it had very nearly been the end of their working relationship. It didn't matter that he could understand that Harriet's role had been exaggerated by those who would seek to shirk their responsibilities, for Drew it was the simple fact that she had lied by omission. He'd learned to move past it, but there were still times when those feelings reared their ugly head and he found himself questioning Harriet's true loyalties.

However, the more time he spent with Harriet, the more he began to understand her true motivations. There was no malice that he could see in her actions, she wanted only to do the very best job that she was capable of doing. Even if that sometimes meant she upset those nearest to her. And that, for Drew, was something that he could get behind.

He understood the desire to get it right. In his line of work, it seemed especially important. One mistake could mean the truth remained hidden, and when that happened it usually meant that justice could not be served as it should.

"You find that hard, don't you?" Harriet paused next to him, her blue eyes searching his.

"I don't need you to analyse me," he said, not unkindly.

Harriet blinked and took a step backwards. "Sorry. It's hard to switch it off sometimes."

Drew's laughter echoed in the office. "Now that's something I can understand," he said. His stomach chose that moment to grumble.

Harriet returned his smile and gestured to the door. "We better get you fed. I know only too well how grumpy you get otherwise."

Drew shook his head. "I don't know what you're talking about."

It was Harriet's turn to laugh, and Drew found himself joining in. It hit him, then, that he'd actually missed her during his convalescence.

He'd thought it was just the job he'd missed, but now that he was standing here laughing along with her as though nothing at all had changed, he realised it was her. Her company, her laugh. He'd missed talking to her, and not just their conversations that inevitably revolved around the work they did, although her understanding on that was definitely a boon.

Freya had never cared about his work in the same way. The thought, when it hit him, was enough to cut his laughter off. Guilt, as sharp as any knife, sliced through him, sealing the breath in his lungs.

Harriet had already reached the door, and Drew went after her, stepping out into the reception as she locked the doors, and turned off the lights.

He remained silent as he followed her into the hall. Years of training allowed him to keep his expression impassive, but inside his mind was in turmoil.

CHAPTER TEN

HARRIET BURIED her face lower into her scarf and gripped the paper cup between her hands. October had seen some of the warmest temperatures on record, but the sudden swing into November had brought with it the first of the frosty mornings and a significant dip in the mercury.

Bianca would have said it was the kind of weather that made make you sick. Harriet had always considered it to be a nonsensical notion. Sudden changes in temperature alone were not a precursor to illness, but as she sat next to Drew on the bench watching the students pass them by, she reconsidered Bianca's theory.

There was no denying the rise in those who sniffed and sneezed—many of them fumbling for pocket sized packets of Kleenex as they went about their day. As she lifted the cup of steaming coffee to her lips, Harriet found herself assessing the tickle in the back of her own throat with a newfound critical eye.

She shook her head, as though the physical action alone was enough to disrupt the neurotic thoughts that had invaded her mind. She'd read a paper not that long ago on the potential effects of collective hysteria, and she found herself wondering if anyone had thought to investigate the links between that and hypochondria.

"So, what did you want to talk about?" she said, deciding a complete change was necessary to rid her mind of the ridiculous notions currently trying to populate her brain cells.

"I heard you weren't asked to join the task force." There wasn't a hint of emotion in Drew's voice as he spoke, and Harriet longed to turn toward him so she could study his expression. Not that she would expect to find much there either. Drew's ability to keep his thoughts concealed was a constant source of consternation for her.

"I wasn't really expecting to be asked," Harriet said, careful to match her tone of voice to his. She sipped the bitter coffee and winced as it burned the inside of her mouth. "*Although*, the university has struck a deal with North Yorkshire CID for training in the area of criminal profiling."

Drew swivelled to face her; the usual mask he wore had slipped to reveal a tantalising glimpse into his inner thoughts. What Harriet saw there took her by surprise. She'd expected disappointment, instead what she saw was rage. Pure and unadulterated rage. In an instant the mask was replaced, and Harriet found herself on the outside once more.

"They've got some nerve," he said, and the level tone of his voice belied the emotions Harriet had seen. Had she been mistaken? It wasn't impossible, reading another's mood wasn't an exact science.

"Did they tell you why they didn't take you on?" Drew glanced back at the cup in his hand, and Harriet found herself wishing she'd kept the question to herself.

"No. Nobody is sharing their reasonings for the choices they made. Not that I can blame them, they don't owe me anything, but it would have been nice, you know? I mean, before Nolan, I was on track to be picked up by the task force when they got it off the ground and now..." He trailed off and shrugged, his gaze fixed on some point straight ahead.

"They probably didn't think it was important," Harriet said. It was an inadequate response, and she knew it. Drew's phone chose that moment to ring, and she felt the tension in her shoulders slowly loosen. A change of topic was for the best.

From what she'd seen of him so far, Drew was in no fit state to discuss the reasoning behind the task force's decision in passing's him over. All she knew for certain was that if she in the same position as he was, she would feel like crap.

Drew stood, the bench creaking as his weight disappeared from the other end. Harriet closed her eyes and let what little heat radiated from the autumnal sun soak through her skin.

"How busy are you this afternoon?" Drew's gruff voice caught Harriet by surprise, and she jolted on the bench, narrowly avoiding the now tepid coffee that sloshed over the side of the paper cup.

"I've got a couple of appointments, but I've got a mountain of marking to do." She sighed and poured out the dregs of the coffee into the grass. "Why?"

Drew's expression shifted to one of disappointment, and Harriet found herself wishing she'd kept her mouth shut.

"Bungled burglary, and they've got a body," he said, tossing his empty coffee cup into the bin. "It's just weird enough that I was hoping you could come and take a look for me."

Pursing her lips, Harriet considered Martha's reaction if she didn't turn up for her afternoon session. "It's fine." Drew shrugged. "I managed before I met you, I'm sure I'll manage again." His smile was tight-lipped and somewhat uncertain.

It hit Harriet then. He was insecure. She'd never thought it was possible that a man like DI Haskell would ever suffer through feelings like that, but there was no denying the evidence in front of her. His experience with Nolan had clearly affected him more than he'd previously admitted.

Harriet knew enough about trauma to know that many people didn't fully understand the depths to which traumatic experiences could impact their lives. Many who were the victims of violent crimes never fully recovered, or at least if they did, they were so transformed by the experience their personalities were unequivocally changed. It stood to reason that Drew would be no different. After all, he was a flesh and blood man who had undergone a life-changing situation.

"No problem, let me contact Martha and tell her I won't be in later."

"Won't she love that?" He raised a dark eyebrow at her.

Laughing, Harriet nodded. "Probably. I've got no doubt that she'll mark my bad behaviour down in the hopes she can use it against me at a later date."

"I don't want you to get into trouble," Drew said, concern causing the corners of his mouth to turn down into a moue of displeasure.

"I'm a grown woman. I'm capable of handling my own affairs." There was a curtness to her voice that Harriet hadn't intended. From the flinching around the corners of Drew's eyes, she knew she'd behaved a little too harshly. "You don't need to worry about me," she said instead. "At the end of the day, the university wants this kind of relationship with North Yorkshire

CID. I'm simply raising the profile of Dr Baig's department as he wants."

Instead of answering her, Drew nodded and took a step back as she slipped her phone from her bag and tapped out a quick email. She contemplated calling Martha, but Drew was correct about one thing, Martha would take far too much pleasure from her change of plans, and the last thing Harriet wanted to do was deal with the other woman's rude behaviour.

"All done," she said, clicking send on the email before she got to her feet. "I'm all yours."

Drew's expression shifted, and Harriet wondered if she'd somehow said the wrong thing again. She breathed a sigh of relief when he said nothing of it and pulled his keys from his coat jacket. Silently, she followed him to where he'd parked his car in the visitor's carpark.

She wanted to broach the matter of his mental wellbeing, but Harriet couldn't find the right words. Or at the very least, the words that wouldn't cause him to turn from her.

Settling into the passenger seat, Harriet chewed her lip thoughtfully as Drew slipped in behind the steering wheel. Perhaps what he needed most of all right now was a friend. And if that were true, then saying anything to him would make that an impossibility between them.

Satisfied she had found a course of action for

now at least, Harriet stared out the window as Drew manoeuvred them out of the car space and joined the flow of traffic from the university. She caught sight of Misha hurrying across the road ahead of them, and Harriet's train of thought on the state of Drew's mental wellbeing was momentarily distracted. When had life become so complicated?

From the corner of her eye, she glanced over at Drew. The answer was obvious. Or at least it would have been if she'd allowed herself to accept the truth.

THE TREES WHIPPED past the passenger window. The silence in the car stretched out infinitely between them. Not that Harriet felt particularly uncomfortable. She enjoyed silence; it gave her overly active mind the chance to catch up with the mental acrobatics it often liked to indulge in when it came to her chosen profession.

"I received an odd phone call this morning," she said without thinking.

"Who from?"

"A Dr Chakrabarti." Harriet turned to face Drew. "She's Nolan Matthew's psychiatrist," she added the last almost as an afterthought. No sooner had the words left her mouth than she regretted them.

The grip Drew had on the steering wheel tightened until his knuckles whitened under the pressure. "Why would she call you?"

Flexing her fingers in her lap, Harriet contemplated keeping the truth from him. Mentioning it to him had been a mistake. He didn't need to know what Nolan Matthews was up to, not after everything he'd inflicted on Drew. She should have known better than to say it to him, but now that she had, there was no putting the genie back in the bottle. "She wanted to talk to me about Nolan."

"Why would she do that?" Drew cast a sideways glance in Harriet's direction, his mouth set in a grim line. "She knows you can't have any contact with him, right?"

Harriet nodded. "She's aware of the situation."

"And she called you anyway?" Drew snorted his derision. "No offence, but that doesn't exactly fill me with confidence for the prospect of Matthews' rehabilitation."

"I wouldn't have thought you were a fan of rehabilitation for offenders in any situation?"

The silence that spread out between them was the uncomfortable kind. Finally, after what felt like an age, Drew cleared his throat and straightened up behind the steering wheel. "I can't say it's all bad. I'm sure it's helpful for some people."

"Just not Nolan?"

"Why do you keep doing that?" Drew asked, his words tinged with anger.

"Doing what?"

"Calling him by his first name?"

Harriet shrugged. "I don't know. Why wouldn't I?" Seeing the incredulous look on Drew's face, she added. "It's his name, Drew. I don't know how else to refer to him."

"By his surname?" His sigh was loaded with frustration. "I don't know, call him scum, call him monster, but don't sit there and so blithely refer to him as though the two of you are long-lost friends." There was a strain in his voice as he spoke. As she studied him, Harriet caught sight of a vein in the side of his neck that throbbed rhythmically.

"Is that how you think of him?"

"What?" Drew cast a look at her, and the action caused the car to drift over the white line. He corrected their course, but the fact that it had happened at all told Harriet the depth to which he was altered by the conversation, and that knowledge made her uncomfortable.

Whoever he'd been speaking to had signed off on his return-to-work, but from her position Harriet found herself doubting if he was truly ready for it. If a mere conversation about Nolan could provoke such an extreme reaction, then what would happen as he found himself interacting with similar situations that his work would inevitably expose him to.

"You said I should call him monster. Is that how you think of him?"

Drew glanced back at her, and Harriet wished she'd chosen to have the conversation with him when they weren't in a moving vehicle. "Are you really asking me that? Of course he's a monster. Are you telling me you don't think he is?"

Harriet glanced back out the passenger window. "He's not a monster, Drew. What he did to you was monstrous, but Nolan is just a man like any other."

Drew jerked the steering wheel to the side, causing the car to slide over onto the hard shoulder. Car horns blared behind them, as gravel and dirt were kicked up around the car. Closing her eyes, Harriet fumbled around for the safety handle on the door and clung to it as the car rolled to a complete stop.

Opening her eyes, she glanced over at Drew, who sat with his face pressed against the steering wheel. He was breathing hard, his shoulders and chest rising and falling like someone who had just run a marathon.

"Are you all right?" Harriet was pleased to find her voice was somewhat steady, despite the hammering of her heart in her chest.

When he straightened up, his face was pale. "I'm fine." He pushed open the car door and stepped out. Harriet watched him go and contemplated letting him go. He clearly needed to clear his head, but the voice in the back of her mind told her to follow him.

Mindful of their precarious position on the side of the road, Harriet slipped out and made her way around the car to where he stood. "You're not fine."

He stood with his back to her, his face buried in his hands. "Is that your professional opinion?" There was an acerbic note to his voice, and he deliberately remained facing away from her.

"No." Harriet contemplated what she should say next. Conversations like this didn't always come easily to her. She was so used to falling back on her profession, it was easier that way, and it allowed her to maintain some kind of objectivity no matter the situation she found herself in.

But this was different. Drew didn't need another professional. What he needed from her, she wasn't entirely convinced she could give him. However, she needed to try. "It's my opinion as your friend."

His hands dropped to his sides, his shoulders rising up as he sucked down a lungful of the crisp November air. "You really don't see him the way I do, do you?" Drew turned to face her then, and Harriet could see the haunted expression in his eyes. "What about Robert Burton? You can't tell me that what he did to those kids, to your friend, what he tried to do to you, doesn't make him a monster."

Harriet shook her head and glanced down at the leaf strewn ground. "I don't, because he's not a monster, Drew."

"I don't understand you."

"Calling them monster makes them more than they are," she said softly. "It turns them into something important, something to be feared. When in actuality they are just two broken, and damaged men who decided to take their grief, and rage out on the world around them."

"That sounds like an excuse to me," Drew said bitterly.

"Well, it's not," she said. "It's just the truth. Hollywood turns them into monsters, an invincible bogeyman we can all fear. The truth is far darker, but also so much simpler than that. They are human, just like you or me--"

"Matthews is nothing like me," Drew practically spat the words out. "I'm not a killer."

"I never said you were," Harriet pressed her fingers to the bridge of her nose and pinched down hard. A headache was beginning to form between her eyes, and the cold air was seeping in through her thin blouse, chilling her to the bone. "You're deliberately trying to misunderstand me," she said.

Drew's laughter echoed off the trees that lined that edge of the road. "What do you expect me to think? You're standing there making excuses for the man who tried to turn me into so much mincemeat. I can't just let that go."

Harriet took a tentative step forward. "I'm sorry he made you feel so much pain," she said softly. "But you know deep down that what I'm saying is true."

He closed his eyes, and Harriet was sure she had lost him completely. It wasn't until he opened his eyes again and met her gaze head on that she realised his reaction wasn't entirely related to Nolan Matthews' attempt on his life.

"He took everything from me," he whispered.

"You mean Dr Connor?"

Drew nodded unhappily. "He took her from me, and then his little mistake nearly cost me my life... Not to mention the fact that his little human *experiment* could have killed you." He pressed his hand to his face and choked back a half-strangled sob. "I had to sit there and watch him threaten you, and there was nothing I could do."

"It wasn't your fault," Harriet said. "You can't control everything in life, Drew. You need to understand that."

"But if I'd been smarter... I didn't realise something was wrong until I was halfway into the living room. I'm supposed to be a DI, and I didn't even know he'd broken into my gaff until I was stood on the plastic. He could have taken an advertisement out on a billboard, and I still wouldn't have realised until it was too late."

"He fooled a lot of people, Drew. You weren't the only one."

"But you knew?"

"And I was almost too late," she said. Harriet sighed and began to pace up and down on the hard shoulder. She needed to do something to get warm, and walking was the only thing she could think of.

"You're not the only one he pulled the wool over on? I looked up to him."

"He got to you when you were young," Drew said. "You trusted him because of what happened with your mother. He made you feel safe..."

Harriet glanced over at him. She'd never allowed herself to think too deeply just why Jonathan had so successfully tricked her into believing him. But now that Drew had spoken the words aloud, she knew it was true.

Jonathan, as much as she hated to admit it, had made her feel safe. For so long, he'd been the one to help her deal with the world and its little cruelties. He'd taught her to handle her mother's condition. Taught her how to take back the control she so badly craved in her life by introducing her to psychology.

She'd allowed him to be her moral compass. What did that say about her judgement? If she could so easily be manipulated by him, then how could she possibly expect her professional opinion not to be tainted by his poison?

"You're right," she said. "He made me feel safe." Harriet placed her hand over her mouth as though that alone could prevent the hysteria from leaking out of her. "I was stupid, incredibly stupid not to see it sooner."

"But you were a child," Drew said. "He was in the wrong."

"That doesn't excuse it," Harriet said, her voice she was pleased to discover was for the most part steady. "I went through the training, all those years in university. All those hours with others who had been manipulated as I had been. I should have seen it sooner." She sucked in a deep breath and squared her shoulders. "If I was going to agree to anyone being a monster, it would be him."

Drew's laughter took her by surprise. "You're not very convincing."

She contemplated being offended by his words, but instead chose to laugh. "I just can't bring myself to use words like that to describe people. It's too easy. It's like saying someone is evil, it stops them from ever having to carry the responsibility of their own actions."

Letting his head drop toward his chest, Drew nodded. "I can understand that." He sighed, scrubbing his hand over his face before he decided to speak again. "Look, I'm sorry about all of this—whatever this is?"

"You don't need to apologise…"

"I do."

His insistence brought a smile to Harriet's lips. "Perhaps we should get back on the road?"

Her suggestion caused Drew to glance down at his watch and swear like a sailor. "They're going to wonder where we are."

"I'm sure they'll have managed just fine without us."

He nodded. "I suppose. It's not like we can do much until the fire officers and SOCOs give us the all-clear."

Harriet didn't bother trying to hide her surprise. "I thought you said it was a bungled burglary. You didn't mention it was a fire."

"Don't look so worried, I haven't lost my marbles yet. It was called in as a burglary, but the whole joint went up in flames. The fire officers don't really think a burglary is the pertinent part. The fire and the body are the headliners." There was an awkward beat before Drew seemed to give himself a mental shake and turn toward the car.

Harriet slipped into the passenger seat and pulled her seatbelt on before Drew spoke again.

"Can I ask you something?"

"Of course."

"That day in my place..." Drew sucked in a deep breath, as though it was a struggle to even form the words. "Why did you save him?"

"I don't understand—"

"Yeah, you do..." He swivelled in the seat to face her. "You had a connection with him. I saw it."

"You were badly hurt, Drew, I don't think you were thinking straight."

"Please don't fob me off on this. I heard what you said to him. You said you understood his darkness. You wanted to help him, and I'm just wondering why?"

"It's my job." Harriet fought to keep her breathing even, and her expression blank. "This is what I do. I try to help."

For a moment, she thought Drew was going to speak again, but he nodded, the expression in his eyes hardening. "Fine." He spun away from her, and started the engine, and Harriet watched as the tension in his shoulders slowly loosened.

He drove the car off the hard shoulder and rejoined the flow of traffic as it tracked toward the coast. Harriet returned her attention to the scenery beyond the glass, studying the trees as they flashed by.

She'd known the risk she'd taken when she'd exposed her vulnerabilities to Nolan. It was a calculated risk, and it had all been for Drew. But that didn't change the fact that he now viewed her differently.

In trying to save his life, she'd driven a wedge between them, and Harriet had no idea how she was supposed to repair the damage that might have caused.

Balling her hands into a fist, she relished the feel of her nails as they bit into the palms of her hand.

CHAPTER ELEVEN

RELEASING the fist she'd formed, Harriet was pleased to see blood well in the half-moon shapes she'd left on her palm.

"How much you want to bet that's where we're headed?" Drew kept his gaze trained on the road ahead.

She glanced up and caught sight of the billowing black smoke that drifted upwards into the otherwise clear sky. "It looks huge."

Drew nodded, and Harriet could practically see the cogs turning in his mind.

"Did you have any indication it would be this big?"

"No," he said. "It seems the DCI left out some of the more pertinent information."

They passed a sign welcoming them to Whitby, and Harriet felt her breath catch in the back of her throat. Drew hadn't mentioned they were heading for the small tourist town tucked away on the east coast. She should have known, but she'd been so engrossed in her own head she'd missed the signposts and landmarks that were a dead giveaway as to their destination.

Drew handled the car expertly on the small, but busy roundabouts, avoiding the centre of town in favour of which considering the traffic moving in that direction Harriet could only imagine how busy it would be. But that was always the case where Whitby was concerned. The sea stretched out in front of them, the vast blue infinitely more unfathomable than some of the minds Harriet had encountered.

She'd visited the town on a couple of occasions when she'd been younger. Bianca had loved the picturesque town, with its rich history, and friendly locals, and Harriet had grown to love it because of the joy it brought her friend.

The road went west, leading them away from the town, and the thick black smoke only got thicker. The Sat-Nav beeped triumphantly, announcing they had reached their destination.

"Well shit," Drew muttered beneath his breath as he pulled to a halt and set the handbrake. They weren't the only onlookers, Harriet noted. Men in hard hats and high-vis jackets—Harriet deducted they belonged to the site in question—milled outside the cordon set by the fire crew.

The chaotic scene filled Harriet with unease as she swept her gaze over the shells of the new build houses that were blackened by what must have been a large blaze.

Judging by the intensity of the smoke damage, which was centred on a town house in one of the long terraces, Harriet assumed it was the point of origin.

As she opened the door, smoke poured in around her, burning her nose and stinging her eyes.

Instinctively, she raised her sleeve and pressed it to her nose and mouth. Her eyes had already begun to water, blurring the scene.

"DI Drew Haskell, and this is my colleague Dr Harriet Quinn." Drew's familiar voice reached her over the noise of the scene. Harriet moved around the back of the car, careful to stay out of the way of those who were working.

"We heard you found a body," Drew said. "We need to speak to the fire officer in charge here."

A uniformed police officer pointed out another man in the familiar attire of a firefighter who was directing the others who were picking their way through the rubble to secure the scene.

Harriet paused next to Drew and continued to stare at the scene. "I think he's a little pre-occupied," Harriet said. Not that it mattered. There was so much noise she was certain nobody could overhear them, even if they had been standing next to her.

Nodding his assent, Drew studied the scene, and Harriet wondered what he was thinking.

"We need to find the site manager," he said. "Find out what he's got to say. Maybe he can tell us who the body belongs to."

"How would he do that?"

"Well, I suppose it depends on how the fire started." He rolled the collar of his jacket up.

"I don't think I understand?"

Drew glanced over at her. "Malicious firing isn't strictly arson until they can prove it put somebody's life in danger."

She cocked an eyebrow at him. "I didn't know there was a difference. But we've got a body, so that means it probably is arson?"

Drew shrugged. "That'll be down to the fire officer and his arson investigation team, and the forensic pathologist will need to determine cause of death. But for argument's sake, if it is arson, what are we looking at here?"

Pursing her lips, Harriet glanced back at the burnt-out husk in an attempt to collect her thoughts. There were many reasons for arson. Many potential psychological profiles. And sifting through them to find the correct one would take more than just a cursory glance at the site.

"It's complicated," she said with a sigh. The

smoke burned the back of her throat as she tried to take a deep breath. "Typically, the reasons for arson fall under a wide umbrella. Vandalism, financial gains, revenge, or extremism. You've also got to consider the possibility that somebody who enjoys setting fires could have started this. It excites them. And also, this could have been done to conceal a crime."

"Burning a building seems a little extreme to cover up a crime," Drew mused as he continued to watch the firemen work with an abject fascination.

"Like I said, there are many psychological reasons for setting a fire. When it comes to concealing a crime, some people panic and think a fire is a simple way of covering their tracks. Usually, they're wrong."

Drew gestured toward the closest uniformed officer and beckoned him over. "Which one is the site manager."

The officer—Harriet noted his apprehension as he approached Drew—stumbled over his words. "He's over there, guv."

If Drew noted the other man's nervousness, he didn't let on. Harriet trailed after Drew, keeping her attention focussed on the other police officers who were working to keep the onlookers a safe distance from the cordon. They all seemed to be a little uncomfortable in Drew's presence, and that realisation surprised Harriet.

"My name is DI Drew Haskell, and this is my colleague Dr Harriet Quinn. I was wondering what you could tell me about the situation here today, Mr..."

"Clarkson." The other man was a good foot shorter than Drew and was forced to crane his neck upwards to meet his gaze. He rubbed his hand back over his head. His hair was so short it was practically non-existent, and Harriet found herself wondering if the gesture was a nervous habit, or if it was a stress reaction.

"I got here this morning first thing." He squeezed his eyes shut, as though that helped him recall the details. "After six am, I think. It was early, the sun was only starting to come up. Soon as I parked up, I noticed the gate to the site was already open. Now I never leave it open. We keep this place locked down tight, insurance demands it."

Drew nodded his understanding, and the site manager took it as a sign he should continue. "I thought it was odd, so I parked up as usual and decided to have a look around, I found the chain on the gate was cut."

"And at that time could you smell smoke, or—"

Mr Clarkson shrugged. "Maybe I could. I can't rightly remember if I'm honest. It all happened so fast after that... I thought at first that maybe it was kids."

"Do you often have a problem with children breaking and entering your site?" Drew asked wryly.

"Well, no, but I didn't think it was anything serious..."

"When did you first properly notice the fire?"

Mr Clarkson glanced back at the site, drawing a deep breath into his lungs. Harriet noted the smoke beneath his nose. Had he tried to enter the property?

"I went around the back of the terrace and saw the broken glass door. It was then I called you lot. But by the time I was on the phone, the upstairs windows blew out and the upper floor of the house was swallowed."

"And you saw nobody coming, or going from the premises during that time?"

Harriet could detect the disbelief in Drew's voice and made a mental note to ask him just what part of the story he'd found unbelievable.

"Well, a few of the men who work here arrived a few minutes after I did."

"And what time did you say that was?"

Mr Clarkson shifted from one foot to the other. "After six."

"And there was nobody here before you this morning?"

Clarkson shook his head. "Not that I noticed."

"Does anyone ever get here before you?"

"No, I'm always the first."

Drew paused and glanced back at the burnt-out houses. "And who locks the site up?"

"I'm usually last out, and first in. If I can't be here, then I let Cain open and shut the place."

"And is Cain here now?" Drew asked, his gaze trained on the other man's face.

"He's over there. Why? You don't think Cain had anything to do with all of this, do you?"

Drew followed the direction the other man had pointed and then shook his head. "At this point, we can't say anything. Do you always start on the site so early?" Drew's tone was deliberately friendly.

"Always on a Monday." Clarkson sighed. "I like to get a jump on it after the weekend." He scrubbed his hand over his practically bald head. "We've already sold most of the houses here, a fire is a huge setback."

Drew gave him a tight-lipped smile, but Harriet noted how he said nothing of the body they'd found. "We'll need you to come down to the station to give a proper statement. But that's all for now."

Mr Clarkson gave a brief nod of his head and started to turn away.

"Just out of curiosity, why did you call it in as a burglary, Mr Clarkson?"

The other man flushed crimson and scrubbed his left hand against the side of his faded blue jeans. "Well, I thought it was. You assume, don't you?"

"Why because the lock on the gate was bust?"

Mr Clarkson nodded. "It seemed the most likely, and then when I saw the door..."

Drew smiled. "Thanks."

"Anything at all. I want to catch who did this," Clarkson added, but Harriet couldn't help but wonder if he truly meant what he was saying. There was obviously something he was leaving out of his description.

Drew moved away and paused, waiting for her to catch up.

"What do you think?" His voice was a low murmur against the backdrop of controlled chaos of the scene.

"I don't think he's being entirely honest," she said thoughtfully. It was the truth, but if Drew asked her to pinpoint exactly why she thought the site manager was lying to them, he would be disappointed.

"Neither do I, but I don't think we're going to get any kind of revelation here. At least not until the fire officer gives us the green light and we can take a look around."

"So, what do we do then, just hang around and wait?"

"We start knocking on doors, get the uniforms and constables organised into some kind of team so they can find out if anyone saw anything suspicious. I don't think we'll get an ID on our body until the pathologist can take a look. Unless we hear of someone who has gone missing."

Harriet glanced around at their surroundings. "I don't suppose you'll find anyone out here?"

Drew scrubbed his chin thoughtfully. "True, but we might get lucky." He fell silent then, and stared out over the cliffs toward the sea.

"What is it?"

"It's a magnificent view," he said. Harriet had to fight the urge to roll her eyes. "You know that's not what I meant."

Drew smiled ruefully. "Before I came to see you this morning, I had another call out."

Harriet remained silent, and Drew took it as the invitation it was intended to be. "Attempted break in down near Newholm."

"That's just down the road from here..."

Drew nodded. "Yeah, seems a little coincidental, don't you think?"

"But why break in here and then set fire to the house?"

"You said it yourself, some offenders panic, and think covering their tracks with fire is the right thing to do."

"Tell me more about this morning's call out?"

Drew glanced down at his watch. "Let me get organised here and I'll see if we can take a trip over there."

"Are you sure that's all right?"

"If the two cases are connected, then I'd prefer to

get you up to speed on it all so we can close these down as quickly as possible."

Harriet nodded thoughtfully. "Fine."

A SHORT WHILE LATER, and they pulled up in front of a stone cottage on the outskirts of Newholm. The two-storey cottage was sat back from the road, the small gravel drive swept up to a bright blue door, and Harriet could almost imagine that under different circumstances the house might even be considered picturesque.

Drew was out of the car first, his face an impassive mask that Harriet recognised as his professional persona. A patrol car sat on one end of the drive, and a young uniformed officer climbed from behind the wheel as Harriet stepped out onto the drive. The gravel crunched noisily beneath her feet. Not exactly an ideal surface for their would-be villain.

"You're still here?" Drew asked.

The uniformed constable shook his head. "No, we were in the area. PC Pearson thought it would be better to swing back by here in order to ask Ms Dunsly a couple of more questions."

Drew said nothing, but Harriet could tell from the flicker of irritation that passed through his eyes that he wasn't entirely pleased with PC Pearson's initiative.

"Anything I should know?" Drew's tone was

conversational, no doubt intended to make the other man feel more comfortable. However, from where Harriet stood, there seemed to be little chance of that happening if the tension in the other man's body was anything to go by.

"You'd have to ask PC Pearson that yourself, sir. She didn't tell me."

Harriet kept her thoughts to herself, but she had her doubts about the constable's statement. There was something he was holding back on, but she knew if she pried, he would only clam up further. Loyalty was vitally important.

"And the SOCOs?"

Pearson's shoulders visibly relaxed. "They left about an hour ago. They've gone over the place with a fine-toothed comb. I'm not sure how much they'll have found though."

"Why is that?" Drew leaned back on his heels.

"They didn't seem too pleased about it. I overheard one of them say whoever it was used gloves."

It wasn't unexpected. Most people who had access to a television knew that wearing gloves was one particularly important forensic countermeasure.

The strain was evident in the set of Drew's jaw as he caught Harriet's eye. "Is there anything you need to see out here?"

"Maybe later," Harriet said, following him as he headed for the front door.

Until she heard from the woman inside, anything

she would look at would form speculation on her behalf; nothing more than here-say. And as damaging to the formation of an accurate profile as rumour and gossip. Nothing more than castles built on sand.

A few moments later, Harriet found herself in the hallway of a small, but orderly house. The books on the shelves in the living room were arranged from large to small, and Harriet quickly realised they were also grouped together based on their topic. The intoxicating scent of cleaning agents hung in the air, and Harriet found herself drawn toward the kitchen at the back of the property.

"And you said this isn't the first time you received a—" The female voice cut off as Drew stepped into the kitchen ahead of Harriet. Two women stood facing each other in the kitchen. PC Pearson was instantly identifiable because of the uniform she wore.

"Ms Dunsly, we spoke earlier," Drew said. "This is my colleague, Dr Harriet Quinn." He made the introductions quickly, his voice deliberately gentle, which belied the tension which held his spine rigid. If he was displeased with PC Pearson's behaviour, then he wasn't signposting it to the casual observer.

Not that Harriet was surprised by any of this. Drew was a consummate professional, especially in situations like this. He would do his best to ensure the victim never suffered because of his own personal feelings.

"I don't want to talk to anyone else about this," Ms Dunsly said. "Why can't you lot just do your bloody jobs and catch the sick bastard responsible?"

Harriet's gaze travelled over the other woman. She wore a pair of dove grey slacks; her cream chenille jumper was only slightly rumpled. Her dark hair was secured at the nape of her neck with several small pins, but small sections of it had escaped and hung around her flushed face.

Drew opened his mouth to respond, but Harriet caught his eye and surreptitiously shook her head.

"Ms Dunsly, I can appreciate this is difficult," Harriet started to speak, drawing the attention of the room. From the corner of her eye, she observed PC Pearson as she stepped back and took up a position near the door.

"What are you, some kind of counsellor? Victim services?"

Harriet smiled and inclined her head in the direction of the other woman. "Am I that transparent?"

"You all have the same look," Ms Dunsly said. "You learn to spot it when you spend enough time..." She trailed off and returned her gaze to the sink of soapy water.

Harriet's gaze travelled to the woman's dry and red fingers. The skin around her nails was peeling, as though they had spent far too long exposed to chemicals that shouldn't ever come into contact with delicate flesh.

She sighed. "How long is this going to take? I'm tired." As though to emphasise her point, she glanced over at the large clock that dominated the exposed brick wall at the opposite end of the kitchen. "The world doesn't stop just because the dregs of society decide my house is a neat little target to support their drug habit, and there's somewhere I need to be."

"Ms Dunsly, is this the first time you've had an attempted break-in?" Harriet tried to keep her tone conversational and light. Most people thought of break-ins as nothing to be overly concerned with; little more than an inconvenience. Their opinion tended to change when they were the victim of a burglary. Home was where you were supposed to be safe, the walls a fortress against those who would seek to do you harm. And when those walls were breached... Well, everyone acted differently. Only time would tell how Ms Dunsly reacted.

Ms Dunsly moved over toward the kitchen table and gestured to the seat opposite.

"Please, call me Caroline," she said, closing her eyes. Harriet took the seat offered and studied the woman on the other side of the table. Caroline's shoulders dropped and Harriet noted for the first time just how exhausted she appeared. There were too many possibilities to attribute to her exhaustion, and it wasn't Harriet's place to jump to conclusions, but she couldn't shake the feeling that something was keeping this woman awake at night. It was this thought that put Harriet on edge.

"That I know of, it's the first attempt at a break-in," Caroline said. "It's always been very quiet around here. The nearest neighbours are a couple of miles that way." She pointed vaguely in the direction of the back garden. "We've never had this kind of trouble around here."

"That you know of," Harriet said kindly.

Caroline stared down at her clasped hands, before she started to pick at the damaged skin on her fingers. "It makes you feel uncomfortable, you know?"

Harriet nodded. "I can imagine it would." From the corner of her eye, she watched as Drew took up an observational position with his shoulder pressed against the doorjamb. He was the picture of ease, but Harriet could sense the tension that kept his body rigid, and his hooded gaze alert.

"I don't know if I want to stay here tonight," she said softly. "I mean, I know I've got Freddy, but knowing someone was deliberately trying to get in here in the middle of the night, well it makes you afraid."

"Is there someone you could go and stay with?" Drew asked, never moving from his position by the door.

Caroline started, as though Drew's question had

pulled her from a deep state of meditation. "And allow him to run me out of my own house?"

"That's not what it would be," Harriet said, trying to get the conversation back on track. "It would be temporary." Judging by the stubborn set of Caroline's jaw, Harriet knew her plea had fallen on deaf ears, and so she decided to try a different approach. "If you don't want to leave, why not have someone come and stay with you?"

"No. That's ridiculous. Why would I inconvenience someone else just because I'm feeling a little jumpy?" There was an edge to her voice that practically dared Harriet to question the meaning of her words. But she was already riled up enough as it was, and the last thing Harriet wanted to do was add fuel to the fire.

A dog started to bark from somewhere deep in the house, causing Harriet's heart to jump in her chest. "You've got a dog?"

Caroline's expression softened. "Yes, that's Freddy. He's feeling a little upset after everything that has gone on. I should go and check on him."

Harriet smiled and watched as Caroline got up and made her way out of the room.

"Is there a reason you came back, constable?" Drew asked, his voice barely above a whisper.

Harriet turned her attention to the uniformed officer on the other side of the room and was surprised to see the other woman return Drew's expression defiantly.

"Ms Dunsly called me."

"Did she remember something else?" Drew pulled away from the wall and moved further into the room.

"She—" PC Pearson cut off as Caroline appeared in the doorway with a small brown and white Jack-Russell on a brightly coloured lead. Despite the relatively small stature of the dog, he pulled Caroline into the kitchen. He huffed and whined as he strained against the leash, desperate to get a good sniff of the strangers gathered in his domain.

"I'm sorry, I couldn't keep him locked up in there. It's not fair." Caroline's lower lip wobbled almost in defiance of the strength in her voice.

"That's fine," Harriet interrupted before either of the others could speak. "He's beautiful."

Caroline seemed relieved. The smile that spread across her face as she beamed down at the small, excitable animal told Harriet just how important the dog was to her.

"So, Freddy was the reason you woke up last night?" Harriet asked, trying to steer the conversation back in the direction she needed.

"I normally ignore him," Caroline appeared chagrined, and glanced down at the dog who was at that moment sniffing around Harriet's shoes. "And now I know he was trying to warn me…"

"Does Freddy often bark during the night?"

Caroline's stubborn expression faltered, and she lifted her hand to self-consciously smooth her hair down. "Like I told your colleague earlier, he's a good boy, but there have been a few occasions..."

"Nights where he's kept you awake?"

Caroline nodded and sighed. "I suppose he is, yes. He wasn't always like this," Caroline added hastily, as though worried Harriet might think badly of him if she didn't set the record straight. "And now that I've had time to think about it, I suppose he knew more about what was going on than I did."

Caroline shifted uncomfortably and glanced toward PC Pearson. "Lyla said—I mean PC Pearson said—there was evidence that whoever tried to break in has been hanging around for a while." Caroline swallowed hard.

"Excuse me?" Drew's voice cut through the silence.

"She said they found evidence—"

"Sir, with all due respect we've got reason—"

"Outside, now." There was no arguing with Drew's tone of voice, and Harriet watched as the constable dropped her gaze toward the floor.

"Oh, dear, I didn't intend to get anybody in trouble."

"You haven't," Harriet reassured her. "Drew..." Harriet cut off as Drew's furious attention focused on her. "DI Haskell, perhaps we could keep things calm?"

He glanced over at Caroline, who had begun to rub Freddy with an almost obsessive zeal. The woman was clearly upset after everything that had happened, and Drew's behaviour wasn't going to put her at ease. After their earlier conversation, Harriet wondered if perhaps he shouldn't be conducting such delicate interviews.

Drew stiffened. "If you wouldn't mind, constable, perhaps we should discuss this outside."

"Of course, sir," PC Pearson said, her voice clipped and angry.

"If you'll just excuse us for a minute," Harriet said, addressing Caroline.

"Don't you need to hear what else I've got to say," Caroline said. Harriet noted the nervous manner in which the other woman twisted her fingers around one another.

"Dr Quinn is far more capable than I could ever hope to be," Drew said. "Tell her everything you would say to me." Despite the smile on Drew's face, there was a sharpness to his tone that Harriet wasn't used to hearing from him. If she wasn't mistaken, Drew was treading very close to dismissing the other woman's fears, and that didn't sit well with her. He was gone before Caroline could respond.

"Could you give us a moment," Harriet said, with a gentle smile. "There's just something I want to address with DI Haskell, but I promise I'll be right back."

Caroline opened her mouth, and for a moment Harriet thought she might argue with her. Instead, her mouth snapped shut, and she nodded miserably. "Fine. What's another few minutes when I've already wasted half the day on this nonsense?"

The urge to reassure the other woman was strong, but Harriet resisted the urge, and got to her feet. She followed Drew out into the hall, catching up to him as he reached the front door.

"What's going—"

"I could ask you the same thing," Harriet whispered, the words tumbling out from between clenched teeth. She glanced back over her shoulder and was grateful for the thicker walls that made up the cottage's structure. "That woman in there is deserving of your time, and respect, Drew..."

Drew nodded his head in PC Pearson's direction. "Could you give us a moment?"

The uniformed constable opened her mouth and then changed her mind and stormed from the hall. Drew waited until she was out of earshot before he returned his attention to Harriet. "I never said she wasn't."

"Then why are you behaving as though all of this is somehow beneath your attention?"

He took a small step backwards, and Harriet could see the shutters come down in his face, but not before she'd caught the wounded expression which had flashed in his eyes.

"I would never—"

"You just did. I'm not sure if it's because I told you about Nolan earlier—"

Drew sucked a sharp, pained breath in between his teeth, and Harriet wondered if she'd gone too far. It wouldn't be the first time she'd misread a situation, but it would be the first time she'd misread one as badly as this.

"I didn't realise I was such a disappointment," Drew said stiffly.

"That's not what I'm saying at all," she said hurriedly. "You're better than this, that's all. And if something is bothering you, then talk to me. We can work through it together—"

He shook his head and stepped out through the front door. "It doesn't concern you, Dr Quinn."

Harriet's heart sank. She'd clearly screwed the conversation up, and he was so bull-headed that rather than correct her assumptions regarding his behaviour, Drew would behave like a martyr and throw himself on the sword of righteous silence.

She let her shoulders drop as she turned her attention back to the situation at hand. Something that Caroline had said niggled in the back of her mind. Was there something here that she was missing? It was altogether possible that they were dealing with a routine attempted burglary, but Caroline had mentioned that her dog had been keeping her awake.

It was probably just her suspicious mind, but Harriet couldn't shake the unease that draped itself over her shoulders.

Returning to her seat at the table, Harriet smiled at the woman sitting across from her.

"Is everything all right?" Caroline asked. Harriet detected an extra note of disquiet that had crept into her voice since their last chat. "I really didn't mean to get PC Pearson in hot water. She's been very kind."

"Everything is fine." She kept her smile fixed in place and did her best to sound as reassuring as she possibly could. "PC Pearson isn't in trouble."

Caroline wrapped the leash around her fingers tighter than before so that the tips of her fingers whitened under the pressure.

"Tell me, what is it you do?" Harriet decided a change in topic might help to ease the tension.

"I work in the bank over in Scarborough." Caroline sighed and rubbed her fingers over the furrow in the middle of her brow. "I fail to see how this is helpful?"

"I'm just trying to find out a bit about you," Harriet said.

"And how does that help you find the man who tried to break in?"

Harriet considered several answers before she quickly discarded them all. It had been said that getting to know the victim was often the key to knowing the criminal, but there were far too many variables at play. And telling Caroline the reason behind such personal questions would only unnerve her further, of that Harriet was certain.

"Does your work see you away from home for long periods of time?"

"We keep regular hours," Caroline said, and then seemed to think better of it. "But I do leave rather early in the morning."

"And Freddy, does he stay here or—"

"I drop him over at my sister's during the day. That's why I leave early. She lives in Scarborough, and by the time I drive over there, and we have breakfast, it's time for work."

"It's good that you can do that. It's important to have connections." Harriet studied the other woman as she continued to stare down at her hands. "Are you sure you couldn't stay with your sister, even if only for tonight? Putting a little distance, both in terms of time, and space might help with the anxiety?"

Caroline nodded slowly. "I suppose." As much as Harriet wanted to believe the other woman was finally coming around to her way of thinking, she had the sneaking suspicion that as soon as they left, she would change her mind.

"Is there anything else you can remember?

Anything at all, no matter how silly you might think it is?"

Caroline pursed her lips. "Well, there is one thing..."

"What's that?"

"It's probably nothing." She hesitated and gave a small nervous laugh. "I'm just being silly."

"I mean it, Caroline, there's nothing you can tell me that I will think is silly. If it's bothered you enough to make you think of it, then you should tell me."

"Truly it was nothing... Lyla said I should be specific and formally report it, but I'm not sure that's a good idea because it can get rather windy up here at times—" She sighed, and pushed her hand back through her hair, and smiled. "Well, I suppose there's no harm in telling you."

Harriet gave her what she hoped was her most open and encouraging smile.

"Some of my clothes went missing from the washing line... But like I said, it can be quite windy, and now that I think of it, we've had a few storms lately and—"

"When did this start happening?"

"Over the last month, maybe two." Caroline's expression grew more concerned. "I'm being paranoid, right?"

"Could you describe the items that went missing?" Harriet deliberately ignored the question in favour of keeping the conversation flowing. It was far too important that she gather as much detail from her as she could. Her fingers curled over on themselves, and it took every ounce of restraint to relax her hand on the surface of the table. But that didn't alleviate the icy concern that slid down her spine.

"Well, it was just a few incidentals. Small items, nothing too important."

"Being as specific as possible always helps us build a picture," Harriet said, tamping down her growing concern.

"Some underwear, a bra, the shorts from my pyjamas. Nothing too vital. And they were all light, they very easily could have blown away..." Caroline trailed off miserably. "You think it's all connected, don't you?"

"I wouldn't want to assume anything, yet," Harriet said, with a warm smile. "But as PC Pearson said, the more specific you are with everything you remember, the more helpful it is for the police officers involved to get to the bottom of all of this. And if it's not connected, then there's no harm in your having told us about it."

Caroline tightened her jaw and nodded. It was obvious, despite her attempts to keep her expression neutral, that she was deeply troubled by everything that had happened. Not that Harriet could blame her. Pushing her any further right now wasn't going to help them. Caroline was fatigued. Anything else she remembered now would more than likely be tainted by that same exhaustion.

"If there's anything else you can think of, Caroline, then you can contact me on my number." Harriet pulled a small card from her bag and slid it across the tabletop in Caroline's direction before she climbed to her feet.

"Is that it?"

"Well, if it's all right with you, I'd like to take a look around outside the property."

"That's fine," Caroline said miserably as she continued to twist the leash around her fingers.

"I'll ask PC Pearson and her colleague to drive you over to Scarborough."

Caroline shook her head, defiance filling her eyes. "I can make my own way there tonight."

"Just the same, I'll have them go with you," Harriet insisted. "That way there's no confusion as to where you are."

Caroline nodded glumly. "I suppose."

Leaning down over the table, Harriet covered the other woman's hand with her own. "It's all right to feel the way you do," Harriet said. "You don't have to be strong or brave all the time. You did all that already. It's time now to let somebody else take care of you. At least for a little while, until you feel stronger."

Caroline gave her the ghost of a smile. "I suppose you're right."

Harriet straightened. "Call me anytime, Caroline. I mean that." Before she moved away from the table, Harriet crouched down next to the small Jack-Russell, who stared up at her with large brown eyes.

"You look after her, Freddy." The dog cocked his head to the side, one brown ear flopping sideways as he gave the appearance of listening to her instructions intently.

"Do you have an alarm system?" PC Pearson's question caught Harriet by surprise, and she glanced up to find the other woman standing in the doorway. She didn't look like somebody who had just been dressed down by their SIO. Then again, Harriet didn't exactly know the woman, so she didn't exactly known how PC Pearson would look under the circumstances.

Caroline shook her head. "I never thought I needed one. At least not while I've got Freddy."

"You can never be too cautious," Pearson said. "An alarm would give you that extra peace of mind. We can put you in contact with a group who specialises in these kinds of things..."

Harriet slipped out into the hall in search of Drew, leaving PC Pearson to give her obviously well-practiced speech.

It was entirely possible that she was just overreacting. That the kind of work she did had coloured her perspective on the world and as a result of that she was now reading more into the situation than she should. But something felt off and the sooner she could share her suspicions with Drew the better. That is, if he wanted to hear her opinions after their earlier confrontation.

Sighing, Harriet stepped out through the front door.

"Dr Quinn!" Pearson's shout followed Harriet as she reached the driveway in front of the house. Turning, she found the uniformed officer hurrying after her.

Harriet returned the other woman's warm smile with one of her own.

"Thanks for earlier," she said as she caught up to Harriet.

"What for?"

The constable glanced down at the ground. "Well, whatever you said to the DI struck a chord with him. I think he went easier on me because of you."

Harriet shook her head. "I don't think so. DI Haskell, is a good man."

PC Pearson raised her hands in mock surrender. "I'm not arguing with you there. I've heard about his exploits, and we all know how he took on the star killer and lived to talk about it."

"Not that he does," Harriet mused.

"Excuse me?"

Harriet shook her head. "Ignore me, I talk to

myself sometimes. Is there something you wanted to talk about, PC Pearson?"

The constable seemed nonplussed by Harriet's admission, and a wry smile crept across her face. "Lyla, you can call me Lyla."

"I'm Harriet."

Lyla glanced back over her shoulder. Satisfied she couldn't be overheard, she turned back. "You think that's weird, right? I'm not just imagining it."

"Without further evidence, I don't think it would correct of me to assume anything from the situation."

Lyla's face fell. "So, you think I'm reading too much into her story?"

Shaking her head, Harriet stepped away from the house and gestured for Pearson to follow. "That's not what I'm saying. I'm sorry if that was how it came across."

She sighed, and let her gaze travel over their surroundings, and was struck by the isolation of the location. "It's possible that it's all just as Caroline explained it. There have been several incidents of high winds this year, and considering how open and exposed the house is, I can imagine any small unsecured items would blow away."

"But it's weird that it was those particular items that 'blew' away?"

"Yes." Harriet found herself agreeing with the other woman. "And when you add to the mix the recent break-in attempt, well, it creates a concerning picture."

Pearson's smile returned. "I knew I wasn't imagining it."

"Excuse me?"

"There are others," Pearson said. "Other calls just like this. Ms Dunsly isn't the first woman targeted in the area."

"Excuse me?"

"I told the DI about it, but I'm not sure he believes me."

"There are others in the Newholm area who have experienced similar attempted break-ins?"

Lyla shook her head. "Not exactly. There have been a few cases York direction of incidentals going missing from washing lines. And we've received a couple of calls about peeping toms, and flashers..."

"I'd expect those kinds of things to be somewhat expected in a city like York?"

Lyla folded her arms over her chest defensively. "You think I'm imagining this too, don't you?"

It was Harriet's turn to shake her head. "No, I don't. But without more evidence of this being the same person, I'm not sure we can say with any certainty that this incident, and those happening down in York are the same. For one, there's the distance involved. And an escalation like you're suggesting is extreme, and far rarer than the television or books would have you believe."

Lyla's expression settled into a grimace. "I understand all of that, Dr Quinn, but I'm telling you there's more to this than meets the eye."

"Then give me something?"

Lyla swallowed hard. "We found several cigarette butts down near Caroline's fence."

The sliver of ice Harriet had felt when she'd spoken to Caroline returned and traced down her spine.

"They were all the same brand. We've had them collected and sent off for analysis, but you know what these things are like. And even if we do get something back, there's no telling if our guy is in the system already."

Harriet shifted position. "It would be unusual for someone like this to have escaped detection."

Closing her eyes, she drew in a breath. If she was wrong about this, and Lyla was correct to assume there was a connection between the crimes in York and the one that had nearly occurred here, it could have deadly consequences.

Somebody like that wouldn't just stop. He would not be deterred by Caroline's disruption of his plan. He probably wouldn't come back here... But he would re-group, and the next time he struck he would be better prepared.

"You agree with me," Lyla said, excitement colouring her voice.

"I'm not going to rule out the possibility," Harriet

said carefully. "You could be right, and I'm not willing to take the chance that you're wrong."

"Then what do we do?"

Harriet glanced over toward Drew, who stood talking to the other uniformed constable. "Leave it with me, and I'll discuss the possibilities of this being more than it seems with the DI."

Lyla practically bounced on the spot. "I'm right, I know I am."

"Will you make sure Caroline gets to her sister's house?" Harriet said, ignoring Lyla's excitement. There was a sourness in the pit of Harriet's stomach as the other woman agreed to do as she asked.

She couldn't get excited about a prospect like this. In fact, the idea of it made her sick to her stomach. She wanted Lyla to be wrong, because being right meant that something much worse was coming down the track. And without the necessary evidence, Harriet knew her own thoughts and ideas would not be sufficient to stop this particular horror show from tearing the North Yorkshire community apart.

DREW PARKED in front of the university, and Harriet listened to the sound of the engine as it cooled.

"I'm sorry about earlier," she said softly.

Shaking his head, Drew grinned at her. But it

was, Harriet noted, a smile that didn't quite reach his eyes. "I guess I need you around to keep me honest."

"No, Drew, it was unprofessional of me."

"Neither of us were top of our game today," he said quietly. "There's no need to beat yourself up about it."

Chewing her lip, Harriet grabbed her bag. She knew when he was changing the subject. "We shouldn't dismiss PC Pearson's theory," she said.

Drew snorted next to her, the sound loud and obnoxious in the confined space of the car. "You can't be serious? We've got enough on our plates with the body over in Whitby, without adding imaginary bogeymen to the list."

"And if you're wrong?" Harriet didn't bother to keep the challenge from her voice. She was pleased to see him swallow hard, his face unreadable in the fading evening light.

"We'll keep an eye on it, but I don't have the resources to devote to a wild goose chase, Harriet. The new task force has gutted us."

"I understand that," she said. "Send me over any files from York and I'll see if I can discover any correlation between the two."

"You don't—"

"I know I don't have to," she said. "But I'd sleep better at night knowing I didn't drop the ball on this one."

"I'll request the files."

She pushed the car door open, cold air flooding in around them. "Are we all right?"

Drew glanced down at his hands, and Harriet wished the overhead light had come on so she could read his expression. "We're fine. I'm fine..." He sighed. "Or at least I will be fine. I just need a little time to find my feet again."

"If you need me, for anything at all you promise you'll call?"

"I promise."

She stepped out of the car, and slammed the door shut, as the voice in the back of her mind screamed at her not to let him drive away.

It was stupid, really. She needed to be able to trust him, to trust that he would ask for help if he needed it. But Harriet wasn't a fool, she'd seen the look in his eye, and she knew enough about DI Haskell to realise that in his world asking for help was akin to admitting weakness.

"You're not his keeper, Harriet," she murmured beneath her breath as his taillights disappeared around the bend. But if that were true, then why did she feel so bloody responsible?

CHAPTER TWELVE

NERVOUS ANTICIPATION THRUMMED in his stomach, made all the worse by the knowledge of how close he had come to getting caught. He contemplated crossing over to the café and getting the key to their toilet. With the way his stomach was twisting, it wouldn't be a prolonged visit; more of a pit stop.

Revulsion gripped him by the nape of his neck at the crude direction his thoughts had taken. He had to be smarter than this. There was far too much at stake. Too much riding on his ability to keep his shit together, in more ways than one.

He stared down at the payphone in front of him. This probably wasn't what dear ole dad had in mind when he'd told him to get right back on the horse after the rejection. Sad bastard was more to be pitied now, and yet his father still had the ability to reduce him to a snivelling pile of snot.

He pushed the destructive pattern of thinking aside. He'd show that old codger who held the power now.

Sighing, he watched his breath fog against the grubby window of the Perspex box around him.

Next time he would be better, faster, more prepared for any possible outcome. If there even was a next time.

It was easier to stay on the fringes. To watch from afar, and never actually interact with them. But whether they knew it or not, he was leaving his mark. Indelible on their lives. His, for all time.

They dismissed his presence. Brushed it aside as nothing more than imagination.

But in the dark, when they settled down for sleep, he knew that was when they thought of him. An incorporeal menace that hung over their heads, the veritable sword of Damocles. Only he held the power.

Chewing his lip, he raised his gloved hand to the telephone receiver. Leather clad fingers slid over the shiny plastic surface before he snatched it into the air. The familiarly flat dial tone mingled in the air which was tainted by his flop sweat. His moist tongue protruded out from between his teeth, before making a quick swipe at his cracked lips.

His hand shook as he dialled the number and raised the phone to his ear, all the time careful to keep his hood between the receiver and skin. He'd watched enough episodes of Crimewatch to know everything he touched left a trace.

Not that he really understood any of it. School hadn't exactly been a piece of cake. Not because he wasn't bright, though. All his teachers had said if he'd just applied himself, he could have the world at his feet. What they didn't understand was the sad fact that if your parents didn't feel the same way, then you never really stood a chance.

Squeezing his eyes shut tight, he felt a squeal rising in the back of his throat, but he crushed it down where it belonged. He held his breath as he listened to the ringing in his mind, imagining her as she hurried across the kitchen to the telephone.

The bloody dog was probably barking again, a fucking menace if ever there was. Next time he'd come prepared to deal with the mutt.

"Hello?" Her voice, a little breathless, took him by surprise when it curled down the line and into his ear. It was muffled by his hood, and he longed to brush the fabric away, to hear the terror in her voice as realisation settled around her shoulders.

He let go the breath he'd been holding onto, more a sigh of satisfaction.

"H-Hello?" There was a hitch in her voice which hadn't been there before. That simple catch was enough to tighten the knot in his gut. He'd been so close... Just what he'd been close to, well, he hadn't quite worked that out yet. It had felt more like autopilot as he'd tried to pry open the glass doors at the back of her house, need thrumming in his veins.

But what that need really was, he couldn't say. He could imagine how it would have ended, imagine the taste of her terror.

She would be different from the others. Whores had a tendency to expect the worst, and when it happened, they were utterly unsurprised by it all. It led to disappointment all around, and he'd had enough of that to last him a lifetime.

When the best part had become the concealment of his actions—convincing everyone the scratches he wore like a badge of honour really were from the neighbour's cat—well, he'd known then it was time for a change of scenery.

"Who is this?" There was no mistaking the command in her voice now. He'd been right about her. Always so coiffed, always so in control. And he'd very nearly stripped her of that. He contemplated driving over again, just so he could watch her hard won control crack, his presence chipping away at it steadily until she was exposed for what he knew her to be.

Excitement made his breathing heavy, and he could practically taste her terror as it wound through the phone line. Discomfort tainted his pleasure as the stitching in his pants dug into him, and he was made aware of the physical reaction to her terror. He shifted, shielding his body against anyone who might pass at that moment and catch sight of him as he adjusted the bulge in his trousers.

"Who is this?"

Laughter slipped out past his lips before he could stop it. There was a sharp intake of breath on the other end of the line and he knew he had her. He put the receiver down carefully and took a moment to compose himself before he stepped out of the phone box.

The rain was heavier now than it had been when he'd stepped inside, and he kept his head angled down inside his hood as he darted across the road and headed for the car park where he'd left his car.

As he rounded the corner, he felt his excitement shrivel as he spotted the familiar hulking figure of his grey Ford. Sitting like a squat toad in the middle of the carpark.

He picked up his pace and tugged open the driver's door; heat rolled out to greet him as he slipped in behind the steering wheel. The other part of him—satisfied, at least for now—was quiet, and for that he was grateful. When it was quiet, it was easier to compartmentalise the different facets of his personality.

"Daddy! You were gone for *ages*." The voice of his five-year-old daughter cut through the last of the darkness which clouded his mind. Turning in his seat, he noted the pout of her lips, and the way she folded her small delicate arms over her chest. So much like her mother...

He grinned at her. "Did you finish that picture for me?"

The pout slipped, replaced by a shy smile as she reached down to the paper's scattered across the darkened back seat. "I did two!" She held one finger up and then seemed to catch herself and lifted a second finger. Counting was still a work in progress.

She passed the two pictures through the gap in the seat, and he carefully took them. Holding them up to the light, he dutifully admired them. "These are beautiful."

"It's me, and mummy, and you. Mummy is fat because of the baby in her tummy."

He grimaced and swallowed the bile in the back of his throat as he noted the rotund figure with straw-coloured hair she'd indicated as her mother. From his point of view, it was a pretty accurate likeness. The blob of yellow which sat over them also had a face.

He assumed it was supposed to be a smiling sun; with its black beady eyes sitting askew, the smiling mouth which gaped large, filled with what could only be described as black pointed teeth lending the otherwise sunny picture a slightly more grotesque atmosphere.

"It's beautiful, sweetheart, I love it."

She beamed at him from her booster seat in the back of the car. He passed the pictures back over the passenger seat and tugged his seatbelt out of its holder as she began to hum in the backseat.

Starting the engine, he pulled out of the carpark, and turned onto the road where the payphone sat. It was an unnecessary risk, but he enjoyed the tingle that traced down his spine as he spotted the phone box where he'd made the call.

"How about McDonalds for dinner?"

The tune she'd been humming cut off abruptly and was replaced by an ear-splitting whoop of joy. Catching sight of her as she bobbed in the back seat, it brought a smile to his lips, as he drove them out of town toward the drive thru.

CHAPTER THIRTEEN

BACK IN THE STATION, Drew contemplated heading home. It wasn't as though there was anything else he could do for the night. There was still no word from Dr Jackson on when the post-mortem would be conducted on the body they'd found in the burnt-out house. Not that they'd even got around to moving the body yet. Until the SOCOs scoured every inch of the place and came away satisfied there would be no getting in or out of the property. But the thought of actually packing up and going home left him cold.

He hadn't been back to his place since Nolan had very nearly gutted him and left him for dead. Instead, he'd gone back to his childhood home. Not that it had been any easier. His mother was a good woman, but she had a tendency to smother him over time.

"I'm heading home, sir," Green's voice cut through Drew's contemplation, and he jerked in his seat.

"Fine."

"Is there anything else you—" The young constable cut off as Drew's phone started to ring.

"It's fine. You head home," Drew said, as he reached for the receiver. "DI Haskell."

"Haskell—" The monk's voice broke up as the connection stuttered.

"Sir, I wasn't expecting to hear from you."

"I know you're busy Haskell, but I could do with your assistance—" The DCI's voice crackled as the phone coverage stuttered. "Girl... Whitby—"

"Sir, you're breaking up. I'm not getting everything—"

"For Christ's sake," the Monk's voice grew clearer. "I need someone to get over to Whitby. They've pulled a girl from the water."

Drew's heart sank as the DCI's words sank in and conjured an image of Freya in his mind. Despite the doctor's concerns on his condition, Drew had discharged himself and a few hours later he'd found himself back on the water's edge. Her body, thrown free of the vehicle on impact with the icy water which had very nearly taken his life, had been recovered a few days later.

Even now, he could remember the divers as they signalled that they'd found something. The feel of his heartbeat as it thundered against his ribs as a part of him—an irrational part—had hoped she was still alive. It seemed grief, and shock had no dealings with the harshness of reality. That ridiculous hope had quickly faded as they'd pulled her from the water and brought her lifeless corpse back to the shore.

"Haskell, are you listening to me?" The Monk's voice cut through the painful memories, and Drew very nearly dropped the phone. His hand shook, and he swallowed past the painful lump which had formed in the back of his throat.

"You said a body had been pulled from the sea, sir?"

"Not a body, Haskell. A girl. She's alive. Barely, but hanging in there. I need you to get down there and secure the scene. The fishing boat which picked her up is due in any minute now, and you're the closest senior officer."

The line went dead, leaving Drew with no chance to argue. He set the phone down and sighed.

"Green!"

The young constable halted in the doorway, the smile on his face fading as he noted Drew's grimace. "I'm not going home, am I?"

Drew shook his head. "Sorry, I need you out on a call with me."

CHAPTER FOURTEEN

SITTING BACK in her office in the university, Harriet stared blankly at the computer screen in front of her. She was supposed to be working. It wasn't as though she had lots of free time on her hands, and yet she couldn't shake her unease regarding everything Lyla had told her.

No matter how much she tried to keep some distance between herself and that side of Drew's job, she was still exposed to the grisly outcomes more times than she cared to count. But that was the deal. In order to preserve life, he had to go where the criminals were, and by extension Harriet found herself along for the ride. It was inevitable really—and terribly ironic—that in saving lives they were surrounded by death.

But this case was different. Nobody was dead.

Yet, at least. Harriet's fingers itched with the urge to reach over to the beige plastic landline that sat on her desk. It wouldn't take much to call Drew and prod him into action regarding the case files.

A knock on the office door caused her to jump, and she stood as Dr Baig strode into the room. Shuffling the papers on her desk about, Harriet did her best not to look as guilty as she felt. She half expected him to launch into a tirade about the hours she was spending with the police. Instead, she was surprised when he dropped into the chair opposite and waved her to do the same.

"Come on, Harriet, you know we don't stand on ceremony around here."

This was definitely news to her, but she took the seat and waited for him to share the reason for his unexpected visit.

He glanced around the room, his gaze lingering on the few books she had on the shelves opposite her desk. When he returned his attention to her face, Harriet could tell he was unimpressed with her selection. It brought a small smile to her lips. Dennis was definitely the type of personality who wanted those who stepped into the small confines of his office space to feel impressed. He did this by filling his shelves with hardbacks that wouldn't have looked out-of-place in Dr Freud's library.

His lips compressed as he spotted the DSM-5

open on her desk among the notes, and as yet ungraded papers. "Is there something in particular you were looking for?"

"That's not what you came here for, Dennis. So, what can I help you with?"

He sighed, but there was something not quite honest about the gesture. Harriet's stomach constricted as she considered all the possible reasons for his visit. They'd spent a lot of time back and forth on the idea of her working with the police in the past, but as far as she was concerned, they had finally come to a mutual agreement on the many ways they both benefited from her continued relationship with North Yorkshire CID.

"You know I don't like to interfere with the many little projects and assignments you seem to take such pleasure in," Dennis said. Clearly whatever he was about to say wouldn't be pleasant, and Harriet schooled her features into an impassive expression. "But when it concerns the reputation of this establishment, you know I have no choice but to get involved."

"What is it you need to say to me?" She leaned back in her chair and hoped she was projecting an air of nonchalance instead of the internal panic that was slowly creeping up the back of her throat.

The last time she had considered leaving her work with Drew behind her, had left her skin cold and clammy. She might not find herself capable of helping people in a clinical setting, but the work she did alongside DI Haskell was important. At least that was what she had convinced herself of. And despite enjoying her job in the university, Harriet knew she would be willing to give it all up if she was forced to choose.

"I received a call from the psychiatrist who has been assigned to Nolan Matthews."

It took her a moment to register the fact that Dennis had spoken to her. She tried to wrap her mind around the words he had spoken, but she found herself incapable of doing so.

"I'm sorry. What did you say?"

Dr Baig sighed dramatically. "Dr Chakrabarti contacted me here at the university. She was hoping I might have a word with you about Nolan Matthews and convince you of the benefit for everyone involved if you were to visit him in prison."

"I told her I wasn't interested," Harriet said, feeling the vague stirrings of anger in the pit of her stomach. It wasn't just anger she felt, however; it was at least partially overlaid with the faintest hint of guilt. She had told Nolan she would help him. Teach him to control the dark impulses he was driven by.

Of course, that had been before he had plunged the knife into his own throat, and she had been compelled to press her hand against his neck in an attempt to prevent him from bleeding out.

No, she had had enough of Nolan Matthews.

She wouldn't visit him in prison, at least not if she could help it, anyway.

"Well, she obviously isn't the kind of woman to take no for an answer," Dr Baig said. He didn't bother to hide the admiration he obviously felt for her from his voice. Harriet struggled not to roll her eyes.

Any worry she might have felt for Dr Baig, and the rejection he'd suffered by Dr Katerina Perez in her returning to America, was clearly misplaced. He'd obviously moved on with his life, just as easily as Katerina had. Harriet envied their easy ability to pick up and drop personal relationships. Was that what it looked like to have healthy attachment behaviours?

"I've discussed it with her, and we both agree that an opportunity like this would be an excellent boon for the university."

"Excuse me?" Harriet tried to keep the irritation from her voice. Judging by the sharp expression Dr Baig shot her, she'd failed in her attempt.

"You're not thinking of the possibilities for research, Harriet. If Nolan Matthews was willing to submit himself to study, we could find ourselves standing on the precipice of a tremendous breakthrough."

"We?"

Dr Baig's countenance suggested self-depreciation, but when he spoke his words were laced with condescension and arrogance. "As your superior, and the head of this department, I would obviously take the lead on any papers published on the subject. It would be done under the guidance of the university, and it's our belief that it could open the university up to a broader audience."

"As I said to Dr Chakrabarti this morning, my answer is no."

"Harriet, think of the funding opportunities."

"I have far too much on my plate right now, Dennis. And anyway, wouldn't my visiting Nolan constitute an ethically grey area."

"Not as far as I'm concerned." Dennis reached up and readjusted the position of his dark glasses on the end of his nose. "And Dr Chakrabarti doesn't think there would be a conflict either. Really, Harriet, I thought you of all people would have jumped at an opportunity like this."

"What would make you think that?"

"Because it was you who flung yourself headlong into your work alongside the police. And I admit, I was initially sceptical, I thought it would distract you from your work here far too much. But once I could see the bigger picture," he sighed, "well, now it's a different story. And look at us all. We're peas in a pod; the university, and the new task force. When they need you, I let you help. And when training is required for their officers... My department steps in seamlessly and picks up the slack. It's a symbiotic relationship..."

Harriet wouldn't have considered the process seamless, but she kept that to herself. Dr Baig looked so pleased with himself as he sat on the other side of the table. However, for Harriet the word symbiotic conjured images of something dark and parasitic in her mind, and she suppressed a shudder. Choosing instead, to fix a polite smile on her face.

"This would work in a similar way." He sighed and leaned back in the chair. "When you first came here, you told me all you wanted to do was help people. What changed?"

Surprised, Harriet's shoulders stiffened. It hadn't occurred to her that anything in her mindset had changed, at least not in the manner he seemed to be suggesting. "As far as I'm concerned, nothing has changed."

"And yet, when you're offered the chance to make a difference — a real difference, you turn it down point blank." There was an awkward beat before he continued. "I suppose what I'm getting at here, Harriet, is that you've got the opportunity to make a difference not just here in the university, but in Nolan Matthews' life, and by extension the wider world."

"I fail to see how—" He held his hand up, effectively cutting her off.

"If Matthews is willing to speak to you, candidly... well, as candidly as somebody with his disposition can; isn't it our job — your job to listen? Most people are afraid to delve into the darker sides of society, I never considered you as one of them."

She laughed, a nervous sound that hurt her ears, and she dropped her gaze to the papers on the desk before her. "I don't see how I could help in this situation. His wanting to talk to me, only convinces me further that he wants to continue to play games. Giving him that satisfaction wouldn't lead to any meaningful kinds of breakthroughs on our behalf. He needs somebody impartial, someone untainted by the machinations of his mind. My answer remains unchanged."

"Promise me you'll at least think about it?"

She shook her head as Dr Baig pushed onto his feet. "Harriet, please, just think about this. You owe me this much at least."

It felt to Harriet too much like a quid pro quo. Nonetheless, she smiled, and bit back the sharp retort which hovered on the tip of her tongue.

"Good, good, great!" He clapped his hands and rubbed them somewhat violently together; the sound echoed in the small room. "How did you get on today with the police?"

Harriet stared at him and swallowed the discomfort that gnawed at her guts. "Fine. DI Haskell, needed my input on a case."

Dr Baig's smile broadened. "Peas in a pod." He paused and looked her over. "You like it here, don't you?"

"I don't understand?" Harriet asked, surprised by the sudden change in conversation.

"Well, you're not falling behind on your duties here?" Dennis straightened the cufflinks on his crisp white shirt.

"No, not at all."

"Because you know if you're struggling, we can always look to lighten your schedule here. We don't want you falling behind in your other work."

She shook her head but felt grateful for the offer. Clearly, he was trying to butter her up into accepting the proposal regarding Nolan Matthews.

The last thing Harriet wanted was to feel somehow beholden to the other man, because she had a feeling it would irreparably skew the relationship they currently had.

"It's fine, really."

He studied her face for a moment, leaving her with a vaguely uncomfortable feeling. When he stepped back and smiled, she fought the urge to sigh in relief.

"Well, I'll leave you to your evening then."

He hurried to the door and slipped out, leaving Harriet to bury her face in her arms on the desk. It seemed there was always some complication just waiting to pop its head up above the parapet these days. She sat up and wished—not for the first time—that she kept a bottle of something stronger than water in her desk drawers.

Closing her eyes, Harriet leaned back in the chair and let the exhaustion she felt wash over her.

CHAPTER FIFTEEN

DREW KEPT his eyes shut as Green directed the car toward their destination. When they finally drew to a halt, it was, he discovered, at a scene of abject chaos.

"What are we doing here?" Green asked, as he glanced over at the DI next to him.

Drew gripped the door handle, his eyes widening as he took in the unfolding scene. If Green noticed the pallor of his skin or how he was gripping the door, then he said nothing, and for that, Drew was grateful. There was something about the scene laid out before them that was particularly triggering for him, and without ever having to think about it, Drew knew exactly what that was.

Green had parked the car sideways on the road which ran alongside the harbour in the centre of the small town. People milled about, their curiosity evident in the way they jostled to get a clear view of the events unfolding.

From the corner of his eye, Drew spotted a flash of colour through the crowd. Focusing on it, the air in his lungs stalled as he realised the colour came from the coastguard's boat which had just arrived.

The last time he had seen a boat like that had been when... He cut his own thoughts off, but not before they could conjure an image of Freya's body as it was recovered from the wreckage of their car.

With a small shake of his head, he turned his attention back to the man next to him. Drew had not made peace with his fiancée's passing, but that didn't mean he had to allow the spectre of his lost love to loom all too large because of the situation they found themselves presented with.

"Sir, what are we doing here?"

Drew opened his mouth to speak, but found the words stuck in his throat. He coughed, and Green's expression shifted to one of curiosity.

"Are you all right?"

"I'm fine," he said, as though by saying the words they were enough to banish the painful emotions that plagued him. He swallowed hard, his Adam's apple bobbing harshly in his throat. "They've pulled a girl from the water," he said. The sound of sirens cut the air, and he glanced over his shoulder in time to see an ambulance struggling to pass through the throng that seemed to swell with each passing moment.

"We're going to need help down here," he said, eyeing the eager crowd. "We won't be able to get them all back from the edge on our own. And considering how crowds behave, we could end up with more people in the harbour before the night is over."

Green nodded, and he was relieved to see the DC's attention had been commandeered by the unfolding events.

Drew shook his head as he grabbed the radio and made a hasty call to dispatch for uniformed officers to join them at the scene. As the radio quietened, Drew climbed from the car and was jostled back and forth by the growing crowd.

The screech of hungry seagulls overhead cut the air as they wheeled back and forth, searching for an unwary victim upon which to prey. They at least were undeterred by the mass of people. In fact, the more the crowd swelled in size, the louder the gulls became.

It was difficult to break through the group, but when he finally managed it, he found Green directing the already onsite uniforms to push the crowd back. He'd pondered the young man's suitability for the job earlier in the day, but as he surveyed the scene, he found he was grateful to have the help.

The boats along the side of the harbour appeared to Drew's untrained eyes to be nothing more than pleasure boats. But the bright flash of the coastguard's lifeboat sat alongside them, bobbing gently in the mesmerising dark water added to a macabre atmosphere. It was, Drew thought, a stark reminder of the situation unfolding.

"Female, age unknown, found on the rocks around the cliff. She's still breathing, but her pulse is sluggish."

Drew stood back and watched as the lifeboat crew handed over to the paramedics, who had finally managed to break through the crowd. The hiss of the oxygen canister as it was unlocked seemed, to Drew, to be unnaturally loud against the background noise which surrounded them. Was he suffering from a kind of PTSD? Was that why everything seemed to be that much sharper, almost grating on his senses.

From his position next to the steps which led down to the boats, Drew got his first glimpse of the unknown woman—not that woman was the word he would have used to describe someone so young. She couldn't have been more than eighteen or nineteen. Skin white as marble, dark hair slick with water, her blue lips stood out in contrast against the almost supernaturally pale colour of her skin.

The shorts and camisole top she wore seemed too flimsy for the cold weather they were experiencing, and Drew wondered just what could have driven her outside in so little clothes.

Shivering, he buried his face in against the collar of his jacket as wind—icy and cutting—wound its way down along the side of the harbour. It seemed to slip inside his coat, chilling him to the core of his being.

The silver blanket they'd wrapped around the girl shifted, and Drew spotted the various bruise patterns which decorated the girl's upper torso.

"Do you think this was self-inflicted?" Green's question pulled Drew from his own quiet contemplation.

"I don't think she could have caused bruising like that," he said. "But until we get a name, some background information, or she wakes up, it's going to be almost impossible to know if this was deliberate or not."

Drew pursed his lips and watched as the paramedics handled the girl carefully.

"Do we have any idea who she might be?"

Green shook his head. "We've got nothing so far. They found no identity on her person, so if we can't find anything in the *mispers*, then we'll put an appeal out first thing." Green shuddered, as he watched them load the girl into the ambulance. "Was she out there long, do you think?"

Drew glanced out at the sea and shrugged. "I don't see how anyone could survive long out there. The water is freezing." He sighed. "We need to have a word with the blokes who found her."

"The uniforms have taken initial statements from

a few of them already. They've left the main blokes for us."

TEN MINUTES LATER, and Drew found himself standing on the edge of the harbour. His fingers were numb from the cold. The wind that buffeted against him cut into his face like needles, and he suddenly wished he'd got a cup of something hot before they started talking to the fishermen.

"What time did you leave this evening?" Drew's voice carried over the call of the seagulls who had gathered to pick over the scraps left by the people on the street.

"We went out just after five, I like to get back in early in the morning if I can." The man wrapped in a thick blue coat stood with one hip propped against the black railing that lined the street.

"Why is that?"

"His missus wants him around more often on his days off." The tidbit of information was volunteered by a ruddy faced man who stood on the small boat deck which had made the emergency call to the coast guard in the first place.

"This isn't your job?" Drew cocked an eyebrow as he pushed his hands into his pockets.

"Nah, we can't keep up with the ships that come in and clear out the waterways. Competition is fierce these days. We fish for pleasure more than profit now."

"And where did you first see the woman?"

"We were circling for a good spot, and James spotted something wedged in the rocks at the bottom of the cliffs. Thought it might be a seal or something, and I was only going to get a picture of it to take back to my Sylvia. We weren't expecting it to be human. Gave us the shock of our lives she did." He sucked in a deep breath through his teeth and rocked back on his heels. The events had evidently shocked him, but Drew could tell there was something he was holding back.

"Did you see anyone else around?" The question when Green asked it seemed innocent enough, but Drew could hear the underlying tension in his voice. It was something the young constable would have to work on if he hoped to improve his interviewing skills.

"Not when we found her." The omission in his words was plain.

"But there was somebody before that?" Green interrupted. The eagerness in his voice was a dead giveaway for the fishermen, and Drew stifled a frustrated sigh.

"Well, yeah, but it'll have had nowt to do with the woman in the water."

"What makes you say that?" Drew's voice

remained impassive, as though what he'd just heard was of no importance to them and their investigation.

"It was just one of them pleasure boats you sometimes see going out. It's not the first time I've seen it out and about."

"But the timing seemed odd?" Drew couldn't help but interject. There was no doubt in his mind that there was something the man was holding back on. Was it possible he recognised the boat, and its occupants? It wasn't implausible.

"It did. They rarely go out so late, especially in winter." He pursed his lips and glanced down at his crew mate. "You thought it was odd too." It wasn't so much a question as it was an accusation, and even from his vantage point Drew could see the other man stiffen.

"I said nothing of the sort. It's not the first evening I've seen them out—"

"You know them?" Drew asked.

The other man shook his head. "Not by name. But it's not the first time I've seen them."

"And what time did you say this was?"

Drew could practically feel Green's eagerness to do a good job and get them an answer they could use.

"They were coming in as we were going out."

"The boat returned to the harbour here?"

The fisherman nearest Drew shook his head. "I don't think so, but it was dark so I can't be certain."

"Do you think you could identify the boat again if you saw it?"

"I'm not sure..." The men glanced at each other, leaving Drew with the suspicion that there was more to the story than they were willing to share. That knowledge alone was enough to bring his frustration bubbling to the surface. He opened his mouth to speak, but Green beat him to the punch.

"Are you certain? If the girl doesn't make it, this could potentially turn into a murder enquiry, and—" Drew touched him gently on the arm. The air seemed to go out of the other man, and his shoulders slumped.

"Thank you for your help," Drew said. "My uniformed colleagues will take your details down, and if you could make your way to the station to make a statement, it would be a great help."

Drew tuned out the men's grumbled complaints as he followed Green back toward the car. There was a subtle tremor in the young constable's fingers as he ran his hands down over the front of his jacket.

"Why stop me back there?" He demanded, struggling to keep his voice quiet enough so that the stragglers on the roadside didn't hear them arguing.

"Because until we know a little more about everything here, there's no point in barging in. For all we know, those men have told us everything they can."

"And if they haven't?" Green rammed his glasses back up his nose somewhat viciously.

Drew cocked an eyebrow at the constable, letting him know he'd crossed the line.

Green subsided into sullen silence, as Drew leaned back against the car, and blew warm air against his numb hands. Green wasn't entirely wrong.

Drew closed his eyes. What was wrong with him? Why was this particular case worming its way beneath his skin? What he did know was that if he didn't take a step back and remain objective, he would be of no use to anyone.

Of course, deep down he knew the answer to his own question. It was the fact that the case reminded him of Freya. It was bound to make him feel antsy.

No sooner had he thought of it, than Drew realised that wasn't all that was bothering him. The argument with Harriet earlier in the day had definitely knocked him for six.

Just why would she want to go and visit Nolan?

She hadn't told him that exactly, in fact she'd said the complete opposite, but Drew was no fool. He'd seen the flicker of eagerness in her eyes as she'd mentioned it. She wanted to visit Nolan. There was something about that psychopathic bastard that pulled her back to him, like a big magnet.

He sucked a deep breath in through his nose, and caught Green watching him "Look, I'm sorry about before. I think you're right, they know more than they're telling us. The problem is, we can't be certain. But all this pressure, and this scrutiny definitely makes them nervous."

"So, you think we should take a second run at them?" The eagerness was back in Green's voice, and Drew sighed. The man was more like an excitable puppy than a DC.

He nodded and jammed his hands into the deep pockets of his jacket as though that alone could force out the icy ache which had taken up residence in his bones.

"You don't think they had anything to do with the girl?" Green cocked a speculative eyebrow at her.

"No. But then again, I don't think it's ever possible to truly know what someone is thinking."

Green glanced out over the water. "Do you know where they found her? They mentioned something about cliffs."

Drew nodded and scanned the horizon. "I'd need to look at the map again, and it's not as though you can see the place from here, anyway."

He pointed out past the headland with its all too familiar landmark of the abbey that stood silhouetted against the skyline. "Out there is my best guess. But with the tide coming in so fast, I don't think the forensic team will get much chance to collect anything of use."

"So, we've got nothing..."

Drew's smile was warm. "There's never nothing, DC Green. We've got a girl who, if she wakes up, can help fill in the blanks of what happened."

"And if she doesn't?"

Drew's smile faded. "Then we do our jobs and find the evidence needed to get us our answers. And if this wasn't self-inflicted, then we use that evidence to take down the bastards responsible."

CHAPTER SIXTEEN

THE SOUND of the phone ringing pulled Drew up from the depths of sleep. He jerked awake in the car, his body shooting bolt upright as he scrambled around for the phone in the centre console. His fingers closed around it and without glancing down at the screen, he answered.

"Drew, I wasn't sure if you'd answer," Harriet's voice was gentle. The gloom inside the car made telling the time difficult, and Drew squinted down at his watch. The digits eventually swam into focus. Six am. And yet Harriet sounded alert, as though she'd never even been to bed.

"Why wouldn't I answer," he said, searching for the coffee cup he'd abandoned in the cup holder three hours before. He lifted it to his lips and took a sip of the cold, bitter liquid. He gagged, but swallowed it down. Anything was better than nothing.

"I've been thinking about the break-in at Ms Dunsly's," she said, ignoring his question entirely.

"Who?" Drew flipped down the visor and slid back the cover on the mirror. He looked older, more haggard than he had the day before. His bloodshot eyes stood out, and the day-old stubble that had taken hold of his jawline was sprinkled with silver.

"The woman from yesterday," Harriet said. "You took me over to see her after the fire..."

Drew swallowed hard. "Shit, yeah. I remember now. The attempted break-in, her dog scared off the intruder."

"Exactly," Harriet said. "Are you still in bed?"

"No," Drew shook his head, and remembered she couldn't actually see him, which judging by the state of his appearance was a blessing in disguise. "I'm in the car." It wasn't a lie. He was in the car. He glanced up at the house he'd parked in front of and sighed.

He hadn't been able to bring himself to set foot over the threshold, and considering he was rapidly beginning to run out of clean underwear and socks, it was a step he would have to take sooner rather than later.

"Good, I thought maybe I'd woken you up. You sounded half asleep."

He didn't answer her. It was easier to lie by omission than it was to speak the words aloud. "You said you had a brainwave about Ms Dunsly?"

"Yes... The more I think about it, the more concerned I am," Harriet said.

"Why is that?" Drew reached over the back of the headrest and tugged the gym bag with his clothes inside into the front seat next to him.

"If there's a link in the cases--"

"That's a really big if," Drew interjected. "We don't know if there's a link yet."

"PC Pearson seemed to think there was," Harriet said. "I don't think she would have imagined it, if it wasn't true."

Drew kept his mouth shut and tugged open the zip on the bag. Clothes spilled out onto the seat and he selected a clean shirt and pants for the day as Harriet continued to speak.

"Anyway, if she's right, and this is the same person, then we are looking at a very concerning escalation."

"Mm-hmm," Drew said.

"Are you even listening to me?"

"Yeah, a concerning escalation..."

Harriet sighed. "I need the files, Drew."

"And I said I'll ask for them..." He paused and pressed his head back against the headrest. "Look, I'm sorry, I had a rough night."

"What happened?"

"They pulled a girl out of the sea over in Whitby."

The sharp sound of Harriet inhaling told him she

hadn't been paying attention to the news. "Is she still alive?"

"Barely," Drew said, and regretted the words as soon as they'd left his mind. For all he knew, while he'd been asleep, the girl had died. "Well, that I know of. The last I heard, she was in critical condition, but she was still in the land of the living."

"What was the prognosis?"

Drew scrubbed his hand over his face before stifling a yawn with his fist. "She'd been in the water for some time, they think. She managed to drag herself onto to some rocks, or at least that's what we think happened."

"Did she fall in?"

"I don't think so," Drew said. "It certainly doesn't look like that. But I can't rule out the possibility that she threw herself in, although if I'm honest I'm not sure about that either..."

"I'm sorry..." Harriet said. "Do you need my help?"

"I'm not going to turn you down on that," Drew said. "But right now, I've got very little information to fall back on. Anything you can tell me about arson and burning bodies would be much more helpful right now." He could practically see the cogs turning in her head as he spoke, and the imagery brought a smile to his lips.

"I'll see what I can dig up," Harriet said.

"Look, I'm going to swing by the office, and then check on the girl..."

"Of course," Harriet said, managing to sound suitably chastised. "I'm sorry for keeping you."

"It was good to hear from you," Drew said, struggling to find the words to express how he felt over the way they'd left things the day before. He'd screwed up, that much he was sure of, but he was blowed if he could figure out a way to fix it without putting his size twelves into it all over again.

"Get some coffee," Harriet said. "And don't forget those files..." The line went dead, leaving Drew alone with his own thoughts. It was the last thing he wanted, or needed. The less time he spent in his own head, the better it was for him.

He stared up at his own house and contemplated nipping in for a shower. It wouldn't take long; he could be in and out before he really even knew he was there...

Without really needing to think about it, Drew started the engine and reversed out of the car space. There were showers at the gym, and his membership had to be good for something.

Besides, there were many things he was capable of right now, but going back into the place where he'd very nearly met his maker at the hands of that psychopath Nolan Matthews wasn't one of them.

A SHORT WHILE LATER, Drew—showered and dressed in clothes that seemed somewhat fresh—

headed into the office. He paused next to the coffee machine and fed it his money before he selected a black coffee.

It wasn't his favourite way to drink it, but after the night he'd had, Drew would have taken caffeine on an IV if he could.

As he stood and waited for the black liquid to fill the waiting cup, he ran back over the scene from the night before.

There was something deeply unsettling about the girl they'd pulled from the water. The more he thought about it, the more he knew she hadn't ended up there because of any choices she'd made herself.

Taking the cup back to his desk, he sat back and closed his eyes.

"I heard you picked something up when you were out today," Maz said, his voice low as he paused at the edge of the desk Drew had commandeered.

"They fished a girl out of the water up in Whitby. She's alive, but barely."

Maz nodded, and Drew caught a flash of the other man's feelings as they flitted behind his dark eyes. "What is it?"

Maz shifted awkwardly, and leaned down, his voice dropping to a whisper. "Fancy a quick ciggie break?" Surprised, Drew leaned back in his chair. The uncomfortable plastic back creaked ominously, making him believe it might at any moment give way.

Maz wasn't a smoker, that much he was certain

of. He'd once admitted to Drew that his mother had caught him with a packet of silk cut when he was a teenager and the subsequent grief, and nagging he'd received had been enough to discourage him from ever picking up another packet. So, the fact that he was now suggesting it made Drew even more suspicious.

"Sure." Pushing onto his feet, Drew watched as the DS cast around furtively as though he expected at any moment to be caught out. Clearly there was something he wasn't supposed to share with Drew.

Reaching the back steps, Maz hesitated, as though suddenly uncertain about where they were supposed to go. Drew moved ahead of him and gestured for him to follow.

Leaving through the exit door, Drew felt inside his jacket for the packet of cigarettes he'd taken to carrying. There had been a time when he'd carried an empty packet, a reminder of the promises he'd made to Freya. But after everything that had happened with Nolan, he'd started the habit up again. Freya would have been so disappointed in him, but she wasn't here anymore, so what he did, or didn't do no longer mattered to her. Death had robbed her of the ability to care about such trivial matters.

Simply thinking about her caused a tightening in his chest that he struggled against. For so long he had been caught up in the memory of her, of everything he'd lost. And now... Well, it wasn't that he had pushed her aside. Quite the opposite, in fact, because now he felt angry. A rage he hadn't known he could feel towards her.

As they reached the bottom of the steps, Drew took a cigarette from the packet and twirled it between his fingers. It was stupid to feel like this. Freya had been ill. It wasn't her fault, but that didn't mean he didn't still feel anger every time he thought of the choice she had made. The choice she had tried to make for them both.

Harriet would tell him it was natural, normal even to feel the clenched fist of rage in the middle of his chest. One of the many stages of grief, no doubt. But he hadn't told her. He didn't want to know that what he felt was normal, because as far as he was concerned, there was nothing normal about any of it.

"So," Maz said, edging toward the corner of the building. The way he was behaving made Drew think of all those spy movies he'd watched as a kid growing up. Drew lit the cigarette and inhaled deeply, allowing the bitter taste to coat his tongue and spread down into his lungs. It brought him instant relief, and he held the smoke-filled breath inside for a beat more than was necessary before he let it go and followed Maz.

"There's something I think you should know." The DS had never been very good at keeping secrets, and it seemed just because he was working on the task force with DCI Templeton it would be no different.

"Oh, what's that then?"

"He has us working on something big."

"Who?"

"Templeton," DS Arya said, lowering his voice to a gruff whisper. "DI Appleton said he was working a similar line in Southampton before he came up here with her."

"DI Melissa Appleton?" Drew asked, surprise causing him to almost choke on the cigarette smoke.

"That's the one," Maz said. "Wait, you know her?"

"It was a long time ago. Anyway, what does the DCI have you working on?" Drew kept his expression impassive as he absorbed the information. He'd known Melissa had gone south to further her career.

What he hadn't known was that Templeton had come from the same place. Had he brought her with him? It wasn't impossible. Melissa was a damn fine officer, and there was no doubt in Drew's mind that she was now a first-class detective.

"Are you even listening to me?" The words were a hiss from between Maz's clenched teeth. "I'm trying to help you here."

"Sorry, right, I'm all ears." Drew took another drag of the cigarette.

"Trafficking." Maz sucked in a deep breath and grinned at him triumphantly.

"What has that got to do with anything?"

"That's what he was working on down south. And now he's come up here to carry it on."

"Don't be ridiculous," Drew said, a wry smile playing around his lips. "Why would Templeton agree to come up here to chase a trafficking angle? It makes no sense."

Maz shook his head and took a step forward. "And that's what I thought, but it ain't what Melissa said."

"Go on then, spill it."

"She says there are rumours of enormous problems up here with trafficking, and human slavery. Everyone thinks of London, but those sly bastards know how to slide under the radar, and apparently they do it successfully here, and further north."

Drew took another drag on his cigarette, only to find he'd finished it. "And what has any of this got to do with my picking up a probable suicide?"

Maz's eyebrows disappeared toward his dark hairline. "Suicide? Nah, mate. The reason I'm telling you all of this is because as soon as Templeton got wind of what you'd found, he started throwing his weight around demanding the task force get jurisdiction. That's when Melissa tipped us off about his actual interest in moving up here."

Silence settled between them as the enormity of the situation pressed down on Drew. If it were true, then they'd stumbled across something huge. Of course, the fact that he'd been the responding detective would only piss Templeton off even more.

That thought sent a thrill through Drew, and a grin spread across his face as he considered the apoplectic reaction of his SIO.

"Do you and Templeton have a history?" There was an innocence to Maz's tone that suggested he'd picked up on the oddity of Drew not being picked up for the task force.

"No. Never met the bloke."

Maz nodded and scuffed the toe of his boot against the ground. There was obviously more he wanted to say, and Drew knew if he probed, the DS would break down and share every last thought that crossed his mind.

But Drew wasn't in the mood for fielding questions he didn't have the answers to.

No, Maz had given him something else to concentrate on.

"We should head back inside," Drew said, jerking his thumb toward the back door.

"I—"

"You know, before they notice us missing and send a search party out." Drew was adept at cutting the younger DS off. He'd worked with him long enough to know exactly the buttons he needed to press to get a reaction, and his suggestion that the others might have noticed their absence had the desired effect.

"Don't say I told you," Maz said hurriedly, falling in step beside Drew.

"My lips are sealed. But you know if you hear anything else you think I might need to know."

"I'll pass it along," Maz said, with a sideways grin that lit up his dark eyes.

Maz picked up his pace and disappeared up the stairs ahead of Drew.

Leaning back against the wall, he let his mind wander back to the incident that morning. The girl had been so very pale as she lay on the stretcher. The blue undertone of her skin made him shiver to just remember it. But at least she'd still been alive.

Where there was life, there was hope. It was a naïve thought, but one he'd never been able to shake free of. Not even everything that had happened with Freya had knocked that from him.

Sliding the phone from inside his pocket, he stared at the blank screen before he changed his mind and shoved it back into his jacket. Calling the hospital would only lead him down a rabbit hole, and he would surface with nothing to show for it.

Far better to swing by the hospital and check in with the uniforms he'd sent down there.

If he was lucky, he'd find a doctor or nurse willing to share more than was strictly necessary.

The idea that there might be more to the case than the usual run-of-the-mill scenarios they faced caused his heart to thud in his chest, and he paused on the stairs to suck in a deep breath so he could steady his nerves.

The police appointed counsellor had said it might take a little time before he felt more in control of himself.

As far as he was concerned, now that he'd been signed back to work, he was one hundred percent back to his former self. Or at least that was the lie he told himself.

After all, he'd faced death and come out the other side. What more could happen?

CHAPTER SEVENTEEN

ARRIVING BACK AT HIS DESK, Drew picked up the still full cup of coffee and took a mouthful. Cringing, he swore beneath his breath as the cold coffee washed down the back of his throat. He was desperate for caffeine, but he wasn't that bloody desperate.

Tossing the cup, he made his way over to the machine, and repeated his earlier actions. If the girl was part of a larger trafficking scenario, then he was going to need the help of Dr Quinn. Traffickers were definitely outside his usual remit, and he didn't have the first clue about how they thought, or what he should do to pursue them. But if anybody could get inside their heads, it was Harriet.

"Haskell, in here!" The monk's voice cut through the noise in Drew's head. Glancing over his shoulder, he caught sight of his SIO standing in the door to his office. It took him somewhat unawares. When he'd arrived in the office, there had been no sign of the DCI.

He'd probably arrived while he'd been outside speaking to Maz. Snatching his cup from the tray, he lifted the cup of scalding black coffee to his mouth and took a sip. It burned all the way down, but the strength of the caffeine had the desired effect on his senses, and he felt some of the exhaustion that plagued him slowly ebbing away.

A moment later, he popped his head around the door to the monk's office. "You wanted to see me, sir?"

"Don't 'sir' me, Drew. Come in and take a seat." The monk set his pen down and shoved the files he'd been perusing out of reach.

As Drew took the indicated seat, he caught sight of the name Nolan Matthews across the top of the pages and a knot formed in the pit of his stomach. "I want a full report on the girl they pulled from the water. Don't hold anything back from me. The last thing I want is to get caught with my trousers around my ankles when I speak to the press."

"I didn't know you were holding a press conference," Drew said, before he sipped at the coffee.

"I wasn't planning on holding anything," the monk said, before he sighed and pinched the bridge of his nose. "But Templeton has left me with no choice."

Drew straightened in the seat, tension singing in his veins. "Oh?" He was pleased to find his voice didn't betray his feelings regarding the leader of the task force.

"Don't give me that," Gregson rolled his eyes. "I know you detest that prick as much as I do. Thinks he's so much bigger, and better than all the rest of us up here. Well, between you and me, I know his SIO down south was only too happy to offload him on us."

"I didn't know he left under a cloud?" Drew asked, struggling to keep the curiosity in his voice to a minimum, when what he really wanted to do was to demand the monk tell him everything he knew.

Instead, he settled back in the seat opposite his SIO. If he could just get the other man to relax, to open up to him, then perhaps he would find out something useful.

Especially after the conversation he'd just had with Maz. The more he knew about Templeton, the more leverage he would find himself with.

"Well, he did," the DCI said. "Got himself pulled up on sanctions for going all vigilante on some bloke."

Drew cocked an eyebrow and swallowed down the bitter coffee. "Why would he do that?"

Gregson narrowed his gaze and glared across the piles of files at Drew. "Why would you care?"

Drew shrugged. "I wouldn't, it's just idle curiosity, sir, that's all." For a moment Drew was sure the monk had figured out his ulterior motives. It wouldn't be the first time his SIO had outmanoeuvred him in regards to a case.

"What do you know?" the monk asked, leaning his elbows on the piles of paper in front of him.

"Sir, I--"

"Don't give me that, Drew. I know you, and I know when you're onto something. So, you either tell me or I do exactly what Templeton wants me to do and I pass the case of the girl in the sea over to his crew."

"Sir, you wouldn't," Drew said, horrified. If he lost this, he would lose all hope of ever moving up onto the task force.

"I just might, unless you can tell me one good reason why I shouldn't..." When Drew wasn't forthcoming with an immediate answer, Gregson sighed, and sat back in his chair. "I don't like that bastard any more than you do," he said with feeling. "And despite us holding the same rank, his team holds all the cards on this one. If he really wants this, he can take it. Unless you give me a reason why he shouldn't."

Drew swallowed hard. Telling Gregson everything Maz had told him was a risk, but it was a risk he was going to have to take. "Has the DCI told you what he thinks the girl is connected with?"

Gregson shook his head. "No, just that he thinks it's a case his team should handle."

"I spoke to DC Arya, and it's his belief that the

interest in the case is because the girl might be a trafficking victim."

"Well shit," the monk mumbled. "That puts a different spin on things."

"Why so?"

"Because we don't have the resources here to go chasing down an angle of that magnitude."

"Sir, I don't mind putting in the hours. I'm more than--"

"Drew, no offence, but you've just come back after a stint in the hospital because a complete lunatic decided to try and turn you into a human lampshade. I'd be remiss as your SIO to agree to you working on something like this on your own."

"With all due respect, sir," Drew said, not bothering to hide the irritation in his voice. "I've been signed back onto work by a trained professional. I don't think it falls within your remit to make me take it easy. If they didn't think I was fit for work, they wouldn't have sent me back here."

Gregson's expression had soured as Drew spoke. "Watch your step here, Drew. There's only so much insubordination I'm willing to accept. And if what you're saying about the girl is true, then it's not really up to me anymore. The task force was developed for that exact purpose. They've got the budget, and the personnel to track down the kinds of people involved in that sort of organised crime. The home office has given them the scope needed to get convictions that will stick. We don't have that same support."

Drew nodded. "Understood, sir."

As much as Drew hated to agree, he knew the monk was right. They didn't have the budget, or the manpower required, but that didn't mean there couldn't be some kind of inter-force relationship formed.

"I think until we have a clearer picture of what happened with the girl, removing me from the case and handing it over to Templeton and his team would be a mistake."

Gregson's expression was thoughtful as he glanced down at the files in front of him. "Fine. I can agree to that. But if this turns out in Templeton's favour, then you'll just have to let it go."

Drew gave the monk a tight-lipped smile. He didn't have to like the answer, he just needed to give the appearance of a team player in order to buy himself the sufficient time he needed to crack the case.

"Now, what about this body in the house over in Whitby?" The monk's brow creased as he shuffled through the files on his desk. "What do we know so far?"

Drew swallowed hard. He'd intended to get a full rundown from the arson investigation team, but with everything that had been happening, he simply hadn't found the time. "Sir, I--"

"I want you to get on that, Haskell. You said it yourself, a professional gave you the all clear for coming to work. So, I expect you to be top of your game."

"Of course, sir," Drew said, feeling somewhat foolish. "Sir, there was something I was hoping to get your approval for?"

Gregson raised an eyebrow in his direction, giving Drew the go ahead he needed. "Dr Quinn was hoping to have a look at some crime reports from York, and--"

Gregson sighed and buried his face in his hands, the gesture effectively cutting Drew off. "Why do you do this to me?"

"Excuse me, sir, I'm not sure I understand."

"I tell you not to bite off more than you can chew, and you then want me to sign off on a request for Dr Quinn, which would see her reviewing every case file involving some form of theft, or--"

"No, sir, just the attempted breaking and entering, some petty theft, and a couple of reports they've had about indecent exposure."

"Do you know how many case files that is?" Gregson replied, looking incredulous. "You might as well just ask me to hand the keys over for the file room in its entirety. We'd find ourselves buried under a mountain of potential dead-ends..."

"Dr Quinn thinks yesterday's attempted breaking

and entering could hold the potential to escalate into a series of much more serious crimes."

"Dr Quinn has a lot of thoughts," the monk said. "And not all of them are good. Without some sort of proof that what she's saying is true, I can't authorise an investigation like that."

"And if she's correct, sir?" Drew balled his hand into a fist in his lap to keep his temper under control.

"We're not in the business of being psychic, Drew. If she's correct, then the proof will turn up sooner rather than later, but we'll cross that bridge when we come to it. In the meantime, I want you to concentrate on the crimes we can actually do something about. If you swing by the hospital, I want a full report on the condition of the young woman. We need something we can start circulating to the public, somebody has to know who she is."

"Of course, sir," Drew said, as he pushed onto his feet.

"And Drew, in regards to the burned body, I want an ID by the end of the day."

"Sir..."

Gregson cocked an eyebrow at him and leaned back in his chair. "Is there something the matter?"

Shaking his head, Drew started for the door. "Of course not, sir. I'll do my best."

"Just make sure your best gets me the results I need. I don't want to spend my time playing catch up. I thought Templeton did me a favour leaving my best DI behind, prove me right."

Escaping the confines of the monk's office, Drew crossed the floor and slammed his cup down on the desk, jarring the few officers who sat pouring over reports.

The last thing he needed was the monk breathing down his neck, but it seemed that was exactly how it was going to be. With a sigh, Drew spotted Perry across the space struggling with the vending machine.

The monk had said he should leave well enough alone, but Drew had never found that useful. It had certainly never helped him to solve a case in the past.

Not to mention the fact that Harriet wouldn't stop her crusade. If she truly believed there was a connection to be made in the cases, then she wouldn't stop until she had her answer.

Sighing, Drew got to his feet and sauntered over to lean against the wall.

Perry swore violently and thumped his hand against the machine as though that alone would get it to give up its treasure.

"I've always found feeding it money to be more useful," Drew said with a wry smile.

"What do you want?" Perry asked, keeping his gaze studiously trained on the machine.

"What have forensics said about Ms Dunsly's

attempted breaking and entering," Drew asked, folding his arms over his chest.

"I heard you weren't working that anymore," Perry said with a smug smile.

Drew's stomach dropped, but he kept his smile fixed in place. The monk's odd behaviour suddenly made sense. It wasn't like him to dismiss a potential case, especially if it meant preventing the crime statistics from climbing. The monk was many things, but he wasn't a bad DCI.

There wasn't a chance in hell that he would have dismissed the notion of an escalating criminal so thoroughly unless somebody had got there first and filled his head with a bunch of crap.

"You spoke to Gregson, I see," Drew said, keeping his tone even.

"I did," Perry said, slamming his hand into the vending machine a second time. "Why won't this bloody thing give me my crisps."

"It probably doesn't like you either," Drew breathed, finally drawing Perry's attention.

"What did you say?"

"I don't know where you got the impression from that I was off the b&e. Gregson assigned the case to me, and as a DI I outrank you."

"So, this is a dick measuring contest, is it?" Perry asked, keeping his tone mild despite the flinching around his eyes. "I didn't realise it was so serious between you and the good doctor?"

"Perhaps we should discuss this somewhere more private," Drew said, straightening up.

"Why, are you worried that the others will hear how you've been screwing around with the help?"

Drew's fingers closed into a fist. "The conference room, now."

Perry's eyes widened, but the smile that swept across his features was one of those shit-eating grins that Drew had always detested. If he could have wiped the smirk from the other man's face, there and then he would have.

But Drew knew anything he did would only come back to bite him in the arse later. He might be Perry's senior officer, but theft, and breaking and entering were Perry's domain, and he ruled it with an iron fist.

As far as the monk would see it, Drew was nothing more than an interloper who didn't fully understand the rules of engagement.

Drew stepped into the conference room and waited with his arms folded across his chest for Perry to join him.

"Look, I don't mean to be such a complete prick," Perry said, his tone showing that he did in fact have every intention of being as irritating as he appeared. "But Gregson and I both feel that this case is best off in my capable hands. Now, the minute someone turns up dead, I'll happily hand it over to you, but for now it's mine."

"Rather than letting it ever get to that point, Dr Quinn and I both feel a second opinion on the unsolved cases mounting up around you would be of benefit to everyone," Drew said, propping himself up against the edge of the large desk that dominated the centre of the room. "She thinks your flasher in York, and the other cases involving items of lingerie that have been stolen are all the work of one man." As the words left his mouth, Drew felt himself cringe inwardly. It seemed a little far-fetched. Perhaps Harriet was grasping at straws.

"Look, I can appreciate that you want to help your lady friend out," Perry said. "But like I said before, there's no connection between the flasher in York, and your bloke who tried to break in Dunsly's back door."

"Perry, I know you don't think this is important, but I'm asking you—" Drew cut off as the door into the conference room slammed shut, and he turned to find Harriet standing there.

"I didn't think you were coming down here?" Drew raised an eyebrow in her direction, communicating his irritation at her refusal to stay away.

"I thought I might best argue my corner if I could speak to the DS involved…" She trailed off, as Drew stepped aside to reveal the short stocky middle-aged DS Perry.

"The infamous Dr Quinn," Perry said, making it

sound like the most despicable insult he could dream up.

"And you must be the detective holding up the files I asked DI Haskell for?" Harriet shot the small man an icy smile, and Drew was pleased to see him wither beneath her wintry gaze. "Why would you have a problem with me looking them over?"

"It's not that I object to you particularly, it's just I prefer to keep my cases out of the papers."

"I'm a forensic psychologist, not a reporter," Harriet corrected him, unable to keep the irritation from her voice. "What if I told you there's a chance the attempted burglary and the cases you've been seeing around York are linked. That if we intervened now, we could stop a—"

"That's a chance I'm willing to take," Perry said, making to move past Drew.

"Well, I'm not," Harriet said hotly, suddenly hating the note of desperation in her voice. "We cannot ignore this. It's too important. The risk is too great. Ms Dunsly has had a few items stolen, and it's my belief that—"

"I thought she interrupted the bloke trying to break-in?" Perry interrupted, directing the question toward Drew.

"She did. Nothing was stolen that night."

"Then what are you on about? I'm interested in the attempted break-in, not the one she thinks might have happened in the past, but she never bothered to report."

The condescension that practically dripped from Perry's words set Drew's teeth on edge, but he knew if he interrupted now, Harriet wouldn't thank him. And it wouldn't do her any favours where coppers like Perry were concerned.

"She thinks someone has stolen personal items from her washing line—"

"She thinks? I need certainty, Ms..."

"Dr Quinn," Harriet corrected, her tone brusque.

"Well then, Dr Quinn, I need certainty. We can't solve crimes based on what might have happened. As I'm sure you're aware, we deal in facts."

"PC Pearson was telling me there have been other crimes happening in the area, which are similar in nature. I'm sure if—"

"I'm sure PC Pearson means well, but you don't need to worry about any of the other cases currently being investigated. I can assure you the job we're doing is more than thorough. And I tell you what—" He leaned closer. "If there's a connection to be made, then my team will find it."

"Look, I'm not trying to step on your toes here." Harriet sighed.

Drew could tell Harriet was struggling to keep her temper under wraps. Not that he could blame her. Perry was particularly behaving like an arsehole.

Obviously, their presence had bothered him more than he had let on to Drew.

"But this is important. If this is the same person, then he is escalating. I need to see the files..."

Perry laughed, the sound booming and obnoxious as he almost doubled over at the waist and struggled to catch his breath.

"Escalations? Can you hear yourself, Dr Quinn?"

"Mike, there's no need to—"

"No, Haskell, she needs to hear this. What we're dealing with here is some low-life scum who saw Ms Dunsly's house as an easy target to score a little fast cash. You don't get escalations in break-ins. Maybe in London, or if you're working with the FBI, but not here. This is God's country, Dr Quinn. All you have here are your run-of-the-mill criminals. We're just not that exciting."

"I don't think you understand what I'm trying to say..."

"I think I'm understanding you perfect. You want to turn this case into another of your circuses."

"You're bang out of order, Mike," Drew said, taking a small step forward. "Dr Quinn is giving you the benefit of her wisdom—"

"What out of the goodness of her heart?" Perry let go a snort of derision. "She's got you well and truly trained, Haskell. She's here to raise her own profile. Ever since she got involved with our boys, her career has taken an upward trajectory. So much so, she's been brought on to work with that fancy team they dragged you onto. I'm not the only one who thinks it—"

"I didn't accept that offer," Harriet said. Her words took Drew by surprise, and he felt his breath catch in the back of his throat. "And anyway, I think I've more than proved myself. If I say I need to see those files, then I'd thank you to hand them over."

Drew had a million questions that he wanted to ask her, but he swallowed them down. There would be time for that later, once Harriet had what she'd come for. "It was with Dr Quinn's help that we could finally stop the Star killer. Without her I'd be dead." It was difficult to admit, but it was the truth and Drew wasn't too big to admit it. If Harriet hadn't arrived when she did, he'd have bled out in the middle of his own living room. It was a sobering thought, and it was enough to bring him up short. There was no point in standing around arguing with Perry. "Give her the files, where is the harm in it?"

"The harm is that this is my investigation, and I'll run it how I see fit. And if I say no to your girlfriend going through confidential police files, then my word on it is final."

Drew opened his mouth to speak, but Perry cut him off. "We've both got our orders here, Haskell. You got your marching orders from your DCI, and I've got mine. Now drop it."

Drew nodded, and rather than meet Harriet's eyes, he let his gaze drop to the floor. He couldn't bear to see the betrayal there. If she'd just listened to him on the phone, then none of this would have been an issue.

"Good." Perry huffed. "Now, if you'll both excuse me. I've got work to do."

"But—" Harriet said before Perry could walk away.

"Leave it, Harriet, he's right. We've got other things to concentrate on."

She dropped into the nearest chair and let her hands drop into her lap. "I don't understand."

"I'll explain later... Give me a minute."

Drew went after Perry, catching up to him as he reached the hall. "I'll be filing a report on this, Perry," Drew said.

"About what?"

"Your conduct. The way you spoke to Dr Quinn—"

"Oh, bugger off, Drew. Chase after your little girlfriend and leave the job of actual policing to those who still understand what it all means."

Drew contemplated lashing out at the other man, but quickly changed his mind. It would only result in a tit-for-tat argument, and he didn't have time for that right now. Instead, he swallowed down the rage that tightened his chest.

"You used to care about this job, Mike, what happened?"

The other man swore under his breath, his face apoplectic, and Drew half expected him to strike him. When he didn't, Drew turned on his heel and returned to the office to find Harriet sat at his desk.

CHAPTER EIGHTEEN

"HE DOESN'T WANT to help, does he?" Harriet raised her gaze. She didn't need to ask Drew the question, she could already tell from the look on his face that Perry had no intention of budging. Drew shook his head anyway, and Harriet sighed. "Can't we appeal to DCI Gregson, I can--"

"He agrees with the DS," Drew said. He dropped into the seat opposite her. "Maybe they're right. We're probably just seeing crooks where there aren't any, jumping at shadows because of our past..." As he spoke, Drew reached out to touch his fingers to the back of her hand that rested on the desk. Without thinking, Harriet withdrew from his touch, and clasped her hands together in her lap.

"You think I'm imagining things, don't you?" Strain threaded through her voice.

"That's not what I'm saying," Drew said, frustration colouring his voice.

"Then spit it out."

"We've got bigger fish to fry," Drew whispered furiously. "The girl we pulled from the sea last night, Templeton wants the case." Drew dropped back against his seat. "That bastard wants to leave me with nothing."

It wasn't like Drew to dismiss her views. She knew he could be stubborn, but past experience had told her she could talk to him, and he would eventually see sense.

His practical nature made him the perfect candidate for the scientific nature that was so very persuasive in forensic psychology. But this was different.

From the set of his jaw, Harriet knew if she continued to push him on this, he wouldn't just see Templeton as the enemy, she would become one too. An outcome like that wouldn't help either of them.

"Why would he do that?" Harriet asked. "What reason would he have to steal your caseload?"

"Why did you turn them down?" Drew asked. Despite expecting him to ask her that very question sooner rather than later, it still took her by surprise.

"It just didn't seem to be the right time," Harriet stalled. How could she possibly explain to him without it sounding like pity?

"Why not?" The ferocity in Drew's voice pulled her attention upwards to his face.

"I've got a lot on at the university, and--"

"Bullshit," Drew said crossly. "Don't lie to me. Your Dr Baig was practically champing at the bit to get this task force together. You and I both know he'd love to see you leading the charge on behalf of the university."

Harriet shook her head. "I don't think he'd like to see me doing exactly that." She sighed, it was a complicated mess, and despite thinking of what she might say to him if he ever discovered the truth of the matter, Harriet found all of her good ideas had fled her brain, leaving her with nothing at all.

"Please, just tell me you didn't do this out of some twisted sense of loyalty." Drew's voice sounded wrong, and in his eyes, she could see some raw vulnerability exposed there. He blinked, and it disappeared as quickly as it had arrived, leaving her to question whether she'd seen it at all.

"If you must know I didn't trust Templeton's judgement," Harriet said stiffly. "He struck me as far too impulsive, and reckless beyond measure, and those are two traits I don't believe should be rewarded with the power he now finds himself in possession of."

Drew sat in silence. She half expected him to laugh in her face and tell her to give him the real reason, but when he didn't, she hoped she'd actually given him an answer they could both accept.

"We should go to the hospital," he said finally. "If

Templeton is sniffing around the case, then I need to be in possession of all the facts."

"Why is he trying to take the case?"

Drew grabbed a file from the desk before he pushed onto his feet and slid into his coat. "He thinks she was the victim of a trafficking ring, and according to Maz, that's all he's interested in investigating."

Harriet felt her mouth drop open. Drew was halfway across the office before she gathered her senses enough to follow him. "You can't be serious."

Drew nodded. "As serious as a heart attack," he said. "Templeton thinks we've got a huge issue regarding trafficking, and if he's right, then this could be one of the biggest cases North Yorkshire CID will ever get to handle."

Harriet said nothing as she followed him out of the office, but already her mind was whirling over the potential possibilities. She knew little about human traffickers, but what she did know was that those who were motivated by financial gain were some of the most ruthless psychopaths out there. And they would stop at nothing to go undetected.

THE SCENT of bleach tickled the back of Harriet's throat as she waited for Drew in the hallway. Patient confidentiality meant she could not be privy to anything regarding the young woman's care. Despite his status as a DI, not even Drew was allowed to breach doctor patient confidentiality, but the consultant in charge of her care had agreed to speak to him in more general terms.

Drew appeared a few moments later and dropped down onto the plastic chairs that lined the wall.

"What did they say?" Harriet settled her handbag more securely on her lap.

"She woke up a little over an hour ago, but she's very distressed so they're trying to keep her as sedated as possible." Drew scrubbed his hand over his face, giving Harriet a glimpse into just how exhausted he was. "One of the uniforms said she was calling out to a Dimitri, and Marissa, but they couldn't understand her."

"She's not English?"

"Nope, best guess we've got is she's Albanian. But not even that is certain."

"And I take it we don't know who this Marissa, and Dimitri are?" As Drew shook his head, Harriet made a mental note of his appearance, and realised the tie he wore was the same one he'd had on the day before.

"Did you get home last night for some sleep?" The question, although framed innocently enough, had been asked to give her as much insight into his state of mind as possible.

"Yeah," he said evasively. "I could do with another coffee though."

Harriet smiled and schooled her features into a blank expression. He was lying to her, but what exactly he was lying about, well that she hadn't quite worked out yet.

"So, what do we do now if she's being sedated, and we've got no way of asking who those people are?"

"I've contacted someone to come in," he said. "Someone who can translate. Her not speaking a word of English causes us some enormous problems. I've got Tim Green going through a list of potential translators, but so far he said he hasn't found anyone suitable."

"Tim Green?"

"The new Maz," Drew said without missing a beat. Harriet gave him a confused look, and he smiled in response. "He's not the worst. Pretty nice, actually. Just not the brightest bulb on the street, if you catch my drift."

Harriet said nothing. "So, this is a dead end already?"

Drew's expression fell. "It's looking that way..." There was something so defeated in the way he spoke, that Harriet wanted to help pick his mood up.

"After everything Maz told you this morning, do you really think this is connected to Templeton's case?" she said impulsively.

"The more I hear, the more inclined I am to

believe it is. I mean, finding out the girl is Albanian... It doesn't look good."

"So, what if we spoke to somebody who deals with this kind of thing, wouldn't that help?"

"Templeton deals with this kind of thing," he said, irritation colouring his voice.

"No, I mean someone outside the system. Who mediates these kinds of situations, I'd imagined there would be a pretty significant conflict of interest if the police were to mediate?"

Drew's expression shifted to something more thoughtful. "There might be someone... That is, if you're willing to take a drive?"

Harriet nodded. Martha had left her schedule blank. Whether it had something to do with Dr Baig's impromptu visit or not, wasn't something Harriet was going to examine too closely. All that mattered was that she had the time needed to help Drew, and that was far more important than anything else.

"Where did you have in mind?"

"Let me make a phone call first," Drew said. "I'm pretty certain the Monk has a connection in the Home Office, and if anyone can get us the info we need without tipping off Templeton, it's him."

CHAPTER NINETEEN

"I STILL DON'T KNOW what we're doing out here," Maz said, as he slid lower in the driver's seat, and repositioned the camera in his hands. "We should have brought the specialist surveillance team in; this is literally their job."

"You can't beat a bit of legwork," Melissa said. "Anyway, it's nice to get out of the office for a while, don't you think?"

Maz glared over at her. "They don't want to talk to us."

"They won't keep saying no," Melissa said brightly. "You're not used to this kind of policing, are you?" She glanced over at him, and Maz felt her narrow-eyed gaze probing at him. He was supposed to be the one doing figuring her out, not the other way around.

"No," he said curtly. "Like I said, specialist

surveillance teams are hired for this specific purpose..." He sighed. "What makes you say that?"

"Because when you don't get your own way, you sulk like a small child." Her grin was intended to soften her words, but Maz felt his hackles rise instead. He folded his arms over his chest and glanced back out the window.

"Perhaps, we should just pay attention to the surveillance," he said mutinously. She didn't answer him, and Maz took the opportunity to take a quick look at her over his shoulder. Her gaze was fixed on his, and Maz turned back to the street they'd parked on.

"Seriously, what is your problem?" Melissa asked finally, breaking the silence between them.

Maz sighed. There was no way he could tell her what was really on his mind, it would only give her the opportunity to weasel out of the truth, and he couldn't risk that. "Nothing," he said sharply. A flash of movement caught the corner of his eye, and he sank lower in the seat. "We've got movement," he said.

Melissa's demeanour changed instantly. "Who is it?"

"One of the grunts," Maz said, as he watched the large muscular man in the black leather jacket cross the street toward the nail-bar.

It still surprised him now to think such a benign business could disguise such a nefarious practice like human trafficking. "He's been seen hanging around some working girls, and intel suggests he's got an in with one of the leaders involved in the trafficking of young women for sex work."

Maz had taken a course in trafficking at the request of Templeton—they all had; it was a requirement for joining the task force—and it had been there he'd learned some darker truths behind such innocent looking businesses.

Of course, they didn't have proof that the newly opened nail-bar in the back streets of York was a haven for traffickers, but the intel had pointed in this direction. And now that they were here, and a known suspect had just entered the premises, it was looking a lot more concrete, but they still needed some kind of proof.

"I'm going to go over there," Melissa said, beneath her breath as she pulled her navy hoodie up to cover her hair.

"I don't think that's a good idea," Maz said, shifting uncomfortably in his seat, as he kept his gaze locked on the pink building with the flashing neon sign in the window.

"I'll go in and find out how much to get my nails done," she said, pushing the car door open. The light popped on overhead, illuminating the inside of the car, causing Melissa to swear violently.

She slammed her hand against the light, knocking it off, so they faded into obscurity again. "I told you to switch the overhead lights off," she said crossly.

"I forgot," Maz said, by way of an apology. It had been a genuine mistake, he'd been so keyed up about the whole surveillance op, he'd forgotten half the things she'd advised him to do. It was one reason he was now sitting here while his stomach protested loudly.

"What if someone is watching us," she hissed the words from between gritted teeth. "I'm so fucking tired of working with amateurs."

"They you should have done as I said, and hired bloody surveillance," he said, irritation colouring his words. "I don't think you should go in there," Maz repeated. "If they've made us, then you could endanger yourself, and me," he said.

Melissa rolled her eyes theatrically. "I'm a big girl, Arya. I can look after myself." She slipped from the car and sauntered across the road toward the nail-bar.

Maz's eyes blurred with exhaustion, and irritation curled in the pit of his stomach like a pit of vipers. He readjusted his grip on the camera, careful to make sure it was still recording everything necessary. Drew would be interested to hear what he'd learned on the little fishing expedition, but only if they could learn something truly useful.

As Melissa disappeared into the building, a second car pulled up alongside the curb. The navy

Audi looked brand new, and Maz made a note of the number plate as the driver climbed out and made for the door next to the nail-bar.

From the bit of work they'd already done, they knew the flat above the nail-bar was owned, and presumably occupied by the one who ran the bar.

A couple of moments later, Maz watched as an older woman escorted a young eastern European girl from the nail-bar. The flip-flops she wore caused her to stumble, and her escort jerked her by the arm harshly, forcing her to walk a little faster.

The girl wrapped her arms around her torso as they stood on the doorstep, the thin camisole top, and the tiny powder blue shorts she wore did nothing to conceal her slender frame. The door leading to the flat above the nail-bar opened, and the older woman ushered the younger woman inside.

Watching the events unfold didn't sit well with Maz. It was one reason he'd never wanted to go into surveillance work. They did wonderful work, and it was an important part of it all, but for him he needed to feel as though he was actively making a difference.

Sitting in the dark car, as the evening drew in around him, and he watched the building across the street with the knowledge he possessed, he couldn't shake the feeling that he was allowing a terrible crime to unfold directly beneath his nose.

Melissa appeared in the doorway of the nail-bar. When she stepped out onto the pavement,

Maz watched as she turned and grinned, giving a cheery wave to someone just beyond the camera frame. She jogged across the road, and pulled open the car door, and this time the light didn't come on.

She slipped inside, and Maz never moved his gaze from the building they were watching.

"Anything?"

"It's definitely a front," Melissa said quietly. "No doubt in my mind about it."

"But is there any proof?"

"Well, I asked a couple of questions, but most of the girls in there hardly speak English, never mind hoping they could actually understand the questions I'm asking..." She trailed off, leaving the silence to open a chasm between them.

Time seemed to pass infinitely slower than it had, and to Maz it seemed like even the seconds dragged by.

"Somebody new went in while you were inside," Maz said quietly a little while later. "Looked like somebody important."

"You made a note of it?" Melissa asked, barely managing to contain the excitement in her voice. "They brought a girl out of the back room while I was in there, but I couldn't get a good look at her."

"I've got her on camera. They took her into the flat," Maz said flatly. "She looked really young." He glanced over at Melissa then, but her gaze was unreadable. "What do you think they're doing to her up there?"

His words seemed to penetrate her hard exterior, and she blinked several times, as though that alone was enough to ward off the images his words had conjured in her head.

"I don't know," she said finally. "I wish I didn't know the kinds of things they do..."

"There's something you're not telling me," Maz said. "Something you're holding back from the rest of us." He sighed and turned his attention back to the nail-bar. He'd hoped Melissa might choose that moment to confide in him, but when nothing was forthcoming, he gave up all hope of her opening up to him.

Forty minutes later, and the door to the flat opened again. The stranger with the bald head exited and made his way to the car. Maz's stomach clenched painfully as he watched the tall and muscular man adjust himself before he climbed into the car, leaving him in no doubt as to what had happened in the intervening time.

"That's Dimitri Kolokoff," Melissa said, her voice low and urgent.

Maz glanced over at her. "Who is Dimitri Kolokoff?"

"Previous intelligence reports have suggested he's leading the charge in regards to human trafficking up here."

Maz waited for her to continue, and when she didn't, he sighed, and returned his attention to the building.

Ten minutes later, and the older woman emerged. She glanced up and down the street, as though afraid of being seen, before she ducked back into the flat.

When she stepped out onto the street, she was pushing the same young girl from earlier. Maz froze, his gaze locked onto the girl who hobbled out through the door.

She held herself, as though if she loosened her grip, even for a moment it would cause her entire fragile existence to crumble into dust. Red, angry marks dotted the tops of her arms, and from where Maz sat, he could see the marks that seemed to extend down over her thighs.

"Christ," Melissa said next to him, exhaling the word out in one long breath.

"I think I know at least one thing that happened to her up there," Maz said, studying the new tattoo that sat on the back of the girl's shoulder blade.

"What?"

"He tattooed her," Maz said, gesturing to the string of numbers just visible on the bony protuberance. "We could go in there now." He turned to face Melissa. "Just put the camera away and go in there."

"And do what?" she asked scornfully. "They'd deny everything."

"We'd ask to speak to the girl," he said.

"And if we even got near her, which I really doubt by the way, we'd get spun a bunch of horseshit. I know you want to go in there all guns blazing, but we need evidence."

Maz shook his head. "We've got evidence, how much more do you want?"

"What we've got is nothing," Melissa said. "We've got supposition, and hearsay. That won't put any of these bastards behind bars where they belong."

"And in the meantime, what do we do?"

"We do our jobs," she said, her voice as hard as ice. "We do our jobs, and when we've gathered the evidence we can then we go in there and we take those women out."

"So, we just leave them to those monsters?" Maz couldn't keep the incredulity from his voice, and he hated it. Deep down he knew she was right, but that didn't mean he had to like it.

"That's right."

He started to close the camera down, but Melissa's hand stopped him. "What are you doing?"

"I'm getting the fuck out of here," he said harshly. "You might be able to stomach this, but I sure as fuck can't." He tried to shake free of her, but she held his hand.

"Don't," she said gently. "Think of the girls in there."

"I am," he said, his voice sounding half strangled.

"Then stay. Let's get what we need so we can take them down. Help me end this..." There was something in her voice that touched him deep down. She wasn't as uncaring as he'd thought. Perhaps there was more to the situation than he'd first suspected.

"Tell me why," he said, not needing to elaborate.

Melissa sighed. "And if I do, you'll stay?"

He contemplated turning her down and then changed his mind. "I'll stay."

She nodded. "Fine." She reached out and flipped the camera off.

"Hey!"

"What I'm about to tell you, can't leave this car..."

"And if something happens that we need to record?"

"Then we'll switch the camera back on," she said, sounding as exhausted as he felt.

"Ok then."

Melissa stared out the window, and he wondered if she was going to keep her word.

"I had a friend," she said. "An undercover police officer who was working on a trafficking case... like us." She swallowed hard and knotted her fingers together. "And Dimitri Kolokoff killed her..."

CHAPTER TWENTY

TWO DAYS. Two whole days since she'd last heard from Jacob. Zara sat on the edge of her bed and stared down at the phone, willing it to do something, anything to prove that she wasn't alone in the world. Instead, it continued to sit there utterly uselessly.

She flicked back through the messages. He'd told her to delete them, but she just hadn't been able to bring herself to do that. And now she was glad she hadn't.

Yesterday, she'd been so angry at him. Noah had been a complete asshole, telling everyone in the school that she was nothing more than a slag, willing to throw down for any guy who so much as looked at her with pity. It wasn't true, of course, but that didn't stop some of her classmates from looking at her differently and whispering about her behind her back. But despite all of that, she didn't care what Noah said, because he didn't actually matter.

None of them did.

The only one she cared about, the only one who actually mattered to her, was Jacob. He'd promised her the world, and now, because she'd got a touch of cold feet, he'd basically cut her off.

The screen went black, reflecting her own swollen and blotchy face back at her. With her free hand, she scrubbed the tears aside. What if she told him she was sorry...? Not that she hadn't already tried that.

The bottom section of messages was just the same word repeated over and over, sometimes interspersed with an emoji or two. But still it had elicited no response from him.

Desperation crawled up the back of her throat like a rabid animal intent on destruction. She contemplated screaming... but changed her mind at the last second. Glancing up, she caught sight of her own reflection in the vanity mirror and cringed.

Just what did Jacob see in her, anyway?

Getting up from her spot on the bed, she crossed over to sit on the stool. Leaning toward the mirror, she examined her face a little more closely. In her mind, her nose was a little too wide, and her brown eyes were lacklustre.

And then there was her hair... Frizzy, black, and boring... She grabbed a fistful of it and eyed the scissors that sat next to her abandoned mascara and then changed her mind.

If she did something reckless, then Jacob definitely wouldn't want anything to do with her. He was probably busy... He wasn't ignoring her deliberately. He wouldn't do that. She scrolled up through the messages. He wanted to meet her. Wanted to kiss her. He wanted to be with her.

He'd asked her for a photo the week before, and while she'd known the kind of picture he was asking for like most things in her life, she'd bottled it at the last second and sent him a boring selfie. Zara glanced up at her reflection in the mirror and grabbed her beauty sponge.

Smoothing the last of her make-up into place, she applied the final touches. A hint of gloss, and a slick of mascara... It wasn't perfect, and she definitely wouldn't be starting a YouTube channel anytime soon, but it was enough. She could always edit the picture with a filter.

Getting up, she crossed the carpeted floor to the door and flipped the lock into place. No way was she having creepy Matthew sneaking in on her. Zara drew in a deep breath and crossed over to the bed.

Nervous anticipation made her fingers shake as she slowly unbuttoned her school blouse. She pushed the arms of it down, so the neckline framed her shoulders and she caught sight of her reflection in the mirror again. It wasn't enough, he'd given her so much already, the least she could do was show him how much he meant to her.

Closing her eyes, Zara slipped out of the blouse and unfastened her bra. Cold air prickled against her skin, a stark contrast to the heat that burned her cheeks. Noah would have shit his pants if she'd sent him a picture like this.

Of course, knowing how childish and immature he truly was, he'd have shared it with the entire school. Jacob, on the other hand, wasn't like that. He wouldn't betray her like that.

Raising the phone up, she angled her head down. A hesitant smile crossed her lips as she pressed the button. The phone clicked, indicating she'd taken the photo. She took a couple more pictures, angling her body this way and that, moving her head and experimenting with several facial expressions until she was finally satisfied. She slipped into a sweatshirt and sat back on the bed, drawing her knees up toward her chest as she set about making her selfie picture perfect.

She would never actually look perfect, of course. She was under no illusions. But Jacob had said she was beautiful... Even if she didn't believe it, the fact that he'd said it at all meant the world to her. She attached the photo to a hastily typed message.

I miss you. xxx

And hit the send button. Flopping back onto the bed, Zara pressed the phone against her chest. Her heart beat hard enough that she could feel the vibrations through her hand.

The minutes ticked by, and her mood darkened. She'd screwed it all up. He was never going to—

Her thoughts cut off as soon as the phone buzzed a response. Trepidation made her hands shake as she flipped the phone over, promising herself not to be too disappointed if it just turned out to be another inane message from Poppy.

Jacob's name glowed up at her from the screen, and her heart stopped. She grabbed the phone in both hands, and quickly opened the message, her eyes welling up as she read his response.

U R so beautiful.

It was such a simple statement, but as far as Zara was concerned, he may as well have told her she'd just won the lottery. The phone buzzed again, and she glanced down at the screen.

U drive me wild.

Zara's fingers flew over the screen as she typed out her message. *I'm sorry bout the other nite. Didn't mean 2 upset u.*

U didn't. Not really. I woz just hurt cuz I thought we trusted each other.

Zara chewed her lip. He was right. She did trust him, so why was she being such a prat? Sure, she'd heard the horror stories, but Jacob wasn't like that. He cared about her, maybe even loved her... She loved him.

The realisation hit her like a bolt in the dark. She loved him. And not just some silly schoolgirl crush, neither. She really and truly loved him.

I do trust u. She typed back. "I love you." She sent the message and waited with bated breath for him to reply. The three dots appeared on the screen and then disappeared again.

The seconds turned into minutes, and Zara felt her heart slowly breaking. Finally, when the message pinged back on the screen, it made her jump.

Then why not meet?

I want 2. But how?

The three dots appeared immediately, and then the message flashed up onto the screen. *4 Real?*

Yes.

Come 2 my uncle's work. I'll meet u there.

Ok. Drop me a pin.

A couple of seconds later, a link for a pin appeared on the screen. Zara clicked on it, surprised to see it opened a map of York. Zooming in on the picture, she discovered the pin was for a nail-bar called *Pretty Miss*.

Ur uncle owns a nail salon?

Yeah. He has a flat over the shop. We can hang out there if u want. Get 2 know each other proper.

Zara's heart flipped in her chest as she read the message over again, before she replied.

When?

Tomorrow?

After school, ok?

C U then!" A couple of seconds later another message flashed through.

I love you too. xxx.

Setting the phone down on the bed, Zara rolled over onto her side, as excitement thrummed in her veins. It was all happening, finally happening. She'd taken the plunge and soon she would see Jacob in the flesh. No more watching and re-watching his Tik-Tok videos. No more pining over his lack of messages. Tomorrow she would get to spend the afternoon with him. And it would be magical.

CHAPTER TWENTY-ONE

THAT EVENING DC Olivia Crandell sat back in the chair and studied DI Appleton from across the room. There was something innately confident about the woman that she couldn't quite put her finger on. She carried herself as someone who had the confidence of their convictions, but Olivia herself was almost certain that she did the same thing.

No, it was definitely more than that. Perhaps the secret to her behaviour lay in the way Melissa held her own among the older SIOs, who would have loved nothing more than to treat her as just another Doris. Not that Melissa was going to give them that option.

Twirling her biro between her fingers, Olivia studied Melissa as she leaned closer to the DCI, their heads practically pressed together as they covertly conversed with one another.

"Penny for 'em!" Maz said, dropping down into the chair next to Olivia. She jumped, the sudden intrusion into her thoughts breaking her chain of thought.

"I wouldn't bother," Olivia said. "I'm more than certain they're not worth it."

Maz shrugged and shuffled the papers clutched in his hands. Even though they weren't the same rank, Maz didn't treat her the way the others did. As far as the rest of the team seemed to be concerned, she was just a glorified skivvy, only good for making the tea when they were too lazy to get off their fat arses and do it themselves. Olivia sighed and glanced over at the rake thin man next to her.

"What have you got there, then?"

"Just a list of working girls in the area," he said nonchalantly.

"Why have you got that?"

"Because I was thinking we could speak to them about any potential newcomers trying to muscle in on their turf..."

Olivia straightened up, jamming the pen into the corner of her mouth so it forced her to speak around it. "Go on, let me have a look."

Maz held the papers close to his chest and eyed her carefully. "How do I know you won't just run off and claim the glory for yourself?"

Rolling her eyes, Olivia settled back into the chair and shrugged. "You don't."

Maz glanced down at the list before he sighed and handed half the sheets over to her. "Fine. It's not like I've got anyone else I could work with this on, anyway."

"So, you think they're a bunch of uppity arseholes too?" Olivia cast him a speculative look before she perused the list. One or two of the names jumped out at her as being regulars out on the street. She'd spent long enough working with traffic to know all the ins and outs on the street, and the working girls were just another piece of the colourful tapestry that made up the county they lived in. "I know a couple of the girls listed here," Olivia said thoughtfully, without giving Maz a chance to answer her previous question. "Maybe we should start with them?"

When she glanced up at Maz, he was grinning down at her. She felt colour flush into her cheeks. "What?"

"Nothing," he shrugged, and pushed onto his feet before he grabbed his jacket off the back of his chair. "Come on, then. We don't want the uppity arseholes to notice us, or they'll only have us looking at more maps so they can pick our brains on the locale."

Grinning, Olivia followed suit. As she slipped out through the door of the office, she caught sight of Melissa as she finished up her conversation with Templeton. The DI raised her head and scanned the room. Jamming her papers into her mouth, so she could slide her arms into her coat, Olivia let the door click softly shut behind her.

"I'M BEGINNING to think this is a dead end," Maz said grumpily as he followed Olivia up another set of winding stairs to the flats on the fifth floor.

"You can always go back to the station if you'd prefer," Olivia said. "It's just a chat, I can do this myself."

"No. You know we're supposed to do this in twos. People like this are only too happy to cry foul over the least little thing, and I'm the senior ranking officer. If I left now, Templeton would have my arse in a sling."

Olivia shrugged her shoulders. "Suit yourself." They climbed a couple more steps in companionable silence, before Maz spoke again.

"Why don't they ever fix the lifts in these places?"

"Not enough money put into the community," Olivia said. She'd grown up in a block of flats much like this one, and she was acutely aware of how the lack of public funds affected communities.

"What do you make of Templeton?" Maz's question took her by surprise, and Olivia stumbled on the edge of the bare concrete step. "Well, aside from thinking he's an uppity arsehole like the rest of them."

"I think he's fine," Olivia said cagily. It was one

thing making a passing comment, and something else entirely to say something about a specific officer.

"But do you think he's acting..." Maz seemed to struggle to find the correct word. They reached the fifth floor, and he leaned back against the wall, drawing in a deep breath. "Do you think he's acting the way a proper DCI should?"

"You mean do I think he's anything like the monk was?" Olivia shook her head and shoved her hands into the pockets of her leather jacket. "But I suppose it takes all sorts."

"I don't think what he did was right," Maz said with a measure of ferocity in his voice.

"What?"

"Passing over Haskell. That bloke took down the Star killer, for fuck's sake, and Templeton thinks having Drew on the task force would be beneath him."

Olivia nodded. She had to agree. Haskell's circumspect absence from the task force hadn't gone unnoticed. The man was practically a hero. And then there was Dr Quinn.

Olivia had never thought she'd root for someone like that, and yet on more than one occasion since they'd started working the trafficking angle, Olivia had wished they had the doctor's brain to pick. She was pretty certain if Dr Quinn had worked with them, they'd be much further down the line than they were.

"You won't hear an argument from me," Olivia said. A door further down the corridor creaked open, and three small children, and a woman manhandling a pushchair erupted into the hall. The kids didn't wait, and started down the stairs, their whoops of joy echoing off the blank walls of the stairwell.

"Need a hand?" Maz asked the woman as she paused on the top of the steps. She gave him a once over, her brown eyes hard and assessing, before she shook her head, and began the treacherous descent with the pushchair in tow.

Olivia waited until the sound of the lower door slamming shut signalled they were once again alone. "Maybe we should just get this over with?" She gestured toward the doors that lined the hall.

"Fine," Maz said. "But if another person slams a door in my face today, I swear I'll--"

"You'll go home and cry into a tub of Ben and Jerry's?" Olivia teased, drawing a scowl from the DS.

"No," he said defensively. "What number is it supposed to be?" The sudden change of topic brought a smile to Olivia's lips. Maz was far too easy to wind up.

"Number fifty-eight," Olivia said, gesturing toward the end of the hall. "Judging by the numbers, I'd guess it's probably the last one."

Maz took off ahead of her, and she followed at a much slower pace. By the time she caught up to him, he'd already rapped smartly on the worn wooden front door.

There were paint chips on the ground, and as Maz raised his fist to knock a second time, a flake of blue paint came away on his hand.

"Ugh, this place is a shit hole," he sneered. Next to him, Olivia cringed inwardly, but was relieved as the front door swung open to reveal a woman in her mid-thirties wearing a thin bathrobe.

"What do you want?" Her bright red hair was piled on top of her head, and the loose top knot rocked back and forth as she spoke.

"Are you Jessica Tambyln?" Olivia asked, pulling her warrant card from her pocket.

"Fuck this," the woman in the doorway said, attempting to close the door in their faces.

"We're not here to cause you any trouble, Jessica," Olivia said, hastily taking a step forward and jamming her foot in the doorway. It definitely wasn't protocol, and Olivia ignored the incredulous look Maz shot her as she tried to keep the front door open.

"I could have you for that," the woman said. "Don't you need some sort of warrant or whatever to come in here? I watch Line of Duty; I know my rights."

Olivia kept her smile in place and struggled not to roll her eyes. If she had a pound for every time she heard something similar, she'd be sitting on a beach somewhere hot, sipping something with enough alcohol to knock a horse out, instead of standing here in this bloody block of flats.

"We don't want to cause any trouble," Olivia said gently. "We just want a quiet chat."

"Yeah, bloody right," the woman said, her voice gradually rising. "When have you lot ever done anything for me? I'm just trying to make a living like the rest of you."

"We don't care about that," Maz said, finally getting in on the action. "We just want to speak to you about a group of people we think might have tried to move in on your turf recently..."

Olivia knew they had her as the pressure on the door released slightly. "What sort of people?" Jessica asked, suspicion lacing every word.

"They'd be managing a mix of eastern Europeans," Olivia said. "Mostly brothels, but we were thinking they might have tried their luck at getting in on the street action."

Jessica eyed them both over. "And you swear you're not here to bust me on some bullshit?"

Olivia shook her head. "I promise we're not interested in you, Jessica. We just want to know anything you might be willing to tell us."

Jessica sighed and raised her hand to scratch at her scalp with glittering nails Olivia couldn't help but think belonged on some kind of exotic big cat. "Fine, you can come in. But if you're fucking with me, I won't tell you nothing."

Olivia nodded. "Of course, we understand."

As Jessica stood aside and held the door open, Olivia felt some tension slowly release from her shoulders. Maybe they were finally going to get something they could work with.

CHAPTER TWENTY-TWO

THE ODDLY SHAPED building on Market Street that housed the Costa Coffee they'd agreed to use for their meeting was typically busy when they arrived. As they stepped in through the doors, the blast of heat that enveloped Harriet was a welcome reprieve from the lower temperatures that had closed in around them more recently.

"Do you really think this is the best place for such a sensitive conversation?" Harriet asked, as she followed Drew up to the counter.

"The woman is doing us a favour, meeting us at all. If she suggested the middle of Time's Square right now, I'd have made it my business to get there."

Harriet kept her mouth shut. Since they'd left the hospital, Drew's mood had improved, or at least it seemed to.

As far as Harriet was concerned, his constantly

shifting moods were merely a symptom of a much larger issue, but she couldn't help but feel that it wasn't her place to pass comment on it. After they'd ordered two coffees and found a small table that would seat three in the back corner of the room, Harriet took a breath.

"How are you?" She gripped the cup in both hands as she waited for Drew's reaction to her loaded question.

"I'll feel better when I know we've got something more concrete," he said, and Harriet wondered if he'd deliberately misunderstood her question, or if he really was that preoccupied.

"I don't mean about the case," she said softly, careful to keep her voice at a level where none of the other patrons sitting at the tables surrounding them could hear. "How are you?"

Drew glanced over at her then, surprise widening his usually dark and unfathomable eyes. "I'm fine. Why would you ask that?" There was a note of suspicion in his voice that made Harriet wary. Saying the wrong thing now, at such a critical juncture, had the potential to damage their relationship beyond repair.

"I just wanted to ask after our conversation the other day," she said, struggling to find the right note between concern and nonchalance.

Drew's lips compressed into a thin line, but movement at the door of the coffee shop pulled his attention away. "I think she's here."

Harriet glanced up in time to see a petite woman, with short dark hair hurrying across the room toward them. She scanned the faces, as though she was searching for something, or someone in particular, and when her gaze came to rest on Drew her shoulders relaxed.

"DI Haskell?" the stranger asked, as she paused next to their table.

Drew stood, extending his hand out toward her in one fluid movement. "And you're Kelly Evans?"

The woman nodded and turned her hundred-watt smile toward Harriet. "I didn't know I'd be meeting two of you," she said. "Although, I'm going to go out on a limb here and say you're not a police officer..."

Harriet's smile was warm as she took the preferred hand of the woman opposite her. "My name is Dr Quinn, I'm a forensic psychologist, I work with North Yorkshire CID on some of their more complicated investigations. But you can call me Harriet."

"Great," Kelly said, dropping her scarf and jacket down onto the wooden seat opposite Drew and Harriet. "If you give me a minute, I'll grab a coffee and then we can have a chat."

Harriet kept her thoughts to herself as she watched the other woman cross the coffee shop with a quiet, assured manner. She didn't bother to even glance at the board above the till, suggesting to

Harriet that either this wasn't the first time she'd come to this particular coffee shop, or she was the type of person who rarely strayed from the familiar and well-trodden path.

A couple of moments later, and Kelly re-joined them. The scent of warm spices drifted from her cup to tickle Harriet's nose. Catching her curious stare, Kelly grinned and gestured to the drink she'd chose. "It's Chai. I'm a sucker for these when I come here. Nowhere else seems to make them like this."

Harriet smiled and made a mental note to try one the next time.

"My co-ordinator said you had a bit of a situation," Kelly said, taking a small sip of her drink before she settled back in her chair. "Something about there being a potential victim of trafficking?"

Drew nodded, and from the corner of her eye, Harriet observed him wrapping his fingers around the base of his cup. "We're not entirely certain of all the details. The girl is in hospital, and--"

"And you didn't think to give us a heads up that there might be a new potential victim? There are things that only we can do, DI Haskell. It would be easier if the police would be a little more forthcoming on these matters so we could all work together more seamlessly."

"Please, call me, Drew. Look, I haven't meant to leave you out of the loop. The girl was only found in the early hours of this morning, and we haven't really had the chance to get on top of everything ourselves yet."

Kelly's expression shifted to one of concern. "This isn't the girl they pulled from the sea, is it?"

Drew nodded. "I thought you knew."

Kelly shook her head. "No, I heard about it on the news, and I guessed there might be a possible connection. But nobody told me anything before our meeting here today. I don't even know if I'll be the one assigned to her case yet, or if they'll have somebody else do the first responder interview."

"You're going to need someone who can speak Albanian," Harriet said. "The girl's English is very broken."

"Yeah, that's not uncommon. We've got people we can ask to come in to translate who can make the process run smoother."

"Any chance you could give us the name of someone?" Drew asked. "Only we've been struggling to find a translator. Apparently, they're not very common."

Kelly's smile was sympathetic. "You'd think we'd have worked out a better system by now, but despite us calling for changes, and reviews happening, the NRM hasn't really changed since its launch here in 2009." She sighed, and took a thoughtful sip of her drink, her hazel eyes sweeping across first Drew, and then Harriet before she set the cup back down.

"I can get you someone, anything if it helps to

ease the burden on the victim. But I don't think you're here because you just wanted my help to find a translator."

Drew shook his head. "Is there anything you can tell us about the situation as it stands here? I want to nail the bastard who did this, but--" Drew spread his hands out. "I'm at a loss where I should even begin."

"There's a large active network at work here," Kelly said, disdain evident in her voice and facial expression. "To them it's purely a numbers game. The more they can bring into the country, either to work in nail-bars, cleaning jobs, the sex industry, or even drugs, the more money the people at the top stand to make."

"But why do people listen to them? I mean, I know you hear stories about the UK being the promised land, and all that. But it's all bull. We've got problems here, just like everywhere else."

Kelly's smile hardened. "I don't mean to sound rude, DI Haskell, but I don't really think you understand the meaning of the word problems. Problems for you or me are deciding whether to have a take-away after work, or use up the veg in the fridge. The people who are lured over here, come because they have nothing at all. Their families live in abject poverty, or their country's education system isn't as accessible as it is here. Or they just don't have any real options to better themselves."

She sighed. "And these traffickers pray on that.

They promise them money, and opportunities, and a future both for them and their families. Tell me, DI Haskell, if you had nothing and somebody promised you a chance at a better future for you and your loved ones, would you take it?"

Drew looked chagrined as he stared down into the depths of his cup. "I suppose when you put it like that, I can see why they're tricked into coming here."

"Make no mistake," Kelly said. "Not everybody is tricked. Some are simply taken off the streets of their home country. They see young girls and boys, and they know they could get a buyer for them, so they take them and sell them into sex, or the drugs industry."

"Does that happen often?" Harriet asked, feeling her stomach clench uncomfortably.

"More often than I'd like to admit," Kelly said. "We try to help the ones we can, but often, we don't find out about it until it's too late." She pushed her fingers back through her hair. "It happens here too. Online grooming of young boys and girls, they lure them out into a place where they can grab them, and they just disappear." She clicked her fingers as though to emphasise the ease with which it happened.

"What can we do?" Drew asked.

Kelly's smile betrayed a bone-weary exhaustion. "I'll find you a translator, and we'll see what we can find out about your girl. If she's a victim, then you must let us do our job first. Get the girl somewhere safe and help get her back on her feet."

"And what do we do?" There was an edge to Drew's voice. "I want to find out who did this to her."

"That's your job, DI Haskell. I'm afraid I only help the victims of these crimes; I don't catch the people responsible too. But if I can help you speak to the girl, and she's willing to do it without it causing her too much distress, then I'll help. It's all I can offer you."

Drew glanced over at Harriet, and she nodded. Kelly was right, it was their job to track down the people responsible, and while it would be nice to have a full statement from the victim, it was also unfair to expect it of her after such a traumatic experience.

They would just have to make do with what they had and hope somewhere along the line it would be enough to nail those responsible.

CHAPTER TWENTY-THREE

ON THE DRIVE to the hospital, Drew's phone rang in the centre console next to him. Glancing down at the screen, he noted the name flashing on the screen and his heart climbed into his mouth.

It hadn't been that long since he'd last spoken to Maz, yet there was no doubt in Drew's mind that his former DS was going to tell him something he could use to his advantage. Indicating, he ignored Harriet's curious stare as he pulled off the road and parked up on the hard shoulder.

"I could have taken the call for you," she said.

The call ended, and Drew shrugged. "It doesn't matter now."

Harriet flinched, as though he'd physically struck her, and Drew instantly felt terrible. What was wrong with him? All he seemed to do lately was hurt those around him, either deliberately, or worse yet without intending to.

"Sorry," he said, grabbing the phone before he pushed open the door and stepped out into the chilly evening air.

Harriet said nothing to him, and Drew knew the simple apology would not be enough. He would need to work a lot harder to help her understand that his short temper and refusal to open up had nothing to do with her, and everything to do with his own personal struggles with everything that had happened.

Simply getting to the point where he could even admit that to himself was an enormous step. Not that Harriet could know that, considering the way he constantly kept her at arm's length.

Sighing, he redialled Maz's number, and waited in the cold as the phone rang. The air chilled his face, and numbed the tips of his ears, so that he tried to sink his face down into the collar of his jacket to hide from the worst of the freezing air.

"Hello mate," Maz said, answering the call in such a way that let Drew know it wasn't safe for him to talk. "Just give me a minute, I can't hear a word you're saying over the noise here."

As far as Drew was concerned, the noise in the background of Maz's location was minimal, but he bit his tongue to keep his impatience from sharpening his tongue.

In reality, it was just a couple of seconds, but in Drew's mind it may as well have been hours, when Maz finally came back on the line huffing and puffing as though he were out of breath.

"Sorry about that," Maz said. "I'm out on the stairs."

"Where are you?" Drew wasn't sure why, but the urge to keep his tone low to match Maz's was overwhelming.

"Just got back into the office," Maz said. "Spent the day out and about, mostly in York." Maz's sigh travelled down the line to Drew, and he could almost imagine the other man leaning back against the wall of the stairwell he was stood in.

"What were you doing out there?"

"DI Appleton had us trace some phones, and one of them seemed to spend a lot of time coming and going and making calls to this place, so we were following up on it."

"Whose phone?" Drew asked, beginning to pace up and down on the gravel outside the car.

"It's a list of phone numbers she swiped from an investigation that was ongoing down south," Maz said quietly. "She and Templeton think that parts of the operation moved out of Southampton and came North after an incident."

Excitement fizzed in Drew's veins. He could tell by the note of triumph in Maz's voice that he knew something big. But whether it would be of use to

Drew was another matter entirely. "Go on, tell me the rest of it."

Maz sighed, and his voice dropped another octave until he was practically whispering. "Templeton had a daughter called Anna Spencer."

Something in the back of Drew's mind lit up as soon as he heard the name. "Isn't that the name of a police officer who was murdered?"

"One and the same," Maz said. "She was working undercover down in Southampton, trying to get them some more evidence on this trafficking ring. They were into all sorts down there; drugs, sex, prostitution, slavery, and human trafficking."

"And she was made," Drew said softly. "They never got the bastard who killed her."

"Nope, and now I know why..."

Silence stretched between them like a taut elastic, and Drew felt his patience wearing thin. "Well, spit it out, man. I'm freezing my bollocks off out here."

"The main guy suspected of the murder was relocated to North Yorkshire. A bloke going by the name of Dimitri Kolokoff. DI Appleton said he's a right nasty piece of work with links to all kinds of murky shit and dealings."

The name caused Drew's heart to leap into his throat. He couldn't be certain of it, but he definitely wasn't a man who believed in coincidences, working in the police force for as long as he had

had taught him that coincidences like this just didn't happen.

"The girl from the sea," Drew said.

"What about her?"

"Son of a bitch..." Before Maz could say anything else, Drew hung up. The last thing he wanted was for his well-meaning former DS to say anything to Melissa Appleton. She was a smart cookie, too smart, and the faintest whiff that Templeton had been right to want to take over the investigation into the girl from the sea would see her shutting him down before he ever got his feet off the ground.

No, this was far too important, and he needed to play it carefully. And if he did, then he had the leverage he'd been searching for.

Climbing back in behind the wheel, he couldn't resist shooting Harriet a wide grin.

"What's got you in such a good mood all of a sudden?"

"I know how to get Templeton to let us in to play for the big boys?"

She raised an eyebrow at him speculatively. "Go on."

"Dimitri Kolokoff."

Harriet stared at him uncomprehendingly. "I don't understand, is that the same Dimitri as the one the girl in the hospital was talking about."

"I think it is, and if I'm right, then Templeton will have no choice but to let me join our investigations."

"Why would that make him do that?" Harriet's voice was loaded with curiosity.

"Because if they are one and the same, then that means Templeton is doing something he shouldn't be doing."

"What's that?"

"Covertly investigating the man he thinks is responsible for the death of his daughter."

CHAPTER TWENTY-FOUR

AFTER HE'D DROPPED Harriet off at the station so she could pick up her own car, Drew had made his way back to the hospital. He'd resisted the urge to check in on the girl from the sea again.

If anything changed regarding her, the uniformed officers he'd left there would get in contact with him. All he needed to do was wait until the morning when they could conduct an interview with the help of the translator Kelly would provide.

In the meantime, Drew had decided to get DC Green to drop in on the post-mortem due to take place on the burned remains found in the house in Whitby. And when he'd got a phone call from a rather irritated morgue assistant who was none too pleased with Tim's reaction to the post-mortem, Drew had decided to go over there himself.

Leaning against the doorframe of the forensic

pathologist's office, Drew eyed DC Tim Green, who at that moment seemed to be more than living up to his name.

"Was this your first post-mortem?" Drew asked, feeling pity well inside as he watched the young DC struggle to keep the contents of his stomach where they should be.

"Kind of," he said, as he held the paper bag Drew had given to him a few moments before back up to his mouth and inhaled deeply.

"I'd like to say you get used to them," Drew said, before he shrugged. "But that would be a lie. You never get used to seeing humans reduced to their constituent parts by the cruelty of another."

Green's face took on an unnatural hue, and he jumped up from the chair, and shoved out through the door practically rugby tackling the pathologist who was at that moment heading up the hall.

"I wasn't expecting you here," Dr Jackson said, eyeing Drew disdainfully. "Come to check up on my work again?"

"Nothing of the sort," Drew said. "I just wanted to see if we were any further along toward getting an ID for the burnt body we found in the house in Whitby." As Drew spoke, the monk's words from the morning rang in his ears.

Dr Jackson pursed his lips and crossed the floor to his desk. From there, he sifted through several files that lay discarded across the otherwise pristine surface. "He came in as a John Doe," Dr Jackson said, sliding his black glasses back up his hawkish nose. "There was some interesting U-shaped fracturing along the long bones consistent with the burning of a fresh body."

He glanced back up at Drew. "That means the body wasn't sitting there for a prolonged period before it was burned. However, I could find no indication of smoke inhalation in what remained of the lung tissue. There was some indication of blunt force trauma to the back of the head, and it would be my opinion that it was the cause of death, not the fire."

"And do we have an ID?"

Dr Jackson sighed. "You're always so impatient, DI Haskell. You don't see me coming to your place of work and badgering you for answers."

"I'll take that as a no," Drew said, feeling dread curl in the pit of his stomach. The monk was going to be pretty pissed off when he got back with nothing to show for the day.

"Then you would be incorrect," Dr Jackson said. "I do in fact have an ID for the body." He pulled a second file from the stack in front of him and flipped it open.

From his position at the door, Drew could just make out the grey and black x-rays within the file.

"Two years ago, our young man was involved in an accident that resulted in quite a severe break to his left tibia. From what I've seen from the x-rays taken at the time, there was a significant splintering of the bone, that resulted in them having to secure the bone with a plate and several large pins. Needless to say, the metal plate and pins survived the burning and from the code I retrieved I was able to find out the name of the patient. A one Levi Jones formerly of Weston down in Southampton. Just what he's doing this far North, I'm not sure, but I suppose that's where your job comes in."

Dr Jackson's smile was predatory as he closed the file in front of him.

"Could he have done this to himself?" Drew asked. His mind was whirling at a thousand miles an hour. It was another coincidence in a long line of them that just refused to make any sense.

"Definitely not," Dr Jackson said. Considering there was no indication of smoke inhalation in his lungs, and blunt force trauma to his head, I don't believe he was responsible for his own injuries."

"And he couldn't have been, I don't know, smoking and fallen and hit his own head?" Drew was grasping at straws, but he didn't want to go back to the monk with only half the story.

"The fire was set deliberately, DI Haskell. They used an accelerant, which is why the blaze was so intense and difficult to control in the first place. If it hadn't been caught when it was, I've got my doubts that we would have had enough of a body left to figure out cause of death."

Drew nodded; it was all he needed. "Thanks, doc," he said as he straightened up and started down the hall. He met DC Green—who was leaving the men's toilet—as he reached the hall outside the morgue.

"Please tell me I don't have to go back in there, sir," Green said. Sweat beaded across the other man's forehead and upper lip.

"No. I'm heading back to the station. There's someone I need to have a chat with."

Green sighed and sagged back against the wall. "We've got an ID on the burned body though," Drew said. "A Levi Jones from Southampton, when you get back to the station, I'd like you to find out everything you can about him."

Green nodded. "Anything particular I should be looking for?"

A smile curled Drew's lips. "See if you can find a connection between him and a Dimitri Kolokoff."

"Sir?"

"Failing that, anything you can get me on who he was, and why he might have been in Whitby on the night he died. When you've done that, contact Southampton and ask them to make the let the next of kin know that he's dead." Drew started down the hall before he'd even finished speaking.

"Do you want this on your desk by morning, sir?" Green called after him, and Drew couldn't miss the note of hope in the other man's voice that he would say no.

"No, DC Green. I want to know the moment you've got something... I don't care how late it is, you call me." Drew glanced over his shoulder at the DC, who had dropped his gaze toward the floor and smiled. He could still remember how it felt to be the one getting the orders.

Of course, he'd learned fast, and it had allowed him to move up through the ranks rather more swiftly than others around him. But that didn't mean he couldn't feel sorry for the likes of Green, who were just learning the ropes.

Pushing out through the swing doors into the main part of the hospital, Drew fished his phone from his pocket and dialled the number for the task force office.

He had enough information to put his case across to Templeton, and there was no time like the present to do it.

CHAPTER TWENTY-FIVE

THREE HOURS LATER, after a tense wait for DC Green to get back to him, Drew stood outside the office. Pulling the packet of cigarettes from his inside jacket pocket, he popped open the lid and stared down at them. Desire thrummed in his veins. Instead of pulling one out, he flipped the lid shut, and replaced the packet in his coat.

For too long, he'd allowed this addiction to get the better of him. The sound of hurried footsteps pulled his attention from his own thoughts. There were far more important things to manage now. What DC Green had told him, along with everything Maz had filled him in on, guaranteed that Templeton would roll over and let him on the task force.

It was that knowledge that filled him with anticipation, as DI Melissa Appleton rounded the corner. She looked up at him, and Drew felt his stomach flip.

"Long time stranger," she said. Her lips—which were a little too thin to be considered attractive, but which only added to her allure—were stretched into a broad, easy smile, reminding him of their shared past.

"There was a time when we weren't strangers," he said. "A time when all of this was your turf as well as mine." He grinned at her as she pulled him in for a tight hug.

"You've lost weight," she said, pulling away to give him a once over. "Too much, in fact," she said, wrinkling her nose. "We've got to start feeding you up, get some of those stotties down your neck."

"Shouldn't I be the one saying that to you?" He asked, raising an eyebrow at her. "After all, I wasn't the one who high-tailed it out of here."

Melissa shrugged and smoothed her blonde hair back down into place. "I didn't exactly high-tail it out of here."

"The moment you got the chance, you ran," he said. "Here today, gone tomorrow." He stared down at the ground, as the memories of her abandonment of their small team came flooding back. "We really missed you."

"And I missed you a lot," she said earnestly. "You

don't know how weird it was starting over down there, but I had to go. I couldn't stick around here and go nowhere fast."

Drew sighed. "Aye, I know what you mean. As much as I hate to admit it, DCI Brockwell was not exactly the most progressive of SIOs."

"Progressive?" Melissa snorted derisively. "He once called me sugar tits, and when I threatened to report him for it, he told HR I was a distraction to the other officers." There was an edge of bitterness to her voice that took Drew by surprise.

"You never told me that," he said softly.

"Doesn't matter now," she said. "He's retired, and I've finally got where I wanted to be. Well, almost." She laughed, the sound bouncing off the surrounding walls.

"Anyway, I thought you said you were never coming back here," Drew said, struggling to keep his grin under wraps.

"I'm allowed to change my mind," she said. "I'm female, after all. But you—" She jabbed her finger in toward his chest in order to emphasise her words. "I heard you were trying to get yourself decommissioned permanently."

He shrugged wryly. "It wasn't intentional, I can promise you that."

"So, tell me what it was like?" She took a step towards him and lowered her voice to a conspiratorial whisper. "Getting up close and personal with the Star Killer and all, you must have been shitting yourself."

Drew cringed, but he couldn't keep his grin to himself any longer. "Something like that," he said. "I had back-up though."

"You were one lucky bastard," Melissa said. "Plenty of others never escaped that wanker's blade."

"I see Southampton didn't soften your love for profanity," Drew said, swiftly changing the subject. As good as it was to reconnect with Melissa after all of this time, he didn't want her poking at wounds—mental as much as physical—that hadn't yet fully healed.

She snorted. "You still afraid someone's going to wash your mouth out with soap?"

When he didn't answer, she sighed. "So why did you want to speak to me?"

It was the moment of truth. Nervous anticipation buzzed in Drew's head as he sucked in a deep breath and contemplated how best to approach what he was going to say next. Melissa's expression shifted, growing darker as he opened his mouth to speak.

"That scummy little bastard," she said vehemently, taking Drew by surprise.

"What?"

"DS Arya," Melissa said. "Don't pretend like this hasn't got to do with what I told him."

"Why would it matter if he did?"

"Because I told him that in confidence, and no offence Drew, but you're not part of the team. I can't have team members running their mouths every chance they get. You and I both know how dangerous that is to ongoing investigations."

Drew scuffed his boots against the ground. "I can understand where you're coming from," he said. "But you have to understand, I've worked with Maz for a long time. We're partners, you can't just expect that to go away because your boss has a bee up his arse over me."

"God, you're so arrogant. I thought time might have sorted you out with that issue, but I can see now that it hasn't. Templeton hasn't got a bee in his arse over you. He just doesn't think you're task force material."

Her words cut Drew to the quick. He'd spent enough time thinking that Templeton hadn't wanted him on the task force because he just wasn't good enough, and the last thing he needed now was for Melissa to confirm it.

"I'm sorry, Drew. I shouldn't have said that--"

"No, if that's the truth, then I'm not going to argue with the man."

"It's not true," Melissa whispered. "I'm sorry, I was lashing out."

Drew glanced up at her and gave her a wry smile. "It's fine, Melissa, I'm a big boy now, I can handle it when someone criticises me. You don't need to try to smooth it over."

"Now you're just being a dick," she sighed. "Look. I don't actually know what his reasoning is. Personally, I thought he was mad not to ask you to come over, and I told him so, but he really wasn't going for it."

"Well, I know something that might make him change his mind," Drew said, his voice low and dangerous.

There was nothing pretty or good about what he planned to do. In fact, if he'd heard somebody else was about to pull the same stunt, he'd have thought they were a complete wanker. But there was a part of him that knew he had no choice.

Yes, it would be nice to get on the task force and prove Templeton wrong, but there was more to it than that. Police officers didn't investigate the deaths of loved ones for a reason.

Too often, personal emotions got in the way, and jeopardised the investigations, leaving loopholes large enough for the scum they chased to escape through. He couldn't let that happen in this case.

"Go on," Melissa said, sounding wary for the first time since they'd started speaking.

"I want in on the investigation," he said.

"But--"

"The girl we pulled from the sea; she's been

saying the name Dimitri. Now I don't know about you, Melissa, but I'm not much for coincidences."

"Give us the case," she said, pushing her chin out defiantly. "Hand the case over to us, and I'll speak to Templeton about getting you on the team when all of this is done."

"I don't think so."

"Why not?"

"Because that's not all I know." He cocked an eyebrow at him and sighed.

"Fine, you know about his daughter, but that's why I'm here. He's not investigating anything he shouldn't--"

Drew shook his head. "That's not all. I want the task force and my team to join up on the investigation. I don't want to just have everything we've been doing, everything the monk, and DC Green have done so far to just get used up and spat out by the task force when Templeton grows bored with us. This is a joint investigation."

"And why would we do that?" There was a coldness to Melissa's voice that hadn't been there before.

"Because I know what Templeton has been up to," Drew said. "Did you hear about the house fire in Whitby," Drew asked, searching Melissa's face for any telltale flicker that she knew what he was about to say next.

"I heard somebody died," she said. "But nothing more than that."

"The body we found belonged to a Levi Jones."

Melissa's face went stark white, and waxen beneath the overhead streetlights. "That's not possible," she said softly.

"Wasn't he one of Dimitri's boys that Templeton tried to flip down in Southampton after Anna's death?"

"That was all cleared up," Melissa said. "He was grieving for his daughter, and Levi had evidence that could have secured a conviction against Dimitri."

"And Templeton knew that," Drew said. After DC Green had called him with the information, Drew had asked the DC to send the files over to him. He'd seen enough in those files to read between the lines about Templeton's activities.

And now that he'd said it to Melissa, he could see that he wasn't the only one thinking the same thing. The proof of Templeton's wrongdoing might be there in black and white, but with enough digging they would find it.

"I find it strange that Levi turned up here... Dead... Not so long after Templeton and Dimitri turn up in the same spot."

"You don't think Templeton murdered him, do you?" Fear tinged Melissa's voice, which Drew could totally understand. If he'd been in her shoes, aiding his boss in a situation that was rapidly spinning out of control, he'd be bricking it too.

"No," Drew said. "Levi got to Scarborough about

a week ago, and from there he made his way to Whitby on the day he died. I've got somebody running through the CCTV from town to see if we can pinpoint Levi's movements over the last week, but I don't think Templeton killed him. I think he could be held responsible for his death, though. I think he sent Levi there to speak to Dimitri, and it went south."

"That's nothing but hearsay," Melissa said, but Drew could hear the doubt in her voice.

"You're telling me when we go through the phone records, we won't be able to make a connection to Templeton?"

"What do you want me to do, Drew?" Resignation filtered over Melissa's face, and her shoulders sagged as though he'd just placed the weight of the world on them.

"Get Templeton to agree to a joint investigation. My team will do all the digging on Dimitri, and Levi leaving him clean as a whistle."

"And what do you get out of all this?" she asked, raising an eyebrow in his direction.

"The satisfaction of seeing the smug smile on Templeton's face being wiped off when I'm sitting in his briefing room at nine am."

Melissa's snort rang out in the air, telling Drew that she didn't believe a word of what he was saying. Not that it mattered to him what she actually believed. He knew why he was doing this.

There had been a time when it all started that he would have gone after Templeton out of petty revenge for keeping him from the task force, but none of that mattered now.

All Drew cared about was nailing the bastards responsible for putting the young girl in the hospital.

CHAPTER TWENTY-SIX

DREW SETTLED into the chair at the back of the briefing room. It creaked ominously beneath him, and he did his best to ignore the curious glances cast in his direction.

The superintendent hadn't been kidding when he'd promised a task force. Sitting there, he smothered the smile that threatened to expose him as he contemplated the monk's reaction to everything he'd told him. Nobody could quite believe that Templeton had had such a complete change of heart. Not that any of it mattered. He was here now. He studied the room, noticing the easy camaraderie among the others. Obviously, they had bonded during the training, and here he was the newbie.

It stank... Drew pushed the thought aside; he couldn't allow such destructive thought patterns to derail him now.

Maz caught his eye from the other side of the room and grinned. Drew nodded in the DS's direction as the tension knitting his shoulder blades together thawed a little.

At least there were some familiar faces among the group. He hadn't yet told Maz everything he'd figured out regarding the DCI; he hadn't even fully decided if he was going to tell Maz the whole story. It wasn't really his story to tell.

If Templeton came clean, then that was his business, he decided.

Drew's gaze was inextricably drawn to the DCI at the top of the room who stood next to the very familiar Superintendent Burroughs. The other man, however, was completely alien to him.

The DCI was whip thin and tall to boot. His suit jacket hung off his wide shoulders and gaped open every time he shifted unconsciously from one foot to the other. In any other man Drew might have assumed the behavioural curiosity was a nervous tic, but as he studied the man who he would be working alongside, Drew was pretty certain the DCI wouldn't know the meaning of the word nervous.

Templeton's expression was unreadable as the Super babbled on about the team pulling together to lower crime rates across the North East of England, or some such media friendly speech, Drew along with a number of the other officers in the room had zoned out. They'd heard it all before.

For Drew, what made the meeting truly interesting was the DCI's hawkish eyes. They roved around the room, alighting on different members of the team, as though by simply staring at them for long enough he could assess their true thoughts.

Christ, what the hell had happened to him? He was starting to sound a little too much like the good doctor Quinn. Sitting here breaking down the strange DCI's character before he'd even spoken to the other man properly. Folding his arms over his chest, Drew concluded he'd been spending far too much time in the good doctor's company, and her uncanny ability to read everyone else in the room.

As though he'd conjured her from his mind, Drew turned in his seat as the door at the back of the room flopped open and Harriet hurried inside. She looked flustered, and Drew tried to hide a smile as her unruly curls flopped over into her eyes.

"Sorry, I'm so late," she said, sounding more than a little out of breath, and Drew found himself wondering if she'd ran up the four flights of stairs to get here.

"Ah, yes, Dr Quinn, so glad you could make it," Superintendent Burroughs sounded almost nervous and Drew snapped his attention back to the top of the room. "It seems we've finally got ourselves a full house."

There was no mistaking the meaning of the Superintendent's words. Clearly, he hadn't been a fan of keeping Drew, and by extension Harriet, from the task force for so long.

However, in all the years he'd known the Super, he'd never once heard him sound so odd. Had Templeton already said something? The DCI caught Drew's eye, and he fought the urge to squirm under the sudden scrutiny.

"My meeting ran over and then my car—" Harriet cut off. The DCI's attention shifted away from Drew and returned to the woman who had interrupted the meeting. "But you don't want to know about my car troubles." Harriet sighed and Drew fought the urge to help her with the papers she juggled precariously.

As well-meaning as he would intend the gesture to be, he knew it would be perceived by the others in the room as possessiveness.

"If you'd like to take a seat Dr Quinn?"

So, he speaks, and he's not local. The DCI's accent had the distinctive twang of someone who had spent their entire life in London.

An officer Drew didn't recognise hopped to his feet and moved toward Harriet.

"Let me help," he said, a shit-eating grin that made Drew's skin crawl, lit up the other man's face.

"Thanks," Harriet said politely. "I can manage." She side-stepped his assistance but took the proffered seat next to him.

"Good, great," Superintendent Burroughs said, clearing his throat awkwardly. "Now that we have—"

"Thank you, Superintendent, I think I can take it from here," the DCI said formally before he turned to the room leaving the Super to flounder.

It was a move Drew knew the Monk would never have made and got away with it. He half expected the Super to correct his mistake.

Instead, Drew was surprised to see him step down and take one of the seats at the top of the room. Just how had Templeton managed to curb the super so thoroughly?

"We've got a lot of work to get through," the DCI said. "But for those of you who are new here today, I'm DCI Templeton, and I've been given the authority to lead this task force."

Surreptitiously, Drew glanced around the room, as far as he could tell Dr Quinn, and himself were the only two new people in the room. DC Green had declined the invitation, telling Drew he still had a number of hours of CCTV footage to run through before he was done.

"As you know, we're currently examining a known group of traffickers in the area," Templeton said. It was interesting to hear him admit to it out loud, Drew hadn't expected him to be so brazen.

"But it seems we weren't the only ones interested in the same bunch of people," DCI Templeton's gaze fell on Drew for a second time. "DI Haskell has graciously agreed to a joint investigation." The DCIs words sent a ripple of interest around the room. "I've asked him here today to take a look at what we've got, and he's going to share his findings with us. Would you care to move up to the top of the room, DI Haskell, you might find it more comfortable up here." There was no mistaking the icy tone in the DCIs voice.

"No, sir, I'm fine here."

There was a distinct tightening around the DCIs mouth as Drew spoke. Just how much had Melissa told him?

"Sir, we've managed to track the location of the encro phones to the nail bar in York," DI Appleton's voice interjected, drawing the Templeton's attention in her direction. "From what we've gathered so far, it's our impression that a significant deal will be taking place in the next few days. Just what they're planning to sell. We don't have confirmation of that yet, but we have received confirmation that the package is arriving today. And we believe it's in our best interests to orchestrate a raid on that premises before they become aware of our surveillance."

"Is there any indication they've been alerted to our presence?" Templeton asked, sounding thoughtful.

"From what we've seen from the surveillance, Dimitri and Oscar are becoming more cautious regarding their behaviour. There has been some chatter regarding Dimitri arranging for a passport under another name. We think it's best we move now, sir."

Drew watched the interaction with interest. Was it his imagination, or was the DCI's gaze lingering a little longer than appropriate?

Shit, now he knew he was spending too much time with Harriet.

Sliding a little lower in his seat, he was determined to ride out the rest of the meeting without drawing any undue attention to himself.

"As some of you already know, my area of interest lies particularly in those cases which seem to elude our esteemed colleagues," Templeton said. "Which is why we've joined the investigation with DI Haskell. He and his team have been made aware of a case he's working and it's connection to our current operation here." Drew silently seethed as the DCI spoke. It was a cheap shot, but there wasn't much he could do about it. "A young girl who we believe has fallen victim to being trafficked by Dimitri Kolokoff and his group was pulled the sea near Whitby on Monday—"

The energy in the room seemed to fizzle out as the DCIs voice droned on. By the time he'd finished, Drew had very nearly nodded off twice. Shifting in the chair, he winced as pain lit up across his abdomen. Despite healing up nicely after the Star Killer's attempt on his life, there were still certain things that pinched. He had been working particularly hard lately, and sleeping in the car outside his house was slowly beginning to take its toll. He was going to have to make up his mind about the house sooner rather than later, because he couldn't keep going like this.

With his eyes closed, his mind dragged him back to the moment he'd believed his life was going to end at the point of Nolan's wickedly sharp blade. He could feel the cold steel against his naked skin, the kiss of it as it bit into his flesh. The plastic beneath his feet crinkled, and he drew a ragged breath in through his nose as he opened his eyes to see the other members of the team getting to their feet. His team, he corrected himself.

Drew shuffled his shoes across the carpeted floor as though to reassure himself that it was just a traumatic memory and that he hadn't somehow slipped backwards in time. He'd contemplated selling up, but it wasn't until that moment in the briefing room that he'd given it any truly serious thought.

"Good to see you back in the saddle, DI Haskell," Superintendent Burrough's voice cut through his quiet contemplation and he snapped his attention toward the older man who had come to stand directly in front of him. He hadn't noticed his approach. Christ, he really was tired.

"Just glad to be back, sir," Drew said, pushing slowly to his feet. He hid the discomfort that speared through his body. The last thing he needed was for one of his superiors to notice he was still in some considerable pain. "I was beginning to go a little stir-crazy staring at the same four walls every day, so it's nice to be back in the thick of it all."

Burroughs laughed, the sound booming in the intimate conference room. It seemed to draw the attention of the other officers, and Drew smiled tight-lipped at the man in front of him.

"Well, you just try to stay out of the hospital from now on. We need good men like you." He slapped Drew's shoulder, the blow sending reverberations down through every cell in his body.

"Of course, sir. I'll do my best."

Burroughs stalked away, seemingly pleased with the conversation. Drew let go of the breath he'd been holding onto as he straightened up.

"So, you came then," Melissa said. She stood with her arms folded across her chest, her lips a thin line.

"You knew I would," he said quietly.

"You don't have to do this, you know. You don't know everything."

"Is that what he told you?"

Melissa sighed. "I've worked with Anthony for a long time. He's not a bad guy."

"Just a misguided one," he said.

"Well, he has a right to be," Melissa said. "I'd like

to see how the rest of us would cope if the same had happened to us..."

"DI Appleton, you haven't come to collect your case files," the DCI's voice cut through their conversation. Drew found it disconcerting that Templeton had managed to get the drop on him too. He took a step backwards, giving the other man a chance to join the conversation.

"I've left them out on the desk for you," DCI Templeton said. Drew knew a dismissal when he heard one, and one glance at Melissa's face said she knew it too. "I'd like a word here with the new boy."

Drew bristled beneath the perceived insult. Without another word, Melissa left, but as she stepped behind the DCI, she shot Drew a pleading look. Just what she expected him to do was beyond him. Templeton had made his bed as far as Drew was concerned.

Facing the older man, Drew schooled his features into an expression of utter indifference.

"I'm glad we could be of assistance to one another, sir," Drew said.

The DCI looked him up and down, his gaze inscrutable.

"I've read your file, Haskell," the DCI said. "You did some good work on the Star Killer case. I was sorry to hear about your stint in the hospital."

"Thank you, sir," Drew said, keeping his face impassive.

"There's just one problem in this," the DCI continued as though Drew had never spoken at all. "I don't want you here. You don't fit in with the team I've pulled together."

"Excuse me, sir?" As much as he wanted to say he retained his cool, and even temper, Drew knew he'd failed when he saw a flash of triumph in the DCI's eyes.

"You heard me, Haskell. It wasn't my choice to have you here. You and your pet psychologist are a match made in Hell. I heard about your insubordination in regards to the suicide case."

"Sir, with all due respect, those weren't suicides—"

"That's beside the point, Haskell. You ignored a direct order from your superior officers to shut the investigation down. Instead, you went off playing rogue hero, and involved an outsider where she didn't belong. People like Quinn see a monster lurking in every cupboard."

"Sir, I—" Drew struggled to find the correct words, or at least ones that wouldn't land him in hot water.

"Your kind is poison, Haskell. Given the first chance, I will have you off this team and back where you belong. You and Quinn both."

It struck Drew then, that perhaps Melissa hadn't told him everything. It seemed odd that she would keep such important information from him, especially when it involved the potential future of his career.

"Sir, I don't think you understand the seriousness of the situation you find yourself in," Drew said quietly. "I know about your daughter. I know about Dimitri Kolokoff, and I know about Levi Jones..." Drew expected to see some flicker of fear in the other man's eyes, but what he got instead rocked him to his core.

DCI Templeton stared at Drew, much the same way he might stare at a beetle he planned to crush beneath the heel of his boot.

"You don't know the first thing about me, or the things I'm willing to do in order to serve justice to those who deserve it," DCI Templeton said, his voice like a frozen tundra that turned Drew's blood to ice in his veins. "Whatever you think you know, or understand about me DI Haskell, forget it." He leaned closer, and the musky scent of his aftershave swamped Drew's senses, turning his stomach and reducing the oxygen he could breathe. "But mark my words on this, Haskell, I'm a powerful enemy to have made, so you would do well to stay out of my way."

Drew fought the urge to take a step back. He stiffened his spine and met the DCIs gaze head on. There was no point continuing the argument. He could see in the set of the other man's jaw that he'd already made up his mind, and no amount of trying to persuade him otherwise would see him waver.

"No, run along, and for once do something useful and get me the information I need from that girl you lot pulled from the sea."

"Of course, sir." Without waiting for further insults, Drew turned on his heel and strode away. As he passed the chair he'd been sitting in, he snatched his coat from the back of the seat.

Maz caught his eye and quirked an eyebrow in his direction, but Drew subtly shook his head.

If Templeton considered him to be poison, then everyone associated with him would receive the same treatment and Maz didn't need that. He was a damn fine officer, and he deserved a break like this.

No, he would not let Templeton screw that up for him.

With a last cursory glance at the room, Drew left.

CHAPTER TWENTY-SEVEN

A FEW MOMENTS later Harriet caught up to Drew in the main reception.

"You're in a rush," she said. "I thought you would have wanted to stick around and see what the others are working on..." She trailed off as she noted the thunderous expression Drew wore. At the best of times, controlling his temper wasn't exactly his strong suit. In fact, if she was being perfectly honest, he was a bit of a belligerent grump. He wore his rage like a suit of armour; one designed specifically to keep everyone at arm's length.

She had a feeling that it was created by a combination of residual trauma after Freya's death, and his line of work. When you spent your whole life meeting people on the very worst day of their lives, it was bound to have a detrimental impact on even those with a saintlier disposition. Not that she believed Drew had ever been a saint.

But this felt different to the usual facade he wore to keep others from getting too close to him.

"What is it?"

He shook his head. "Outside," his voice was a mumble of displeasure.

She followed him outside the building and watched as he fought the urge to take the packet of empty cigarettes he always carried in his inside jacket pocket out. The urge to reassure him was strong, but Harriet bit it back. She wasn't a fortune-teller, and telling people things would be all right when you couldn't predict the future was a disaster. All it did was get their hopes up.

Sometimes hope was a good thing; judging by the rage that bubbled beneath the surface of Drew's eyes, it wasn't what he needed to hear right now.

"That arrogant bastard," he said. "He really thinks he'd above it all." His words rushed together as he jammed his hand back through his hair, causing it to stand to attention on the top of his head.

"Who?"

"DCI Templeton," Drew said, sounding more than a little frustrated.

"What happened? I saw you two talking."

Drew sighed and tipped his head back toward the grey cloudy sky. "I could murder a proper brew right now. But instead, we've got to get ourselves over to the hospital for the meeting with the translator. DCI's orders."

The emphasis he placed on the word little told Harriet that whatever he was about to say next was probably the root cause of his foul humour.

"What did he say about everything you've uncovered?" When Drew had called her up the night before and filled her in on the final pieces of the puzzle, Harriet had found herself feeling a rush of empathy for the DCI. Now that she'd seen what he'd done to Drew after one short conversation, she was beginning to think that the last thing he required was empathy.

Drew sighed and glanced down at his watch. "We really do need to get over to the hospital," he said. "I'll fill you in on the drive."

Keeping her thoughts to herself, Harriet followed him to the car and slid silently into the passenger seat.

From the corner of her eye, she observed Drew's tight-lipped expression as he manoeuvred the car into the flow of traffic. She couldn't blame him for his mood; in fact, the more she contemplated it, the more she wasn't feeling particularly charitable toward the DCI herself.

"He reckons we're poison," Drew said softly.
"Who, us?"

"Yeah," Drew said. "You and me both. We're poison, apparently. And I've got no idea the lengths he's willing to go to for justice."

Harriet fell silent, allowing Drew's words to sink in. Something about it all just didn't sit right with her. That wasn't the decree of a man who was willing to face up to his wrongdoing. It sounded more like somebody who felt they had nothing else to lose. And a man like that was dangerous.

WHEN THEY REACHED THE HOSPITAL, Kelly was already waiting for them. Sat next to her was another woman in her forties, who Kelly introduced as Lule Wilson.

Lule's golden blonde hair was tied back in a ponytail that brushed against the collar of the leather jacket she wore.

"Kelly has told me there is a young woman you wish me to speak with?" There was the vaguest hint of an accent in Lule's voice as she spoke.

"Kelly has explained that we're looking for somebody to translate from Albanian. Or at least we believe it's Albanian," Drew said, sounding a little more clipped than Harriet was used to. Clearly his conversation with DCI Templeton was still playing on his mind.

Lule nodded. "Yes, Kelly, told me a little of the story. You think this girl was trafficked?"

"Yeah, we think she escaped, or was dumped. That's what we need you for," Drew said. "We need as much information as we can get from her so we can stop this happening to other girls."

Lule glanced over at Kelly, who seemed to nod her encouragement. "Ok, I will help."

"Have you done this before?" Harriet interjected before Drew could lead them down the corridor.

"Yes, many times I help with the translation process. I came here from Albania when I was twenty-four, and I was learned English so I could work." There was a slight flinching around Lule's eyes as she spoke.

"Did you come here of your own volition?" Harriet regretted the question as soon as she'd asked it. It was unfair of her to pry into other people's lives when they hadn't volunteered the information in the first place. Lule stared at her for a moment before she smiled.

"I was not trafficked, if that is what you mean? But I did do things when I got here that I am not proud of." Lule's gaze dropped to the floor. "The world can be a cruel place for a young woman who has nothing to offer it but her own body."

There was a starkness to Lule's words that took Harriet unawares. There had been a time when Harriet was used to listening to those who were willing to share their stories with her. A time when she had sat and talked people through their trauma in order to help them process their grief, or shame, or sometimes their guilt.

But it was so long ago now that it felt like another lifetime, so hearing Lule speak took her back to that place.

"It can be," Harriet said. "But you are a survivor."

Lule shrugged. "Some days I don't feel much like a survivor. Some days I feel like I am still powerless and broken." Lule sighed. "But this helps. Helping those who cannot help themselves yet comforts me, because then I know my brokenness is not a permanent thing. I can put the pieces back together, by reaching out to help them find theirs."

"That is a beautiful way to look at it," Harriet said. "Thank you for sharing that with me."

When Lule smiled, it lit up her face, making her appear far younger than Harriet had first assumed. Taking a step back, Harriet allowed Lule and Kelly to take up the lead down the corridor. So engrossed was she in her own thoughts that she didn't realise Drew had fallen into step next to her until he cleared his throat.

"Sorry, I was a million miles away," she said.

"What was that about back there?" There was a curiosity in his question that took Harriet by surprise. It had been so long since he'd been genuinely curious about anything that she hadn't realised how much she'd missed it until now.

"I think Lule is a survivor of some kind of

violence," Harriet said, studying the other woman. "She's very strong."

"It seemed more than that," he said. "I think something she said to you struck a chord. Or maybe I'm misreading the signs."

Harriet shook her head. "I don't think you're misreading anything," she said. "Everything I do is so clinical and academic these days, that I'd forgotten what it was like to just sit and listen. To bear witness to the pain of others, and in doing so to help them to gain a deeper understanding of their own humanity and the traits that allowed them to survive some truly terrible things." Drew's silence settled around her like a warm mantle, and Harriet gave him a small smile.

"I haven't slept in my own house since Nolan tried to kill me..." Harriet chanced a surreptitious glance in Drew's direction, but he was focusing on the floor as though the pattern had suddenly become vital to his existence. "Some days I still don't believe I survived Nolan. Some days I think I'm right back there, in that room with him while he guts me in my own living room."

"You did survive him," Harriet said, reaching out to brush her fingers against his. He flinched, and then reflexively reached out to crush her fingers in his.

"I survived because you saved me," he said, a small bitter laugh escaping him. "You don't know how hard that is for me to say."

"Actually, I can," Harriet said. "I felt the same

way after Robert tried to kill me. I've always prided myself on being strong, on not letting others get the better of me--" She left out her reasoning for feeling that way. Drew didn't need to hear her terrible life story right now. There would always be a time later, when things were more controlled.

"I didn't know you felt like that," he said carefully. "I suppose it never occurred to me that you would."

"Why, because I'm a psychologist?" She tilted her head up to meet his gaze and watched as colour suffused his cheeks.

"Actually, because you're a woman." He raised his hands as a grin slid across his face. "I know, I know, how very sexist of me. But it's true." He glanced up, and Harriet followed suit, both of them realising at the same time that they'd reached their destination.

Kelly and Lule stood by the door to the girl's room, and it struck Harriet then that they still didn't even know her name. She'd gone through so much, and they didn't have a name to give her. It seemed terribly cruel.

But that would soon change. Soon she wouldn't be an unknown statistic. She would have a name, and a voice, and slowly but surely, she would rebuild herself; stronger because of all the places where others had tried to break her.

"Are you ready?" Kelly asked, a strained smile playing on her lips.

"We are," Harriet said, as Lule pushed open the door.

CHAPTER TWENTY-EIGHT

ANTICIPATION THRUMMED in Olivia's veins as she waited for the armed response unit to give them the all clear. It wasn't the first time she'd participated in a raid, but it was the first time she'd ever been a significant part of the investigation and not just an extra body to lend a hand. Her foot bounced on the floor of the van, her knee jostling up and down as they waited in silence.

Radio static sizzled, and a clamour of voices poured over the airwaves. Initially, it was almost impossible to decipher what the rest of the team was saying, but after a moment Olivia heard one of the response unit call for the 'big red key'. This was it, the moment they'd all been waiting for, weeks of preparation on their behalf, and months of prep on the behalf of DI Appleton and the rest of her team came down to these final moments.

"Breach!" The shout went up, and the back doors of the van opened. Olivia poured out along with her fellow officers. She'd never felt more alive than she did in that moment as they crossed the road and joined the others who had already secured their path ahead.

By the time she reached the doorway of 'Pretty Miss' the nail-bar they'd been watching for weeks now it was almost entirely over. In the middle of the floor, the ARU officers had handcuffed four men on their stomachs in the centre of the room. Olivia's gaze fell on a gathering pile of illegal firearms they were collecting in a pile nearby, and her eyes widened. It wasn't that she didn't expect there to be guns, it was just that she hadn't expected there to be so many.

Maz caught her eye from across the room, and he gestured for her to follow. Olivia went without hesitation. Their time on the task force was slowly bringing them closer together, and she was rapidly seeing him as the older brother she never knew she'd wanted.

"They've got an entire room back here filled with drugs," he said, awe colouring his voice. "I think we caught them with their new shipment."

"Is there any sign of Dimitri Kolokoff?" Olivia asked, her gaze wandering back to the men in the front room.

"Nobody has seen him," Maz said. "And the blokes out there allegedly don't speak English, despite us catching them on the surveillance more than once speaking it just fine." He sighed. "There's something else back here you're not going to like," he said, indicating she should follow him further into the shop.

Olivia found herself in a small grubby hallway. The black and white tile floor looked as though it hadn't seen a mop in at least a year, and the walls were covered in what could only be described as suspicious staining. They reached a back room, and Maz pushed the door open to reveal a room full of Asian women and young girls. A small barred window at the back of the room was boarded over, ensuring that no natural light could enter. The people cowered back in the corners of the room, crouching low to the floor as though the very sight of Maz and Olivia filled them with dread.

"Holy shit," Olivia said, her gaze sweeping over the room. "How many people are there in here?"

"Twenty," Maz said, his voice low and filled with pity. "Judging by the bedding on the floors, Melissa thinks they've been sleeping here too."

"Where is DI Appleton," Olivia asked. "I didn't see her when I came in."

Maz swallowed hard, his face taking on a pale sickly hue beneath the natural caramel of his skin tone. "She's upstairs."

"What have they got up there?" Olivia glanced

up, half expecting to see what lay beyond the floorboards overhead.

"More girls," Maz said, letting his gaze drop to the floor. "They caught some bloke up there too, balls-deep in one of them."

Olivia found herself unable to say anything. During the years she'd been working with the police, she had seen some terrible sights. There was a gruesome road traffic incident involving a family of four that even now haunted her dreams. But this... Nothing had prepared her for so much human suffering.

The sound of crying and pleading in languages she didn't understand tore at her ears. She stared back at the women who clutched some of the younger girls to protect them from Olivia and Maz. She felt her heart break.

"I've got to get out of here," she said, making a run for the hall.

"Melissa wants us to start cataloguing as much evidence as we can," Maz called after her, but she was already halfway out the back door. Tears blurred her vision, and a heady combination of shame and guilt burned the back of her throat as she burst out onto the street.

Ignoring the curious glances from some of her fellow officers, Olivia moved to the side of the street, and crouched on the pavement with her head between her knees to keep the nausea at bay.

Minutes ticked by, and still her head thrummed with the sounds of suffering.

"Finding it too rough in there?" Olivia looked up to find Melissa standing over. The other woman crouched down next to her and pressed her back against the wall. "Me too, if I'm honest."

Olivia stared at her in surprise.

"Don't look at me like that," she said. "Of course I struggle. You'd need to be a machine not to be touched by that in there." Melissa sighed and let her head drop back.

"So how do you do it then?"

"How do I keep going back into places like that, you mean?" Melissa kept her gaze trained on the grey sky overhead.

"Yeah. How do you not let it get to you?"

Melissa shrugged. "I don't know, really."

Olivia's frustration rose. How could Melissa be so blasé about it all? "How can you be so cold?"

Melissa's laughter as it cut the air took her by surprise. "If that's what you got to do in order to make yourself go back in there and sort through this shit, then I'm not going to stop you." She cut off her laughter and focused in on Olivia's face. "But understand this everything we've seen in there--", she gestured toward the building they'd both come out of, --"none of that flows off me like water off a duck's back. I'll carry it with me. Everything I've seen in there, I'll bring it home, and I'll do my best to live with it, but every night when I close my eyes, I'm going to see the face of that young woman upstairs who was getting raped by a bloke twice her size in my nightmares. Every single night I'm going to hear her pleading with me—in a language I don't speak—to help her, to save her, to take away her pain..." She blew out a long breath and stared down at her empty hands. "And do you know what?"

Olivia felt compelled to answer. "What?"

"I'd do it all over again if I had to, just so I could get them the help they need. And the sad part is, I probably will do it all over again, because fuckers like Dimitri Kolokoff will keep doing shit like this so long as they know there's money to be made out of human suffering." Melissa fell silent, but the sounds from inside carried on the still air.

"I'm sorry," Olivia said.

"Don't be sorry," Melissa said. "Sorry isn't going to fix this. Getting off your arse and getting back in there is what's going to fix this mess." Melissa stood up and paused, staring over at the building before she held out a hand toward Olivia.

Melissa was right. Sitting out here, feeling sorry for herself, was a luxury those people didn't have. Grabbing onto Melissa's proffered hand, and pushing up onto her feet, Olivia dusted down the back of her black trousers.

"Thanks for that," she said.

"We all need a good kick in the pants now and

then," Melissa said with a sad smile. "Next time, you can do it for me."

Olivia returned her smile with one that was filled with grim determination. "What are we going to do about Dimitri?"

Melissa's face fell, and Olivia suddenly wished she'd never asked.

"Honestly, I don't know. He was supposed to be here, every bit of intel we had said he was here, but five minutes before ARU went in the front door he upped and vanished."

"Do you think he found out we were coming in there?"

Melissa screwed her face up and folded her arms over her chest. "The only people who knew about this raid were the officers on the task force. If he figured it out, then that means there's a leak..."

Olivia shook her head incredulously. "There's no way somebody would leak information like that. Not after everything."

Melissa nodded. "I agree. Everyone wanted this..." She sighed. "And now I've got to break the news to the DCI that Dimitri is in the bloody wind."

Olivia's smile was sympathetic. "I'm sure he'll understand. None of this was your fault."

"It still stinks though," Melissa said, sliding her phone from her pocket. "We've just got to hope somebody picks him up before he flees the country."

Olivia watched as Melissa stalked away with the phone pressed to her ear.

The thought of Dimitri getting away with it all, after everything they'd done, and seen left her cold. But that, as her father would say, was life.

CHAPTER TWENTY-NINE

ZARA PRACTICALLY BUZZED with excitement as she sat in the canteen to eat her lunch.

"What's made you so happy?" Poppy asked, dropping her tray down onto the table across from her. Zara considered telling her best friend about what was going to happen, but seeing the look of thunder on Poppy's face, she changed her mind.

"Nothing," Zara said, shrugging nonchalantly. "What's up with you?"

Poppy rolled her eyes and plopped onto the seat. "Suzie is really getting on my nerves. She can't make up her mind if she wants to come with us to the cinema on Saturday or not because..." Poppy cut off and, scooping up her bread roll, began to tear chunks out of it. "Uh, never mind."

Zara wasn't normally one to tolerate Poppy's histrionics but considering the day and the adventure that lay ahead for her she was feeling magnanimous. "No, go on, tell me."

Poppy shook her head and glanced awkwardly over toward the table next to them. "Are you prepped for Mr Bulman's quiz later?"

"Poppy, what aren't you telling me?" Zara asked, feeling her good mood begin to fizzle out in the face of her friend's dishonesty. Her phone chose that moment to chirp a notification, letting her know she had a new message. Snatching the phone up from the table, she popped it open and scanned the message.

Her heart climbed into her throat as her eyes zeroed in on the sender's name.

Jacob: Something came up for this evening, so I was wondering if you'd like to bunk off school with me?

"Are you even listening to me?" Poppy demanded, and Zara realised her friend had been talking to her the entire time she'd been reading her message.

"Sorry, I've got to answer this," Zara said distractedly.

Wot came up?

The reply was almost instantaneous, and Zara could almost imagine Jacob sitting next to her typing out the responses.

Uncle wants me 2 work. But he said u could cum over now if u want. We're outside now.

Zara's heart hammered in her chest. She'd been

right to think he was practically next to her, especially if he was as he suggested sitting outside.

How do u know my school?

It was such a stupid thing to ask really, but she couldn't remember telling him which school she actually attended. Not that she truly cared, not if he were truly outside waiting for her.

Without thinking, she climbed to her feet and picked up her untouched lunch tray. It wouldn't really matter if she blew off school for a couple of hours. It wasn't as though there was much happening, anyway.

"Earth to, Zara, my god, you're like one of those zombies on that movie we watched last year," Poppy whined, following her a couple of steps behind. "Who are you talking to?"

"Listen, if I leave, do you think you could cover for me?" Zara asked, whirling around to face her friend. She stared into Poppy's eyes and hoped she was pulling her most adorable face.

"Leave school?" Poppy stared at her, dumbfounded. "Bitch, why would you leave school without me? Why can't I come too?" Bitch was Poppy's new go to favourite word, and term of endearment.

Zara leaned in close as a giggle slipped past her lips. "Look, I can't tell you because it's this huge secret. But I swear I will call you this evening and fill you in on everything if you promise to cover for me."

Poppy's eyes were wide with shock. "You're such a dark horse."

A giggle finally escaped Zara. She felt like she could walk on air. Her phone pinged again.

Can't stay here 2 long. Plz come!

"I've got to go, but I love you!" Zara said, drawing Poppy into a tight hug.

"Bitch, you better swear you'll call WhatsApp me tonight."

"I promise."

Poppy released her almost reluctantly and followed her to the school door. It had started to rain, and Zara drew her jacket tight around her body, as she typed out a message on her phone. *On my way. x*

Gr8 we're in black van opposite school gate.

Zara dashed out into the rain, drawing her fleece hood up over her hair in an attempt to keep the water from making it frizzy. While it wasn't exactly as she'd planned her meeting with Jacob, the thrill of the illicit more than made up for the change of plans.

The black van he'd mentioned in his message stood idling opposite the school gates, just as he'd promised. Seeing it sitting there brought the first real wave of unease crashing over Zara. What if this was all some big mistake? What if Jacob wasn't who she thought he was? What if...

Another message pinged through and she glanced down at the phone, swiping away the water droplets that threatened to blur the screen.

UR even more beautiful in reality.

That one simple message was all it took to rid Zara of her fears.

During her short life, she'd spent her childhood reading fairy tales. Cinderella with her stepmother and ugly stepsisters was a firm favourite of hers as she'd moved through the foster system.

The idea that one day someone would come along and sweep her away from all the pain and heartache she'd suffered in her life was more than enough fuel for her imagination.

When she'd been young, she'd imagined that person, or people would come in the form of a loving family. A mother and father who would love and care for her like she was the only person in the world who mattered.

As she'd matured and turned into a teenager, that dream had blossomed into a more romantic notion. The idea that the person who came to save her didn't have to be a parent but could in fact be a prince who would love her for her was intoxicating to Zara.

She wanted that dream... She'd tried to create it with Noah, but he'd turned out to be a toad. An ugly, vicious toad who'd tried to make her life a misery...

But Jacob was different. He loved her, accepted her, and he wanted her for her alone.

She swiped her thumb over the message and glanced back up at the black van. Her prince was waiting for her, she just needed to be courageous enough to take that leap.

Glancing up and down the road, Zara zipped across the street and pulled open the front door of the van. The man who sat behind the wheel grinned at her, the gap in his mouth where one of his teeth should have been unnerved her.

"Are you Jacob's uncle?"

"Zara!" Mr Bulman's voice rang out across the school grounds, and she glanced back over her shoulder at the teacher standing under the big metal canopy at the front of the school.

She didn't register the grating sound of the metal back door of the van as it slid open until it was too late. By then a strong arm had already snaked out around her waist, one meaty hand closing over her lips as she'd opened her mouth to scream.

The man in the back of the van snatched her backwards, dragging her into the darkness alongside him.

She had one last moment to see the grey, overcast sky as it hung low overhead, register the fat raindrops as they fell toward the ground, and then the van door slammed shut with such an air of finality.

"You're so much more beautiful in reality," the voice whispered in her ear. Zara was dumped onto the floor of the van, the plastic beneath her crinkling noisily in her ears as the bald man who had grabbed her came into view.

His lecherous grin caused her stomach to sink, and a second scream to rise in her throat, but any sound she might have thought to make was silenced as he fell on her like a starving animal falls on its first meal.

CHAPTER THIRTY

DREW STARED down at the notebook open in his hands, and the words began to blur together.

"Naomi said he took her to the boat because she had asked someone to get help," Lule said, her voice soft despite the horror of her words. "She said he beat her and injected her."

Naomi nodded enthusiastically and gestured to the needle track marks in the crook of her arm.

Naomi spoke quickly and fluidly in Albanian, and all the while Lule sat there and listened, taking in every word until Naomi was forced to take a breath, giving her an opportunity to speak. "He threatened her sister, Marissa. Said he would use her to recoup the losses Naomi incurred for him..."

Drew's phone buzzed in his pocket, drawing his attention away from the woman in the bed. He reached down to silence the call, but Melissa's name flashed on the screen.

"If you wouldn't mind giving me a minute, I've got to take this," he said, pushing wearily onto his feet.

"This is probably a good time to break anyway," Kelly said wisely. "I think everyone is pretty exhausted, especially Naomi, and well, the more she can rest right now, the faster her body can heal."

Drew flashed her a grateful smile. "You're right, we've got time." He reached the door and pressed the phone to his ear. "I didn't think I'd hear from you," he said cautiously.

"We've got a huge problem," Melissa said, not bothering to conceal the concern in her voice.

"Right, tell me."

"We executed the raid on the nail bar this morning, but before we got there Dimitri was gone." Drew swore under his breath and caught a wrath filled stare from a nurse in the corridor. Pacing hurriedly down the hall, he reached the visitor's room, and finding it empty, he ducked inside.

"Do you think he's going to flee the country?"

"Honestly, yeah, probably..." There was a pause on the other end of the line, and Drew fought the urge to break the silence. Whatever Melissa had to say, she would spit out in her own time. "Right, we've got another problem," she said, her voice softer this time. "Someone matching Dimitri's description, in a van we know belongs to Dimitri's business, was seen earlier today outside a high school. He snatched a thirteen-year-old in broad daylight, Drew."

"Christ," Drew said, shoving his hand back through his hair. "Do we know who the girl is? Have we spoken to her parents?--"

"Easy tiger, the call just came in regarding the girl, and the only reason we even picked up on it is because we've got a BOLO out on Dimitri, and all of his vehicles. But that's not even the worst part..."

"How can scum like Dimitri Kolokoff taking a thirteen-year-old girl not be the worst news, Melissa?" Drew said, not bothering to hide the anger from his voice.

For hours he'd sat in the chair across from Naomi's bed, listening to her cry, and sob over the treatment she'd received at the hands of that monster. The thought of him laying his filthy hands on a child filled Drew with the kind of dread and rage he hadn't fully known he was capable of.

"Templeton is gone missing," she said. Her voice was so low it was practically a whisper.

"Can you repeat that," Drew said. "I thought you said Templeton was missing..."

"He is, Drew. I tried to contact him to let him know about the raid, and the fact that Dimitri was nowhere to be found, but he's unreachable."

"Maybe he went home, or there was an emergency..." Drew could hear the ridiculousness of his own statements and cut himself off before he could even finish. "Who knew about the raid, Melissa?"

"The team," she said, sounding as miserable as Drew felt. "Dimitri isn't that lucky, Drew. We had good intel that said he was supposed to be there today. Which leaves only one option..."

Drew swallowed hard. "Is Templeton capable of something like this?"

"Well, I don't see how," she said. "I mean, why would he? He's wanted to nail this bastard from day one. It wouldn't make any sense for him to completely screw up the operation."

"Do we know where Dimitri would go?" Drew asked, deciding to approach it from another angle.

"He has safe houses, but we know about them all."

"He has a boat," Drew blurted.

"Fuck." It never ceased to amaze Drew how such one simple word could so completely sum up the entire situation so succinctly.

"I've got to go," Drew said as he cut the call dead. The moment he hung up, it started to ring again, but he ignored it.

Turning to the door, he found Harriet watching him carefully.

"What's happened?"

He filled her in as quickly as he could and watched as Harriet paced up and down the floor. She pursed her lips. "I knew there was something off about what he said to you earlier."

"So, you think he's done this deliberately?"

Harriet nodded. "It's the only thing that adds up."

"It's a bit of a leap, isn't it?"

"Is it?" She turned to face him, her face alight with as the words tumbled from her lips faster than he could hope to keep up with. "Think of it logically? He's a grieving father, and what do we know about grieving parents? They're willing to go to any lengths to avenge their loved ones. And that's exactly what all of this is, isn't it?"

Drew waved his hands. "Slow down, please. My brain doesn't move as fast as yours when it comes to emotions, and people's screwed up brain chemistry."

Harriet sucked in a deep breath. "He lost his daughter, and when he tried to do his job, when he tried to follow the letter of the law, it let him down."

"The case over Dimitri fell apart in Southampton," Drew mused. "I guess it sort of makes sense."

"It makes perfect sense. He's an excellent police officer, who follows the rules, and does everything he's supposed to. He raises a daughter who follows in his footsteps, and that makes him so proud, and then somebody like Dimitri Kolokoff comes along and tears all that away from him."

"You're right," Drew said.

Harriet nodded. "And then when he does everything he's supposed to, and the case falls apart anyway because of insufficient evidence, or a failure to get a witness to testify, Dimitri walks away scot free. But Templeton's daughter is still dead. His pride and joy is gone, and now even his job has failed him. That kind of emotional toll is enough to drive any parent to the brink."

"But would it be enough to make him do this?" Drew asked. "I mean, he practically had him bang to rights. All he had to do was wait for Dimitri to get arrested, and justice could finally be served."

"What like it was last time? If you were in his position, would you want to take that risk? Or would you much rather take matters into your own hands and guarantee that justice was doled out to those who deserved it?"

Drew couldn't argue with Harriet's logic. As always, she seemed to grasp the human mind in ways he could only hope of achieving. "So, where is he?"

"Well, I don't know," she said. "He knows where Dimitri is, you can put money on that. And if we don't get there..."

"Dimitri will kill him," Drew said, his stomach lurching over the prospect. He wasn't the DCIs' biggest fan, but the last thing he wanted was for something to happen to him. "We have to figure out where he'd go."

"I heard you telling Melissa about a boat," Harriet said. "And there's one person we know for certain who has been on that boat."

Drew's grin was more of a grimace. "Do you think she'll be able to tell us where it was?"

"I think she can give us enough information for us to make an educated guess. She was found near Whitby; doesn't it stand to reason that Dimitri might be keeping his boat moored up near there?"

"It's a busy place. There are always people about, I'm not sure how he could slip in and out of there without somebody seeing something."

"Well, there's one way to find out."

A couple of moments later, Drew found himself standing back in Naomi's room. "Can you please ask her if she remembers where the boat was moored?"

Kelly shook her head. "I don't think this is right, Harriet. She's been through enough. She needs to rest."

"Please..." Harriet paused, and Drew took the opportunity to interject. "We believe Dimitri has taken a thirteen-year-old girl."

Kelly's face visibly paled, and Lule took a stumbling step backward before she dropped into the chair next to Naomi's bed. Naomi's words collided with one another as she struggled to get Lule to speak to her.

"She wants to know what's happening?" Lule said, sounding a little dazed.

"Tell her," Drew said. "She knows Dimitri, she deserves to know."

"This isn't right," Kelly said a second time. "It's not healthy."

But Lule clearly wasn't listening as she hurriedly responded to Naomi in Albanian. Drew knew the moment she'd been told because the colour faded from her cheeks, and she hurriedly made the shape of the cross over her chest.

"Ask her if she knows where he keeps his boat," Harriet asked, her voice gentle as though she were coaxing a very small child. Lule never even looked up at her, but she spoke rapidly, in hushed tones to Naomi.

The young woman in the bed shook her head and replied. "She says she doesn't know exactly where it is, but that Dimitri often spoke of a place where there is an arch made of whale bones and Count Dracula's castle. Being from Albania, Naomi said it always frightened her because the tale of the vampire was a story she often heard as a child."

"Can she remember anything about the boat?" Harriet asked.

It took Lule a couple of moments to get an answer, and when she did, Drew felt his heart soar. "She thinks the boat had a similar name to the nail bar, but she can't be certain." It was enough to go on, and Drew fought the urge to throw his arms around the women in thanks.

Instead, he backed out of the room with the phone in his hand.

SPLINTER THE BONE

"Melissa, I need you to get ARU over to Whitby."

"Where exactly in Whitby?"

Drew sucked in a deep breath. "I'm not exactly sure, but have DC Green go over CCTV for any signs of Dimitri's van. And get somebody to look into a boat registered under the name of the Pretty Miss."

"Where will you be?" Melissa asked.

"I'm leaving the hospital with Harriet," Drew said. "If we're lucky, we'll beat Templeton to Dimitri before something terrible happens."

"Don't let him get hurt, Drew," Melissa said. "I know you don't like him, but he's one of the good guys..."

"I'll do my best, but you know I can't make any promises."

"I know," she said, as Drew ended the call. He couldn't make any promises, it was true, but he also had no intention of letting Templeton wind up as another casualty of that lowlife scum Dimitri.

CHAPTER THIRTY-ONE

DREW PULLED onto the main road that led toward Sandsend. The sat-nav in the car beeped, and an arrow appeared telling him to turn right at the next turnoff.

"This can't be right," Harriet said, eyeing the small side road that for all intents and purposes more closely resembled the driveway of somebody's house. "Are you sure this was the place DC Green said Templeton's phone signal was coming from?"

Melissa's voice came back over the phone, sounding distorted and tinny. "Templeton's phone has been pinging the nearby towers for the last hour."

"It's almost as though he wants us to find him," Harriet said thoughtfully.

"Maybe," Drew said, indicating to take the turn onto the small road that disappeared alongside the golf course. "Well, the sat-nav must know what it's doing," Drew said, hoping he sounded more convinced than he actually felt. The road was rough, and the car bounced and heaved as he accelerated. They passed beneath a small bridge that connected two separate cliffs, and suddenly the sea appeared ahead of them.

"Wait, is that--" Harriet cut off and Drew was forced to slam on the brakes. The car screeched to a halt mere inches from a body which lay face down in the middle of the slipway. Ahead of them, blocking the path down to the beach, was a black van that matched the description of the van Dimitri had been seen in.

"Do you think he's dead?" Harriet asked, eyeing the body and the puddle of dark blood that glistened in the semi-twilight.

Without a word, Drew slipped from the car and gestured for Harriet to stay put as he crept toward the body. The wind whipped back up off the sea, throwing the voices of two men back towards him. Crouching next to the body, Drew felt along the neck for a pulse, but instead found the body cold and a lack of any life signs.

"They're on the beach," Harriet's voice came from directly behind him and Drew jerked, practically falling back on his arse.

"I told you to stay in the car," he said quietly.

Raised voices reached his ears again, and this time it was followed up by the sound of a gunshot.

Drew froze. With no weapon to speak of, he was practically useless against an armed assailant.

"Get back in the car and ask Melissa how soon ARU is going to get here," Drew said.

"And what are you going to do?" She cocked an eyebrow at him in challenge.

"I'm going to see what's going on down on the sand." He started to move before Harriet could argue further. Stealthily, he crept toward the voices, his heart beating so hard in his chest he was certain whoever stood just beyond the van could surely hear it.

Drew rounded the van and came face to face with a surprising sight. Dimitri was on his knees, hands raised above his head in surrender. Blood had dried down his chin and was dotted down the front of the white shirt he wore. Templeton rose the butt of his shotgun in his hands and brought it down on Dimitri's cheekbone with a bone shattering crunch that drove Dimitri onto his hands.

"Sir, you don't have to do this. We can take him into custody from here," Drew said, fighting to keep his voice level so that it would carry above the wind that whipped around them.

Templeton glanced over his shoulder. "Why would I do that? I've got the bastard right where I want him."

"This isn't what you want, not really," Drew said, edging closer. Templeton swung the gun around and pointed it at the centre of Drew's chest.

"I wouldn't keep shuffling forward if I were you, Haskell. I told you earlier to stay out of my way."

Sucking in a deep breath, Drew shook his head. "You know I could never do that, Sir. And that's why you kept your phone with you, isn't it? You wanted us to find you before it was too late. You wanted us here so we could finally get that lowlife where he belongs."

Templeton shook his head, a sad smile playing around his lips. "You should leave the psychology up to your doctor friend," Templeton said. Drew eyed the distance between them. It was too great for him to cross without Templeton pulling the trigger and blowing a fist-sized hole in him.

"Where is Zara Clemmons?" Drew asked, hoping to distract Templeton from his rage long enough for the ARU to get there.

"She's safe," Templeton said. "I made sure of that. It's all I could do. I might have failed my Anna, but she'd be happy to know I at least got to Zara in time." Templeton swung the gun back, so it pointed directly at Dimitri's face. "Why kill her? Why brutalise her like that? I've never understood it. What did she ever do to you?"

"She was scum," Dimitri said, the words whistling oddly out through his broken teeth. He spat a glob of blood out onto the sand, before sneering up at Templeton. "You're too much like her. With your friends here, you won't kill me. It would be more than your job was worth."

Templeton shook his head, and the gun wavered. Drew took a couple of quick steps, closing the distance between him and his DCI. "She loved life," Templeton said, more to himself than to Dimitri or Drew. "I swore I'd protect her, and I couldn't."

"She begged for you," Dimitri said. "Called out for her precious daddy to come and save her before I slit her throat--"

The sound of the gun when it went off was deafening. Drew stood for a moment, shock momentarily freezing him to the spot as he watched Dimitri's face vanish in a hail of bright red blood and viscera.

"Tell my wife I'm sorry, I couldn't save her," Templeton said, as he swung the gun around and angled it back toward his own chin.

Drew moved, his hand grabbing the barrel of the shotgun before Templeton could place it beneath his face.

It went off again, and the sound of the wind and the sea disappeared entirely as pain erupted through Drew's head.

Still holding the gun, he stumbled backwards, jerking it free of Templeton's hands before he dumped it onto the sand.

Lights flooded the slipway, illuminating them both as ARU swept down toward them. Drew watched bemused as their mouths moved, but no sound penetrated the odd ringing that filled his head.

Seconds ticked by, turning into minutes, and he jerked in surprise as Harriet's hand closed over his arm.

Her mouth moved, but there was no sound. She reached up to his face, and when she pulled her hand back, it was slick with blood.

He took a step and then dropped to his knees as the pain in his head intensified.

Harriet's mouth continued to move, and still all Drew could hear was the rushing of white noise in his head.

CHAPTER THIRTY-TWO

A WEEK LATER, they stood gathered in the office. From his vantage point in the doorway, Drew watched them as they laughed and joked, almost as though nothing at all had changed. When in reality, nothing could be further from the truth. Pain flared for a moment in the side of his head, twinging down through his ear as he flexed his jaw.

"Has your hearing come back yet?" Harriet asked, raising her voice above the noise the others were making.

Drew nodded and regretted the movement instantly. "It's coming back. They don't think I'll have any permanent damage. Apparently, I'm very lucky," he said with a rueful smile.

"Lucky, or stupid?" Harriet cocked an eyebrow at him before she touched his arm. "I'm just glad you're all right."

"Templeton has pled guilty to the murder of Dimitri, and Oscar," Drew said, as he returned his attention to the rest of the team.

"What kind of sentence do you think he'll get?"

Drew shrugged. "No idea. Hopefully, they'll look at the circumstances that led him to that place, but they might decide to make an example out of him."

Harriet nodded. "I've decided to go and visit Nolan," she said, the suddenness of her admission took him by surprise. "I hope you don't mind, but I feel like it's important that I go. I know you don't agree, and I can completely understand why, but--"

"It's fine," Drew said. "I get it. We've all got to fight our demons in different ways."

Harriet cast him a sideways glance, before tucking her dark curls behind one ear. "That's exactly right," she said, with a broad smile. "Anyone would think you'd been hanging around with a psychologist."

"I've decided to move out of my house," he said. The moment the words were out there, he felt as though a weight had been lifted from his chest. "It's not right that I stay there. It isn't healthy, and even though many of my memories of Freya are tied up in that place, it doesn't feel like it belongs to me anymore."

Harriet nodded sympathetically. "I'm so pleased you've made the decision for yourself. A move will be good for you."

Drew nodded. "Of course, that leaves me with the dilemma of finding somewhere in the meantime, and--"

"Stay at mine," Harriet said. "That is, I've got a spare room you can have until you find something of your own..."

Drew grinned at her, but shook his head. "I don't think that would be such a good idea."

"Why not? We're both adults."

"I might crash at yours for a night or two, but anything else and I'd start to feel like I was taking advantage."

Harriet looked as though she was willing to argue further, before she clamped her mouth shut. "The offer is there if you change your mind," she said.

"And I appreciate that."

Harriet glanced down at her watch and sucked a breath in through her teeth. "I've got to go," she said somewhat reluctantly.

"You're not coming down the pub to celebrate the appointment of the monk to the new position as head of the task force?"

She shook her head. "I can't. I've got a meeting to go to with a young student."

"You could always blow it off..."

"Not this one," she said ruefully. "I used to know her mom, and I don't know, I feel like maybe this is important for Misha, and maybe me too. A type of closure."

Drew shot her a sideways look. "Then go, we could all do with some closure around here."

With a backward wave, Harriet grabbed her handbag and headed for the door, as Melissa poked her head into the office where Drew stood. "Quinn not coming with us?"

"Nope, she's got a student to teach," he said, acutely aware of how disappointed he felt. Melissa nodded and slipped into the room with him. "How are you?" he asked, giving her a once over. He noted the dark circles that had sat beneath her eyes were finally fading.

"I'm good," she said. "You know me, I'm a trooper."

"You don't need to be so tough around me," he said gently. "We've known each other a hell of a long time."

She shrugged. "True, but think of it as a form of protection."

Drew nodded. He could understand that. "It wasn't your fault, you know. You couldn't have known what he had planned."

Melissa shot him a grateful smile. "I'm good," she said. "The rational part of my brain knows it wasn't my fault. The irrational part still thinks I should have done more, but it'll soon come around."

Drew stretched his arms over his head. "I can respect that," he said. "Now why are we still here when we should be down the pub?"

Melissa's face broke out into a wide grin. "Now

you're speaking my language," she said, threading her arm through his as she led him from the office. "Who's for celebratory drinks?"

The rallying cry went up from the rest of the team, and for the first time in a long time Drew realised he'd found his way home.

CHAPTER THIRTY-THREE

CONSULTING her notes one last time, Harriet settled back in the mustard coloured, uncomfortable plastic chair to wait for Nolan Matthews.

It hadn't been a complete surprise that he'd requested to see her; in fact, part of her had expected it after their last meeting in Drew's living room. She hadn't been able to shake the memory from her mind of his scarlet blood slicked across her fingers.

It had taken her hours to scrub every last trace of it from the lines and whorls of her hands and fingers. She hadn't wanted even one drop of it left on her skin. Part of her—an irrational part—had considered her almost complicit in Drew's ordeal. There wasn't much that separated her from Nolan, at least not that she could see, anyway.

Traumatic background, check.

Used by Dr Connors, check, and check.

The ventilation system above her head rumbled to life, dragging her from her thoughts.

Sighing, she pressed her fingers to the bridge of her nose and pinched the skin gently. A migraine was rearing its ugly head and sitting here in this windowless room with Nolan would not cure it.

There was a buzz from somewhere deep in the bowels of the building, and Harriet sat a little straighter as the door opposite her chair clicked open. Nolan shuffled inside, his skin the same colour as his grey jumper. The thick bandage that covered his throat brought another wave of memories crashing over her head.

Swallowing them down, Harriet focussed on the man before her to ground herself in the here and now.

His hair was long and shaggy, giving him an overall unkempt appearance. He raised his handcuffed hands to push his hair away from his face, a gesture that happened unconsciously.

The last time she'd seen him, Harriet had thought he was thin, but his time spent in custody clearly didn't suit him and he was now painfully gaunt.

He stared at her. His dark eyes—sunken and red-rimmed—lit up as his gaze came to rest on her face.

"You came?" He sounded hoarse, like a man who had spent a long time screaming. Considering everything she had seen so far of the Category A prison where he was being held, it wouldn't have surprised her to learn that he spent all of his time now screaming into the uncaring void.

"You seem surprised." Harriet kept her voice as devoid of emotion as she could, but considering the pitiful sight before her, she wasn't entirely sure she had succeeded.

"Dr Chakrabarti said you wouldn't come," he said, glancing around the room. "It's nice in here."

It was such an off-hand comment, and Harriet took another look around the exposed room. Aside from the table and chairs, there was nothing else inside the bare block constructed walls. The room was cold, almost clinical.

"Why did you ask me here, Nolan?"

He sighed and took the seat opposite her. "You don't like small talk, do you?"

"I don't see a need for it," she said, quickly.

His tongue darted out between his teeth and he moistened his chapped lips, conjuring reptilian images in Harriet's head.

Nolan cocked his head to the side, studying her quietly before his shoulders slumped. "I need your help," he whispered.

For a moment, Harriet wasn't sure she had heard him correctly. There wasn't a snowball's chance in hell that the infamous Star killer had just asked for her help.

"Excuse me?"

"I don't belong here," he said, leaning forward across the table. The clink of his handcuffs on the Formica surface the only sound to break the silence that stretched between them. "This place isn't good for me."

Harriet fought against the instinctual response that threatened to bubble out of her. He was guilty of his crimes, in her mind there was no doubt on that.

And so, it made perfect sense that he would find himself incarcerated. Not to mention the fact that it wasn't the first time she had heard killers try to shirk their responsibility for the crimes they had committed.

"Why do you say that?" She fought the urge to fidget and instead levelled her gaze at him.

Nolan pushed his fingers against the table-top until the tips turned stark white. His nails were bloody and ragged, no doubt chewed to the quick.

"I'm not like the others in here," he whispered conspiratorially. "I don't belong with the lowlifes they house here."

The urge to laugh in his face bubbled in her chest, and she pushed it aside.

"You're a murderer, Nolan. We both know that."

"Do you see me denying it?" He sat up a little straighter, his shrewd gaze swept across her face. "I can be both guilty, and also not belong with the other prisoners."

"I can ask them to put you into solitary confinement if that's what you mean?" Harriet disliked feeling as though the man before her was somehow manoeuvring her into a corner.

"I don't want to be isolated. I want to be with others like me."

"But that's just it, Nolan, you are with others like you. There are other murderers in here that—"

"You're not listening to me!" He slammed his cuffed hands onto the table, causing the prison guard standing at the door to take a step forward.

"We spoke about this, Nolan." The guard's voice held a note of warning that sent an uneasy shiver tracing down Harriet's spine.

"I'm not going to hurt her." Nolan spoke without turning to face the other man. His voice was flat, his expression suddenly shuttered; it only heightened Harriet's feeling of unease.

"Tell me why you really asked me here, Nolan."

She watched his Adam's apple bob in his scrawny throat, as though the thyroid cartilage it was formed of was trying to scrabble out through his skin.

"They don't understand me in here, don't understand what I need." He sucked in a deep breath like a man drowning. "They won't even let me make my puzzles in here. I don't know who I am without them. The things I've done..." He trailed off, his shoulders rounding over, and reminded Harriet of a small child who had been scolded for breaking the rules.

"They've given you access to a psychiatrist, Nolan, I really think—"

He started to laugh. The sound held a note of hysteria that made Harriet's skin crawl, and the hairs on the back of her neck stood to attention.

"That idiot doesn't know the difference between a psychopath and a sociopath. She can't help me."

"Is that what you think you are?" Harriet kept her tone deliberately mild so as not to make him feel as though she was pushing him.

"I know who I am, Dr Quinn. I've known for a very long time."

Harriet glanced down at her notes. "Nolan, if you're not going to tell me why you wanted me to come here, then I'm afraid I'm going to have to leave. I'm already running late—"

"We didn't get to finish our conversation." He spoke so softly that Harriet wasn't sure if she'd heard him correctly, or if the sound of the ventilation system above their heads had distorted it.

"Excuse me?"

"I know you feel the same pain I do," he said, his words rushing together so that they tumbled over one another excitedly. "You showed me your scars, the physical manifestation of your emotions. And you've seen mine."

"I was—"

"I'm not a fool, Dr Quinn, I know you showed

me your scars to save his life. But that doesn't matter now; I've already seen them."

Harriet pushed her chair back from the table, but she didn't stand

"You promised you would help me control the darkness." There was a desperation to his voice that she hadn't expected. Almost as though he was afraid that if she walked out the door, he would be left alone with the demons—both real and imagined—who plagued his every moment.

"I did," she said, choosing her words carefully. "But how do I know that this is what you really want? Your response seemed pretty clear cut to me."

He gave her a crooked smile. "Pun intended?"

Harriet kept her expression blank and waited for the grin to fade from his face.

"I didn't want to get caught," he said. "I didn't want to end up in here." He gestured to their surroundings. "But now that I'm here, I don't see that I have a choice. Either I get help, or the darkness eats me from the inside out."

It would be easy to walk away. To turn him down; leave him to his darkness. It was what Drew would do. It was what Jonathan Connors would do. But as much as she wanted to follow the easy path and do just that; Harriet found herself unable to get up from the chair and walk out the door. If she did, then Dr Connors would be victorious in his utter destruction of them both.

"Then talk to me, Nolan. If it's truly my help you're after, you're going to have to give me something in return."

He pressed his forehead to the cold tabletop, and she watched his breath fog against the plastic-coated surface. "I don't know how," he said, his voice half strangled. "But I want to learn."

This was something she could work with. So long as he was willing to receive help, he could be reached.

"Time to go," the guard at the other side of the room said gruffly.

"You could talk to them," Nolan said, straightening up. "You could tell them I need my puzzles."

Harriet started to shake her head. "That's not a good idea, Nolan. The puzzles are a part of your pathology."

The guard stepped up behind him and placed a hand on Nolan's elbow. "Time to go."

Nolan shrugged him off and leaned across the table, his fingers clasped together in a gesture of pleading. "Please, Dr Quinn. It's the only thing that quiets my mind. Without it, I'm not sure—"

The guard touched his shoulder, and Nolan twisted his head around to glare at the other man. "Give me a minute."

"Now!"

"Nolan, we can talk about this the next time. I'm sure there's something we can arrange..."

"You're just like him." His words were a vile venom he spat in her face. His expression contorted into one of rage, like a child who couldn't get his own way. Harriet schooled her expression, keeping it as blank as possible. Giving him a reaction now would serve nobody, least of all her, especially if she hoped to help him.

"We'll speak again soon, Nolan," she said assuredly, as he was helped to his feet by the guard.

For a moment, she wondered if he would shake himself free of the guard's grip and launch his gangly frame across the table. When he didn't, and instead allowed himself to be led away toward the door, Harriet felt some tension in her shoulders lessen.

Nolan said nothing else to her as the guard led him from the room, and Harriet glanced down at her pile of notes. Everything she had thought she had known about him seemed to be wrong. It seemed unlikely that her profile for him could be so completely askew, and yet, the proof as they said was in the pudding.

Gathering up her items, Harriet got to her feet before glancing down at her watch.

Great, late for another briefing.

At this rate, she would get her marching orders long before she proved any use to the team. With that thought in her mind, Harriet hurried for the exit.

CHAPTER THIRTY-FOUR

STANDING in the hallway of the block of flats, he pulled the hood more securely down over his face. The CCTV cameras didn't work here, he'd made certain of that, but there was no harm in being cautious.

Pulling the screwdriver from the sleeve of his pocket, he worked it into the frame of the door, twisting it back and forth until the rotten wood gave way, and the door swung inwards to reveal the flat beyond.

He closed the door behind him carefully and slipped the screwdriver back into his jacket.

The soft sound of snoring reached his ears as he crept inside. Excitement built in his gut, making it so he very nearly lost control of his bowels. This was it, his moment of truth. Would he be able to go through with it, finally?

SPLINTER THE BONE

Crossing into the kitchen, he pulled open the fridge door and removed the butter. Heading to the cupboard, he took down a mouldy loaf and stared in at the blue tinged slices before he set them back down on the table. He found a Kit-Kat in the back of the cupboard instead and ripped the wrapper off, savouring the taste of its sweet chocolate as he wolfed it down. There was something so exciting about eating other people's food without them knowing. Something that fed the possessive side of his soul.

When he'd finished, he crept toward the bedroom, ignoring the clenching of his stomach as he crept ever closer to his goal. The soft snoring he'd heard when he'd first arrived in the flat was louder here. Pushing open the bedroom door, he saw her there, pyjama-clad body tangled in the sheets. It seemed strange to think of a whore wearing pyjamas but Jessica it seemed liked her animal print nightwear.

From what he'd seen of her drawers the last time he'd been here, she practically had a whole chest of drawers of the stuff.

From his pocket, he pulled the drawing his daughter had done for him. The straw-coloured hair of the stick figure momentarily illuminated by the light that crept in through the blinds. She wasn't going to be the next Rembrandt, that was for sure, but she definitely had a knack for nailing down the image of her mother with her fat, disgusting belly.

A baby... Another fucking mouth to feed. Like they didn't have enough problems as it was. He must have made a noise because the snoring in the bed next to him came to a stuttering end. Pushing the picture back into his pocket, he slipped the screwdriver from his jacket and raised it above his head as Jessica's eyes opened groggily.

Before she could even register what was happening, he brought the screwdriver down on her, driving it into her body, over and over until her legs stopped kicking.

Exhaustion and elation ripped through him in equal measure, and it was a struggle to keep his eyes open as he sat onto the side of the bed. He could do it. And now that he knew the truth, nothing could stop him.

Grab the next book, Hunting the Silence, Now!

GET THE NEXT BOOK!

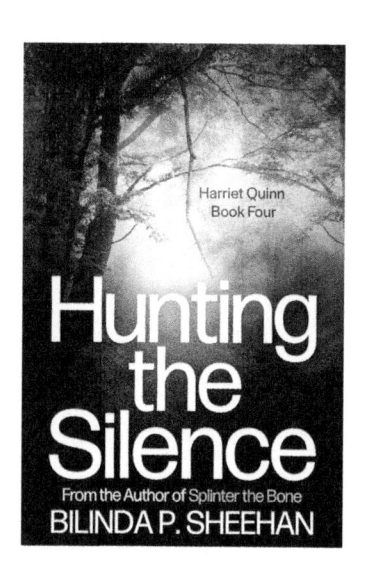

Harriet and DI Haskell return in the next book in the series.
Hunting the Silence

WANT A FREE NOVELLA?

Sign-up to the mailing list to receive Harriet's prequel novella absolutely free when it launches in December

Mailing List

Or Join me on Facebook
https://www.facebook.com/BilindaPSheehan/
Facebook: The Armchair Whodunnit's Book Club

Alternatively send me an email.
bilindasheehan@gmail.com

My website is bilindasheehan.com

ALSO BY BILINDA P. SHEEHAN

Watch out for the next book coming soon from Bilinda P. Sheehan by joining her mailing list.

A Wicked Mercy - DI Drew Haskell & Profiler Harriet Quinn Detective Series Book 1

Death in Pieces - DI Drew Haskell & Profiler Harriet Quinn Detective Series Book 2

Splinter the Bone - DI Drew Haskell & Profiler Harriet Quinn Detective Series Book 3

Hunting the Silence - DI Drew Haskell & Profiler Harriet Quinn Detective Series Book 4

All the Lost Girls - A Gripping Psychological Thriller

Wednesday's Child - A Gripping Psychological Thriller

ALSO AVAILABLE AT AMAZON

At any given time, there are at least three active serial killers in Britain.

A new team has been created to find them…

To get your copy, click HERE

Printed in Great Britain
by Amazon